Sweet and Dirty

Sweet and Dirty

Christina Crooks

APHRODISIA

KENSINGTON BOOKS
http://www.kensingtonbooks.com

APHRODISIA BOOKS are published by

Kensington Publishing Corp.
119 West 40th Street
New York, NY 10018

All Kensington Titles, Imprints, and Distributed Lines are available at special quantity discounts for bulk purchases for sales promotions, premiums, fund-raising, and educational or institutional use.

Special book excerpts or customized printings can also be created to fit specific needs. For details, write or phone the office of the Kensington special sales manager: Kensington Publishing Corp., 119 West 40th Street, New York, NY 10018, attn: Special Sales Department, Phone: 1-800-221-2647.

Aphrodisia and the A logo Reg. U.S. Pat. & TM Off.

ISBN-13: 978-0-7582-3873-3
ISBN-10: 0-7582-3873-8

First Trade Paperback Printing: January 2010

10 9 8 7 6 5 4 3 2 1

Printed in the United States of America

CONTENTS

BARING IT ALL

1

Michelle Gray shut off her car. As she stared at the unusual store before her, the old anxiety rose up.

She pinched herself just below her elbow. Swiftly, angrily. "No. That's done with, that's behind you, that's gone." She focused on the pain until the anxiety receded. An old trick. It was one she hadn't had to use in weeks, not since she'd moved to Los Angeles.

Her new boss, a domineering woman who'd hired her at Dog Day Care and Cage-Free Boarding, clearly had a mean streak. Why else would she send Michelle *here* to buy a dog collar?

The odd store seemed to grin at her, its entrance a mouthful of teeth ready to gobble timid types.

Michelle looked away, small-dog style. Maybe she'd always be the smallest, most submissive puppy in any pack. Human packs, anyway. Fortunately for her dog-training livelihood, dogs knew she was pack leader.

Michelle's gaze crept up to the sign, FANTASY DRESSER, then

to the display window. Her eyes locked on the sight within. This time she didn't look away.

Human figures cavorted. A few wore dog collars. They seemed to be the metal-studded type she'd been sent to buy.

Nearly nude, the mannequins wore an astonishing array of strategically placed bits of material: animal skins, rubber, satin, steel. There were curvaceous female angels with white feathered wings and muscular devils with bright red horns. No plain hairstyles or wavy brunette tresses like Michelle's own, but instead a rainbow of wigs. Silver headdresses glinted under spotlights, and gold headdresses with feathers, too. One intertwined couple was enshrouded beneath a curtain of beautifully real, straight long human hair. It gleamed with an unlikely orange sheen.

A velvet backdrop and the mannequins' beauty acted as a display for the bondage gear. Life-size human cages, fur-lined handcuffs, riding crops, paddles, floggers, small steel jewellike cages the size of Michelle's fist, ball gags, and other things . . . the variety of paraphernalia got her mind to wondering how many of them could possibly be used.

She'd heard of those kinds of things before, of course. She accepted that there were all kinds of strange people in the world, and their sexual preferences didn't have to affect her one little bit.

But now she had to enter such a store. That was another matter entirely. It was a "den of iniquity," or so her ex-boyfriend Ted would label it. The thought made her smile—a little. He'd always been so conservative. So proper, so concerned with what others thought of him, so determined to keep Michelle in his tight little grasp.

Well, she'd slipped away despite his best efforts. And she intended to be everything they'd all said she'd never become. Even if it meant going in that store.

She swallowed, pulling her keys from the ignition without taking her gaze from the store. What kinds of weirdos might pounce on her, thinking she was one of them?

She braced herself to the task and moved. If her boss preferred these collars for the dogs, Michelle would fetch them. Posh wasn't a woman to piss off.

Michelle's hand pushed the store's glass door before any second thoughts could take hold. She moved inside like a hound on the scent.

She collided with a dominatrix. Her purse whacked the taller woman in the center of her tight black leather micromini.

"I'm so sorry," Michelle breathed, feeling herself blush to the roots of her hair. She clutched the offending purse, breathing fast. The woman looked strong. And stern.

"That'll be forty whacks," the woman drawled, amused as she gave Michelle a once-over. The chains and rivets on her top sparkled, but didn't come close to the ruthless glitter in her eyes. She gazed down with a small cruel smile. The woman reminded Michelle of an older Posh.

Embarrassment and envy and admiration snaked through Michelle. The foolishness of her own klutzy maneuver brought a smile to her face. "Forty whacks?"

"Unfortunately I don't have time to explain or administer . . . but Ro is currently giving a demonstration." The woman waved one careless, perfectly manicured hand toward the back corner of the store. She brushed past Michelle not waiting for a response and trailing faint scents of musk, new leather, and the tang of metal and mystery.

"Nice meeting you, too," Michelle finally said. What she wouldn't give for such confidence.

She'd taken only one step farther into the store before jumping out of the way of another dominatrix. Michelle blushed again when her gaze stuttered to the woman's face only to see that she was a display mannequin. The female stood, alabaster white and imposing and half-blocking the main corridor, tassels on her whip draping over the rear of a male mannequin crouched at her feet. Michelle viewed with appreciation the hard roundness of his bottom. Someone had colored his rear pink with crayon crosshatches patterning the otherwise white expanse, lovingly smudged for effect.

The kneeling mannequin's face was twisted in pain and lust. The whip-wielder's face showed amused contempt.

Michelle felt her body respond to the scene, to its simple interpretation of sexual power. A momentary languor, then a haze seemed to descend gently over her, like the distant buzzing of bees. It felt . . . good.

She shook off the sensation, bemused.

"Dog collars." She eyed the collar on the kneeling male's neck as she skirted the two mannequins. It seemed a shame to deface the display by removing the exotic stainless-steel collar. Its red down lining and enormous center O-ring made it the most outlandish one she'd seen yet. She'd like to watch Posh fit the dignified old mastiff with that thing. She was sure the dog's owner hadn't meant an actual collar for humans when the wealthy woman had insisted, over the phone, on "human-quality everything" for her precious pet.

Posh knew far less about dogs than she should, working in the pet industry. Worse, she still hadn't availed herself of Michelle's vast canine expertise. It made Michelle wonder why the woman had hired her.

It made Michelle worry for the dogs.

A gasp came from the back of the store. Then, the slap of leather on flesh.

Flesh?

Scandalized and not a little curious, Michelle followed the sounds toward the back.

The ceiling soared far overhead to give the store a roomy, airy feel. The theme from the display windows continued deeper inside, with exhibition after exhibition of mannequins arranged in dramatically dominant and submissive positions.

Her first impression—that there were many shopping patrons—proved false. Only half of them were flesh and blood,
though some of those fooled her into thinking them mannequins initially. It seemed that pale makeup, contrasting eye-
liner and lipstick, bright wigs or suspiciously black hair, and
exotic clothes were the rule rather than the exception.

Michelle glanced down at herself. Khaki slacks, cotton shirt,
comfortable sandals the same brown color as her belt and
watchband. The clothes went well with her makeup-free face
and her medium-length, unruly brown hair. A natural look.

She belonged in this store like a Chihuahua belonged in a
wolf pack. She should buy the one collar and leave. She would,
just as soon as she satisfied her curiosity.

She reached the source of the sounds.

Seeing the man who inspired the sounds made her forget to
look for dog collars, and also to breathe. She was entranced, her
thoughts replaced by a primal imperative that left her momentarily without the strength to move. She knew she was looking
at the alpha male of the wolf pack.

The controlled rotation of his shoulder showcased muscles
underneath his tight black T-shirt. Strength flexed in his forearm as he brought the paddle down . . . onto a woman's half-
bared rear.

Smack.

The woman gasped as she jerked forward with the force of
his blow. The thin black rubber material of her miniskirt had
been peeled partway down, revealing the globes of her upper
cheeks. They were pinkened darkly, like the mannequin's.

The man waited.

It was his face that made Michelle suck in a long overdue
breath, and then another until she panted like a bitch in heat.
His dark, blade-straight hair and naturally pale skin combined
in a way that hit her viscerally. His too-large brows and nose

and, most of all, those curling lips, gave an impression of straightforward ferocity. Yet he held himself still and disciplined, with only the hint of a smile on his lips. He wasn't traditionally handsome, but she knew she'd never in her life been in the presence of a more compelling man. His mouth was exquisitely carved, cruel and thin and smiling slightly, as if with contempt.

"Thank you. Another, please." The woman's voice sounded ragged, with lust, or pain. Michelle drifted closer.

He brought the paddle down again.

He was magnificent.

Drawing closer yet, as if under a spell, Michelle felt her nerve endings leap to life. She should go about her business, she should leave, but the sexual buzz she felt didn't allow her to turn away. Her mind was full of the stern disciplinarian and his now-whimpering victim.

Primal, and as straightforward as dog pack dynamics. It was beautiful, and simple, and for a moment Michelle felt as if she understood a great many things about herself.

But people weren't dogs. And if they were, Michelle thought bitterly, then that would make her the cringing runt.

Smack.

An unexpected new surge of desire left Michelle weak. She tried to escape the distracting pull of the sensation by concentrating on the logistics of the scene before her. The woman, doubtless a willing participant (*though what if she wasn't?* Michelle thought, the possibility spiking her desire, *what if she'd just been yanked aside randomly and punished, it could happen, it could happen to* anyone), was held in her bent-over position with the help of a contraption clearly built for the purpose. A stringed price tag knotted to one stainless steel strut identified it as one of the store's available products.

It looked familiar.

"Of course! It's a breeding rack for dogs," Michelle said with surprise. Too loud. The man seated his paddle in his other hand, scowling. The woman stopped writhing. Spectators turned, glared. For the second time in a day, Michelle felt her face heat with embarrassment—and some apprehension, seeing the disapproval in the man's eyes. They were a bottomless aquamarine, but steely cold rather than warm. "Oops," she gulped. "Please." She waved her hands. "Keep going. You're doing a great job."

He frowned, then bent in one graceful movement to unhook the woman from the rack. He whispered briefly in her ear. She glanced at Michelle with something like pity.

Michelle's apprehension grew. She backed away. Maybe she could find some clothes to hide behind, or a side door to make her escape.

Tall, white plastic stands held a variety of studded collars. Michelle paused only long enough to scoop an adjustable fur-lined leather collar on her way to the anonymity of the denser clothing section of the store. She didn't think anyone was following her. Hopefully they'd forgotten her faux pas and just gone on with the demonstration. Hopefully—

The man stepped out from behind a display. "And where do you think you're going?"

Startled, she jumped, grabbing at the nearest sturdy object to steady herself.

He was even more gorgeous up close. His deep voice seemed to bypass her ears and zing straight to her nervous system.

"I'm browsing, just browsing," she replied, a little breathlessly. Metal clanked under her palm as his voice toyed with her system some more.

"You interrupt my demonstration, you insult"—he paused for a moment, then shrugged—"pretty much everyone with that 'dog-breeding rack' comment . . . and now you think you can just stroll off without even an apology? It doesn't work that way where I'm from."

If she had hackles, they'd be up. She bared her teeth in a smile. "Where're you from?"

"Somewhere they teach manners. You?"

"The uncivilized backwoods," she replied truthfully. She tugged at the metal piece without looking away from the man's accusing stare, trying to casually add whatever was in her hand to her collection of dog collars. Just browsing. She should tell him she was sorry—lord knew she wanted to, the apology all but strangled her trying to get out—but something held it back.

She tugged at the metal, harder.

"Need some help with that?"

"You have experience with these?" She couldn't believe her ears. Her voice was the human equivalent of a dog's warning growl. What was she doing? She had to disengage, somehow, before she hurt herself.

The sudden heat that snapped to life in his eyes didn't help matters. It took an effort of will for her just to turn her head and look at what she held.

She had no idea what she held. It appeared to be a small steel skeleton, complete with spine and ribs wrapping around empty space, attached to a ring and a small, dangling padlock. The padlock seemed to be hung up on another padlock, from an identical product next back on the hanger. It was caught.

"That's a very personal question," he said with cool dignity. "But, no. I have no personal experience with male chastity cages." His expression softened slightly as he watched her struggle. "Here, I can work that loose for you." He stepped closer, not seeming to notice the way she suddenly sucked in her breath, and worked the padlock back and forth.

She worked hers at the same time, trying to free hers from his. She was not going to back down, not going to run away again, and above all, she refused to reveal how embarrassed she was to be tugging on a cage that evidently fit over a penis. She eyed the cage. A large penis.

"It's stuck. We seem to be tied together," he said at last. Male amusement tinged his voice.

Stuck. A tie, she thought, mad hilarity rising. First the breeding rack, now this. He had no way of knowing the images his words evoked. During mating, a female dog's muscles contracted and the male's penis swelled. The resulting "tie," as it was called in dog-breeding circles, sometimes kept a pair stuck together for thirty minutes to an hour. Michelle had seen it often enough while managing the breeding of her champion studs back in Alabama.

"But if you don't mind me saying so," he added in a tone that indicated he didn't care whether she minded or not, "I don't see you needing this particular tool. Any pet of yours would keep himself ready and waiting for you."

"Pet?" Michelle asked, surprised into letting go of the device. Had he read her mind about the dogs? "Pet of mine?" Michelle couldn't help it. She began to giggle.

"Pet. Or pony boy?" His answering smile warmed his eyes to a glinting green. "The pony gear is over there if you're into pony play."

He was flirting with her. A thrill spiraled through her body. And yet, he was one of the weirdos. "Thanks . . ." Michelle took a hesitant step away from him. *Pony play?*

Then his voice immobilized her. "A dog-breeding rack is for canines, to hold a bitch muzzled and ready for mounting. That structure"—he jerked his thumb over his shoulder—"is a strictly human affair. Though the similarities are obvious."

"You know about dog breeding?" She was surprised enough to stare directly into his eyes for a long moment. He looked back, calm and amused. He was the alpha male of the pack, after all. *Dangerous, dangerous.* She backed away, then sideways, into the corridors of exotic dresses, always keeping an eye on him.

He stalked her, not deigning to acknowledge her comment. He made a quick scan of her, head to toe. "Size six."

"I know what size I am," she snapped. She felt adrenaline amping her up, making her feel more jittery than normal. It seemed important to defend herself from him, from the danger that seemed to radiate from him. From the way he made her feel. "Do you work on commission?"

His voice was even. "It's not often I give a demonstration here at Fantasy Dresser. Not with a club of my own to run." He stepped closer, raising an eyebrow at the way she tensed. His tone became soft and caressing. "You disappointed some people back there. And you still haven't apologized. It's almost as if you want to be punished . . . ?" He reached behind himself and began to pull something out of his back pocket.

"Forty whacks," she said airily, but her nerves shrieked in warning. What was he reaching for? Michelle whirled to grab the nearest dress. Black. Size six.

"Forty-one. Now I'm going to touch you. If you want me to stop, say so."

Something touched the small of her back, momentary and feather light.

She jerked. A moan started in her throat, but she swallowed it, locking it there.

A thick fingertip, or a knuckle, slowly traced her spine up and up. What was he *doing?* The single contact seemed to unfurl, radiating sensuously throughout her body. She was about to start gasping like the woman in the rack when he pulled away, grazing against strands of her hair, tickling the nape of her neck.

She tingled, holding her breath.

"Turn around," he commanded. When she did, he held out a business card. "This is my club. The Dungeon. It's new. I want you to stop by."

"Maybe I will." She took the card, trying to maintain her crumbling reserve. The grin he flashed told her he knew it.

"My name is Ro." He held out his hand. She took it. Large, warm fingers closed around her smaller hand. "And you are . . . ?"

It was too much, too soon. She felt naked under his knowing gaze. All she'd wanted was a dog collar. Inside a store she'd never normally enter, she'd collided with a dominatrix, interrupted a paddling, and now felt her body wanting to fling itself at an assertive stranger who administered punishments. A lusciously dominant male who'd promised her forty-one whacks. She admired his calm authority.

She wanted to possess his calm authority. Not him. Not his forty-one whacks.

Reaching deep for the reserves of determination that had enabled her to begin a brand-new life away from those who'd dominate her into oblivion, a memory was triggered. A nursery rhyme: "Lizzie Borden took an axe / And gave her mother forty whacks. / And when she saw what she had done, / She gave her father forty-one."

Michelle took his hand. "Call me Lizbeth."

He wasn't fooled. "Whatever you say. Lizbeth."

Michelle made a show of looking at her watch. "What's the dress code for your club?"

Ro tilted his head, as if trying to figure her out. "Dress to play. That"—he indicated the latex dress she held—"is playful."

"Indeed. It was nice meeting you, Ro. Maybe I'll see you later?" Initiating the end of their conversation, she felt an odd sense of courage envelope her.

"You, too." Brusque nearly to the point of rudeness, Ro pivoted and disappeared into the thicket of clothing, presumably in the direction of the back of the store. She felt the loss of his presence immediately.

She wanted to feel it again. Soon.

Excitement gripped her. As she backtracked, looking for matching shoes, she felt a nervous smile begin to play about her lips.

2

Ro surveyed his nightclub and felt his heart sink. The lack of bodies packing the place worried him. He prayed the events he had planned would turn the place around before he had to consider his business a failure.

He had to make the club an LA hot spot, and he believed he knew exactly how: offer an oasis of authenticity, where LA's fetish people could romp to their heart's content with the latest and safest toys and equipment.

Killer tunes pleased the ear. Tasteful decor pleased the eye.

He showed a stoic face to his bartender, his waitstaff, and his friends. Especially "Mistress Vivian."

She turned away another group of guys.

Immediately he crossed The Dungeon's too-empty dance floor to where she worked the door. He saw her expression, clearly disdainful even behind the half hood that hid the upper part of her face. Her blood-red lips curled in a feral smile at his approach.

Ro gazed at her appreciatively. He'd known Mistress Vivian for years, knew her past, knew what she did at her day job, knew everything about her vanilla life outside of the club just as well as she knew his. He knew her a little too well, maybe. She drove him as crazy as an irritating younger sister. But, she was a top-notch dominatrix, and she stalked on her six-inch heels with style and menace.

Sometimes too much menace.

"Scaring boys again?" he asked her, giving her a stern look.

"My second-favorite pastime." She didn't spare another glance for the group of guys, even when they howled insults—from safely across the street, Ro noticed.

He sighed. "So, what was wrong with that batch?" They moved slowly away, he saw with both relief and regret.

"Fag bashers. I heard one of them say 'dung-punching ass bandits.' You don't want their kind."

"I want any kind at this point."

He intercepted her sharp look, gave her one back. "You know I trust your judgment, Vivi. But if you threaten their masculinity, they're not going to stay." He saw the cynical quirk of her lips. Lowered his voice. "I want you to let more people in here."

"I will. The right kind."

"Don't be elitist."

She snorted. "More like quality assurance and safety management."

"Please just do it." She was wrong, but Ro didn't want to debate it. Vivian loved nothing more than to pick fights.

She sneered. When he just stared in response, she shrugged, nodded, stalked away. Leaving him to gaze at his nightclub's brick-and-cinder-block columns, at the subtle lighting and decoratively painted walls, at the stockades and strategically placed, cushioned, bondage-themed chairs.

He frowned.

It was a great place. It should be packed.

The Dungeon was his brainchild, a BDSM haven where people could be true to themselves, whatever their consensual kink. More than an enormous investment, it was a labor of love.

People would come. Of course they would.

Ro scanned the club, from the cash room/coat check to Whip It Good Café to the open dance floor and the stage where he would hold his first Dungeon slave auction in a few weeks. He began to walk, enjoying the buzz of satisfaction he felt about owning such a nightclub. The sense of power cheered him and centered him. He evaluated the themed mini-rooms that scalloped the main space. They still looked fun, intimate and inviting.

He couldn't shake the feeling that something stood in opposition to his goal of making The Dungeon a success. Had his father, who'd been irritable since being told Ro wasn't following in his respectable lawyer footsteps, somehow managed to torpedo his dream before it even got off the ground? Or was it something else?

Ro reached the heavy wooden door at the far edge of the club. The faded words stenciled on it, CAGE ROOM, looked far older than he knew them to be. Pondering how to ensure that his first month in the nightclub-owning business wouldn't be his last, Ro turned to see if Vivian had maybe let in a few dozen people while he wasn't looking.

He was just in time to witness a very strange thing. Vivian, always aggressive and capable in her role as bouncer, let in a trio of giggling coeds without even checking their IDs. She was too busy staring, seemingly astonished, at the attractive woman next in line.

Ro instantly recognized the woman from Fantasy Dresser.

Why is that woman staring at me?

Michelle—no, she was Lizbeth now, she had to remember—looked away, then felt her gaze drawn back to the black-clad bouncer woman like some hypnotized puppy. The woman was tall, aided no doubt by the high-heeled leather boots, but her Amazonian presence didn't come from height alone. A steel-riveted black leather hood hid half her face, revealing only a stubborn jaw and hard red slash of a mouth. A bare neck and corseted cleavage showed blinding white skin, and strong shoulders and arms extended from a tight sleeveless top to swing confidently, menacingly. Heavily black-lined eyes bored holes into her. The irises were an unlikely shade of bright purple. Contact lenses, of course, but still . . . Michelle—*Lizbeth, damn it*—felt suddenly anxious and alert, hyperaware of the woman's scrutiny.

Her own outfit, a black vinyl dress, hugged her curves and the high heels weren't so stratospheric that she couldn't walk easily, but it still felt more like a Halloween costume than evening wear. The red lace bra she wore under the peekaboo top had felt especially daring, but now she withered under the other woman's gaze.

Lizbeth reluctantly stepped up, next in line. She couldn't seem to control the anxious tremble of her bottom lip or the wobble in her stride. The woman had more presence than the dominatrix at Fantasy Dresser. It was intimidating. Lizbeth could see the woman's nostrils flare and her mouth open slightly, as if in recognition. For a moment, the woman did seem familiar. Which was impossible, of course. This one was more muscular and young than the other dominatrix.

Lizbeth let her right hand drift over to her left arm. She pinched herself just below her elbow. A measure of relief rushed in after the brief pain, helping her conquer the jittery dance of nerves and adrenaline enough to calmly present her ID. The woman snatched it, checked it against Lizbeth as if she suspected a fake. A smile spread across the visible part of her face. "What is someone like you doing someplace like this?"

Was she flirting? Or challenging? "I'm here to play."

"Are you." Vivian handed back her ID. Her long, red-lacquered nail tapped it, twice. "My name is Vivian."

"I'm Lizbeth," Michelle responded, before remembering there was a different name on her ID.

Vivian simply stood there, blocking the entrance.

Feeling increasingly tense and insecure, Lizbeth peered past the woman. Finding Ro and learning what she could of dominance suddenly seemed a silly dream. She didn't belong here; she was a pretender, and everyone could tell, including herself. What had she been thinking?

But even as she turned to leave, a familiar male form suddenly appeared out of the greater darkness inside the club.

"Is there a problem?"

"Ro." Lizbeth felt the individual thuds of her heart against her breast. His charisma licked out at her.

"You know her?" The dominatrix looked like she wanted to laugh. A flash of irritation shot through Lizbeth.

Under the goad of ire, Lizbeth lifted her head high. She saw the way Ro looked at her, and smiled. She stepped inside, took Ro's offered arm. The cotton of his dress shirt crinkled and slid pleasantly over hard muscle. His body heat and the clean musk radiating from him had her moving closer, as if her body had its own secret plans. Too close; her lace-covered nipple brushed against his forearm.

"You came," he said. Pleased but not surprised.

"Not yet." It was her voice, yet not hers.

Lizbeth's.

A purely masculine laugh vibrated against her. He directed her into one of the darker alcoves off of the dance floor, one equipped with new-looking restraints jutting from the back wall. She turned. Instantly closed off from the rest of the world, with only Ro's broad shoulders before her, she felt safe rather than trapped.

"Are you the Pied Piper? My club was deserted before you

arrived, and now they're lined up. It's a short line, but it's a line. You're incredible."

His look of delight, and appreciation, made her smile. She couldn't remember the last time a man wore quite that expression while looking at her.

Then he spoiled it.

"You don't belong here."

Her calm felt punctured. "You invited me."

"Yes." The appreciation was still there in his face, but she could see he'd pounced on the puzzle of her like a dog on a bone. "You didn't belong in Fantasy Dresser either. Your accent. Your clothes. Your nervousness. It was cute."

"I was a bitch," Lizbeth protested. Did she really have an accent? She moved restlessly and felt the thick dangling leather manacles dig into her back. Chains scraped against stone. It seemed she was in a multipurpose alcove.

Ro smiled, his eyes glittering dangerously. "Perhaps," he said. "And perhaps not. You're an enigma to me, which is unusual. Believe it or not, I'm usually pretty good at pegging people quickly. Part of the job description, running a place like this. How do you identify?"

"You're straightforward, aren't you?" she asked, while parsing his last question. How did she identify? "Hetero?"

"Good." His eyes lit up even more, if that were possible. She suddenly understood what was meant by the phrase "burning gaze."

"Hetero, and . . . ?"

"And I'm not sure." What else was there? She had the feeling she'd find out. She met his gaze, feeling heat swirl in her belly, and up and down her spine. He seemed perfectly at ease with her uncertainty, with her nervousness, which had the strange effect of lessening it.

He gave her a small, purely friendly smile that further reduced her worry. "If I may ask another way . . . please try to tell me what you want out of this."

She noticed it wasn't a question. The force of his personality penetrated what remained of her reservations. She found herself grinning back at him. "You really want to know what I want? What I need? What only you can give me?"

His smile turned speculative as he lowered his head, hooding his irises. A nod.

"I want to learn how to be dominant. I want you to teach me, whatever it takes."

"That's what I thought." Then, shocking her with the sudden sure movement, he secured first one of her wrists, then the other, in the dangling leather manacles. When she only gasped, surprised free of words, he cocked his head critically then tightened the buckle on her left-side manacle. He was close enough for her to smell his scent. He smelled nice.

In the first few seconds of her bondage she felt herself launched into a more intense version of the erotic high she'd experienced at Fantasy Dresser. A languorous, knee-buckling anticipation.

Then she returned to her senses.

"Let me *go*."

With the same startling swiftness, Ro released first one restraint, then the other. He looked at her expectantly but said nothing.

Disappointment cascaded through her. Lizbeth rubbed her freed wrists though they didn't hurt. The stiff leather had only gripped her snugly, like the firm grasp of large hands. "I think you misunderstood," she said. "I definitely don't need to learn about being . . . being . . ."

"Restrained."

Lizbeth nodded, and blushed. She'd enjoyed it. She knew he knew she did. And yet, it wasn't what she needed to learn. He was looking at her inquiringly. She spoke, still confused. "I don't mean to imply I have vast experience with that sort of thing. Not that there's anything wrong with that sort of thing. I don't even want to label it 'that sort of thing.' I'm not a judgmental person. Um."

"Are you finished?"

"Yes, please."

"You want dominance lessons. I can give them to you."

"Tying me up isn't going to teach me how to be dominant."

"You're wrong about that, actually." His honeyed voice sent a pleasant sensation all through her body. "May I show you why?"

"Start by telling me." She was amazed at how badly she wanted him to show her why. She hoped he'd grab her and lock her up again. She certainly wasn't about to *ask* him to put those manacles back on her. And why was she having such thoughts about a near stranger, anyway?

"You can't top until you've bottomed. The top is the dominant person. Controlling, confident, maybe a little aggressive. But always respectful of a bottom's limits. Bottom is the sub, or submissive, person, the one who gives up control, either all the time or only during a session. There's no shame in being a bottom. It's certainly a lot less work." He spoke with the assurance of someone who only had to give half his mind to the topic under discussion. But what he said next seized her imagination with possibilities. "There's a rack in the Cage Room. Similar to the one you saw at Fantasy Dresser. Would you like to know what it feels like?"

A bolt of lust shot through her.

He smiled, a knowing expression. "You're not ready for that. But these"—he flicked a manacle—"maybe these aren't too much? I won't do anything you don't want me to." He paused for a long moment. Then, "Tell me you want me to put these back on you."

As if an invisible string controlled her head, Lizbeth found herself nodding. *I can't believe I'm letting him do this.*

He locked her back in the manacles.

"You're thinking that you can't believe you're letting me do this," he said, securing the straps around her wrists until they held her firmly. She felt the delicious languor suffuse her once more.

"You're awfully sure of yourself." Her voice came out breathless. "Oh god, we just met and I'm letting you do this. Why am I letting you do this?" And yet she couldn't deny her almost painful arousal.

"Because you trust me. Wisely. The most important thing in a relationship is trust. Now, we need a word—"

"We're in a relationship? I don't even know your last name."

"And I don't know your real first name," he retorted. "And I won't ask, Lizbeth. Respect for privacy is common in the fetish scene. However, everyone knows I own this place and that's something that is a matter of public record. I don't use an alias. My name is Ro Kaliph."

"Kaliph? The 'Call Kaliph and Son and your worries are done' law firm Kaliph?"

"I no longer practice law. Much to my father's chagrin. He really should change that commercial. Now, why don't we get back to bondage and domination."

She clinked the buckle of her manacles against the hard wall behind her. "Still bound, here. The domination seems to be missing, though."

Gently, slowly, he cupped the back of her head, cushioning it from the wall. The tender gesture had her expecting a kiss, and she turned her face up to his. But with shocking swiftness and enough force to knock the breath out of her, he pushed his body against hers, pinning her to the wall. His body fit hers perfectly, strong and uncompromising. She felt his cock shoved against her at the juncture of her thighs, and she felt vulnerable. The sensuality of it was unexpected.

As he simply held her immobile, a fiery ache sparked to life inside her. She tried to move against him.

He shook his head. "No." She could see every shaved whisker on his jaw, and each dark lash ringing his eyes. Surprisingly, it took an effort not to grind her body against his, but she managed. She saw the small smile touch his lips.

"Obedient. And responsive. I thought you would be." He eased back with a graceful movement, as casual as if he did that sort of thing all the time. It was only when her feet touched the floor again that Lizbeth realized she'd been lifted entirely off the ground. "Now. We need a word. A safe word for you. When a participant utters a safe word, all play stops."

"That thing you just did." Michelle wished she could tug down her dress. The latex had bunched up, raising the hemline to a risqué height. "That was okay."

"I'm glad you approve." Masculine humor. "But pay attention. I want you to pick a word, any word."

"Collar?"

"Collar, then." Ro smiled, a little bemused. "To be 'collared' is to be a submissive, or slave, who is owned in an intimate relationship. And 'collaring' is a ceremony of commitment. Much like a wedding ceremony. You picked an interesting word."

"Beginner's luck." Ro was giving his attention to a section of the wall next to her. If she turned her head she could just make out previously unnoticed shapes fastened to it, much as she was. Only these were objects. She had a sneaking suspicion she knew what they were.

She wasn't surprised when he ran his hands over the selection, lifting a whip here, examining a paddle there. So that she could see them, she suspected. Crop, flogger, wooden paddle, a single-tail whip, a two-tasseled whip . . . Then he paused and lifted off its hook something that looked like an oversized Ping-Pong paddle. It had a hand's-width of pink fuzz affixed to the back, and the front seemed to be rubber-ridged, black . . . and very hard looking. He turned to her, eyes narrowed, and smacked the black surface none too gently into his palm.

"That's not necessary," she said, remembering the woman being paddled in the breeding rack. She didn't want a paddling. Probably. "I'm just here to learn."

"Who am I to discourage the pursuit of knowledge."

"Am I going to have to say my word?"

"If you like." Ro waited. When she said nothing, he arched an eyebrow, adult to child. "I'm going to show you what it's like to give away control."

Michelle found it hard to swallow.

"I'll teach you how it feels when your body takes over, plea-surably so, putting your senses at the command of another who has the experience to make them leap to new heights."

Michelle's body trembled at just the thought, but she managed a bit of bravado. "You talk big."

"Wouldn't you like to find out if it's justified?"

Yes. Oh yes. "I don't usually do bondage on the first date."

"Does that mean you're ready?" His gaze torched her wherever he looked.

"Maybe." *If he only knew how ready.* But, seeing shadows flicker behind him, she was reminded. Despite his blocking the view into their intimate little alcove, it was still quite public.

He seemed to read her thoughts again. "Don't worry. I won't take your clothes off. Or mine. No matter how much you beg." He positioned himself directly in front of her, with an almost military stiffness. But his eyes still glittered with humor. "The name of this game is, Don't Move."

The devilish glint in his eyes was the only warning she got before he kissed her.

Her body jerked against his, and it took her a moment to re-alize that it was his hand holding the paddle clamped against

the small of her back doing the jerking and not her own delirious reflex to jump him. His lips pressed firm and hot against
hers, his breath sweet as it mingled with hers. And his body . . .
Her heart thundered in her ears as her knees weakened. She
tried not to move against him.

His hard forearm and the paddle, plus her manacles, kept
her centered and upright. His lips curved in a smile against hers.
Her body seemed to open up, becoming sensitive all over. She
heard the sound of a moan, felt the vibration against their lips
and knew she'd made the sound.

When his lips opened and his tongue plundered her, the
electricity forked through her body. Taking effortless possession of her mouth, he cupped the base of her head with his
other hand. He tilted her head here or there as it pleased him.
His tongue slid out, then in again to tease and play with hers.

Then he stopped. Air rushed into the small gap between
their faces, cooling her enough for her to regain a sense of pro-
priety. The low thud of the nightclub's music thrummed through
her, beating in time with her pulse. She felt her lips quivering
with unfulfilled desire. Her eyelids drifted closed to savor it.
She tried to shift in a way that gave her better access to him.

The smart slap of rubber against her rump reminded her.
Her eyes flew open. Ro's expression was stern. "You moved.
You'll notice I'm making a clear connection between your of-
fense and my correction." At the word "correction," the paddle
tapped her again. Hard enough to sting, even through her dress.

"You mentioned your interest in dogs. Swift disciplinary action is good for dogs, and for people too. Rewards also work."
He gave her the briefest of smiles, easing the stern expression as
he spoke over her demurral. "Don't bother trying to deny what
you feel." He rubbed her against him, an obscene jiggle that
made her cry out sharply with surprised pleasure. "Now, tell
me. Why do you want to learn dominance behavior? Is it for
dog training?"

"Training and breeding. It's what I do." The training was for herself too. But she didn't tell him that.

"Thank you for sharing."

His respectful, gentle voice soothed her.

Aftershocks from his kiss kept hitting her, tingling on her skin and vibrating in slow sensual waves to her stomach. Butterflies on steroids. All she had to do was remember Ro's tongue in her mouth and she felt an eager warmth between her legs. It was as if he commanded her very emotions to reject all doubt. Well, most of the doubt. She trembled in her bonds, helpless. She felt a distant dismay at the realization that part of her reveled in the helplessness.

The paddle lifted, and he held it there before her for her inspection. He turned it so she could see every groove on the rubber side, every fiber of material on the fuzzy side. Then he extended it so it stroked her hair. The fuzz felt like the softest brush, light and delicately tickling.

He ran it down her body, over her dress, turning it so that the dangerous side faced her. The rubber ridges nudged her breasts, her belly, continuing down, and he turned it again. Fuzz. Down, past the hem of her dress, and back up the inside of her thighs, hidden underneath. Firm against the juncture of her thighs, and she moaned out loud at the shocking intrusion of the rubber pressing against her most sensitive area. The rubber on one side and fuzz on the other created a wicked sensation. It continued down again.

She trembled more violently as he repeated the movement, up one inner thigh to her panties. Her knees buckled, but the leather restraints held her upright, pulling on her wrists.

Down the other side. Then again, with one variation: his hand accompanied the paddle. Her breath came in short pants. The feel of his large warm fingers gliding against the inside of her thighs tore a whimper from her.

He moved in close, giving himself more leverage and allowing his taut body to brush against hers. His breath felt erotic against her throat. His chest burned against her wherever it touched.

The conflagration was happening lower, where his hands worked. Cool air moved under her dress, contrasting with the heat of his skin. His hand hitchhiked on the edge of the paddle, but the paddle moved too slowly. She tried to move against it, but she couldn't move down; she had to wait for him to move up.

He stopped, began moving it back down again.

No! She groaned, then gasped in gratitude as he reversed it once again.

Waiting for his touch was making a cinder of her. His fingers felt mobile and deadly under her skirt. But he wouldn't use his fingers the way she wanted him to.

He wouldn't be hurried. He continued the rhythmic stroking, the contrasting sensations making her muscles tremble and tense.

"*Please*," she begged finally, the word ripped from her. She thought she felt him grin against her neck, but suddenly her awareness exploded as he worked his fingers underneath her panties. The deliberate invasion jerked a small scream out of her, wordless and primal.

"Hush, love," he said, his voice a million miles away and bursting inside her mind. "They'll think I'm killing you."

He kissed her neck as she tried to remember who "they" were. Ro stepped back to observe her hanging limply, and the direct appraisal made her feel cheap and deliciously violated in her still-hiked-up dress. Others could see her, too, if they looked past him into their alcove.

A flush of shame and pleasure informed her that part of her reveled in the exhibition.

His small smile told her he knew. "That will conclude today's lesson."

"Unlock me," she said in a voice she barely recognized as her own.

He stepped close again. She relished the heat and strength of him as he unshackled her wrists. She wobbled a bit on her feet, then rubbed her wrists. They had faint pink marks.

"Those will be gone in a few minutes." She saw his sharp eyes on her wrists. She lifted her head, ran a shaky hand through her hair and concentrated on standing without swaying. Movement drew her gaze again. Though Ro's large form blocked most of the entrance to their alcove, she could see a woman lead a man, leash attached to collar, past them. The collared man flipped an incurious glance in Lizbeth's direction, then quickly looked back toward his dom when his leash twitched.

The masked dominatrix, Vivian, held the leash. The dark caves of her masked eyes might or might not be watching. Had she seen everything? There probably wasn't much more to see than Ro's backside when he was working on her. It was reason enough to stare, even clothed, Lizbeth had to admit, peeking at Ro's glorious form as he tossed the paddle into a wall-mounted receptacle. "Like a laundry chute," he explained without turning his head. "Some unlucky sub who needs punishing gets to clean the toys."

Now that she was calming down, Lizbeth began to feel overwhelmed by what she'd done. "I hope you don't mind, but I need to get out of here."

Ro turned to her, unsurprised.

"Thank you?" she added. She fidgeted, tugging at the edge of her dress. What do you say when the most sensual man you've ever met ties you up and gives so much pleasure that you can barely stand? What did it mean to him, after all? Probably nothing. Probably did it twenty times a night.

Sudden dismay stabbed at her and she tugged harder, as if

getting her dress down to a respectable length would let her re-claim a sense of control. "Thank you very much?"

His lips tilted up in an almost-smile. "You're welcome?" he said gently, in the same questioning tone.

She liked him. How could she feel such affection for a stranger?

"I hope you'll . . . come again." The devious glint in his eyes made them seem to sparkle.

This time she laughed out loud. Emotions pounced on each other in her head like a writhing puppy-pile. Exhilaration topped by humor, lust trading places with apprehension. At the moment affection took preeminence.

She craved the solitude of her apartment to sort it out.

He seemed to sense it. He stood aside to let her pass. "Until next time, then."

When Lizbeth exited the club, Vivian was nowhere to be seen.

3

Lizbeth negotiated the stairs up to her second-floor apartment while fumbling for her house key. Soon her home would envelop her. She could take off the stratospheric heels that made her feet hurt and her back ache. She could peel off her dominatrix dress in favor of comfortable old overwashed sleepwear. And, most anticipated of all, she could sort out her feelings about the crazy thing she'd just done.

Her ex-boyfriend blocked her front door.

"Ted?" She gaped. "What . . . How . . . ? What a surprise," she finally managed. "I hadn't expected visitors from back home."

"Especially not me, I'll bet," he said in a Southern drawl she still found endearing after so many years. But then he smirked at her dress, and she remembered why she'd left him. Once one of his charms, his smug knowledge of her became constricting when they'd dated, and downright painful once she'd determined to change.

Two rectangular suitcases bracketed him. He'd brought luggage? She allowed a chill into her voice. "I gave my address to you so we could keep in touch, not so you could move in. I'm starting a new life. One without well-meaning friends and family who treat me like the runt of the litter."

"I know we didn't part on the best of terms . . ."

Lizbeth snorted.

". . . but you have to face it. The way you left, right after Sasquatch bit you. It made lots of people worry about your state of mind. Your loved ones just don't want you getting hurt, Michelle."

"It's Lizbeth now," she said, the new name still feeling odd in her mouth.

He shook his head. "You've been a Michelle for your whole life, you can't just up and change it and expect it to mean anything." He shifted. She saw how tired he looked. "Can I come in?"

Lizbeth watched the man she'd once thought she loved pick up his suitcases. Expectant. She felt the old frustration, and wished she had the strength of will to send him away.

He lowered his suitcases again. He gave her a self-effacing shrug. "Please?"

Lizbeth ground her teeth. So much for the time and space to sort things out. But what could she do? It was Ted, and he was a thousand miles from home. Just like she was.

"Fine." She edged by him, poked her key into the lock.

As she opened her door and stepped inside, she felt her dress ride up her thighs.

He whistled. "Wow. You went out like that, huh?" Disapproval laced his voice. She felt a flush of irritation though she'd expected it.

What she didn't expect was his next comment. "It looks good on you." She felt him following her so closely that she could feel his body heat.

Lizbeth turned to stare at him. Ted stood in the middle of her living room, arms folded over blinding white T-shirt, legs positioned enough apart to stake his territory. Which he still seemed to think included her.

He frowned at her expression. "Not that you should be wearing it. It could be dangerous." He looked at her more closely. "You look flushed. Have you been exerting yourself? You didn't say where you've been."

His accusing tone pried at her like fingernails. It made her cranky. "No, I didn't say. How long will you be staying?"

"Just long enough to talk you into coming back home with me. Where we both belong."

He said it with such a loud, certain voice. Almost too certain, as if he wasn't really sure at all. Did he really think she belonged with him? Or belonged back home? She felt the beginnings of a headache. "Sorry you wasted your trip."

She noticed the way his gaze leapt from her dress, to her arm, to the red lace that covered her nipples, and back to her face. Baffled. Concerned. She sighed. He cared about her well-being. They had all cared in their own ways. And maybe he had a point. Her behavior just lately had been anything but normal. Guilt surged hotly in her, and she had to press her lips together to keep from apologizing.

"You can have that room," she said in lieu of an apology, indicating the spare. "There's a futon. Blankets are in the hall closet, as many as you need. I'm going to bed. Got to be at work in six hours."

Ted's voice became grave. "Yes. The dog day care. Michelle, your family misses you. And your clients. Your business is on hold until you get back."

"It's Lizbeth. I'm not going back. I can't." She waved her arm violently at whatever he was about to say. "Please. Not now. I've got to haul myself out of bed at the crack of dawn." She remembered the way the telltale blue glow of his laptop's screen used to emanate from underneath the office door in his old apartment. She supposed he'd set up in her spare bedroom, and she'd soon see the glow in her home, too. She ground her teeth. Why couldn't she throw him out?

"You love working with dogs."

"I used to." Then, seeing the way he blanched, she added, "I still do, I guess. Well, help yourself to whatever you find in the kitchen. Good night." She escaped to her room and shut the door before he could answer.

She could finally take her leisure. She could remember all the titillating details of her evening with Ro, and relive the way he'd made her nerve endings jump to life. He'd transformed her body into a throbbing instrument of lust.

Lizbeth peeled off her dress, enjoying the cool air hitting her bare skin. She let herself fall backward onto her bed.

A total stranger!

Part of her savored the memory regardless. But another part, larger and more familiar, was convinced she'd made a crazy mistake.

"You think I'm crazy?" Lizbeth stared at Posh cuddling a Chihuahua.

Slender, real bones from some exotic animal pierced the knot of the taller woman's elaborate coif. Posh cooed to the dog as if it were a baby, or possibly a plush toy. She held it too tightly. The dog raised its pointed muzzle toward Lizbeth, clearly miserable.

She felt her lips tighten, but didn't tell Posh that a "toy dog" wasn't a literal toy. She waited patiently for her boss to explain her outrageous comment.

Posh rotated her head toward Lizbeth, her eyeballs the last part of her to turn in Lizbeth's direction. Her warm tone and clear good humor was all the worse while displaying such effortless contempt. "I didn't say you're crazy. I doubt very much you're crazy. I asked, do you think you have a split personality?"

"Because I want to change my name to Lizbeth?"

"Not exactly." Posh smiled, and her eyes glinted with mischief.

Lizbeth shifted from one foot to the other, nervous as always under Posh's regard. Posh found humor in the strangest things. "Have I done something to lead you to the conclusion that I have a split personality?"

Posh laughed. "No one leads me anywhere. I found myself wondering if everyone's got a secret side. Or two." She released the squirming lapdog into the enclosure for the smaller dogs. It immediately ran to the low pallet of real grass, hopped onto it, and defecated.

Posh shuddered. "Look at me, for example. Dogs bore me. But just because I brushed and braided some cuter examples of the species, word got out and rich people started paying to leave their purebreds with me. No one knows I loathe the beasts. Except you, now. I've told you my little secret. Do you have a secret?" Posh flashed even white teeth in a smile. With her shining ebony hair tamed to perfection, and her muscular, confident body language, she intimidated Lizbeth utterly.

"I knew you weren't a huge fan of dogs," Lizbeth said. She flipped through the Dog Day Care and Cage-Free Boarding Application, making sure the Chihuahua's owners had attached copies of vaccination dates, spay/neuter certificate, and the pet's personality profile. It didn't surprise her to see the small dog described as "nervous."

Lizbeth could relate. Especially with Posh's speculative, hungry gaze on her, like some she-wolf waiting for a rabbit to poke its head out of a burrow.

"I never did thank you for picking up those collars yesterday," Posh said suddenly. "I half-expected you to bring back some cheap, ugly Petwise collars instead. But you didn't. How did you like Fantasy Dresser?"

"I think we paid too much for dog collars."

Posh waved this off. "People of extravagant means in LA demand originality with a bit of ostentation. They don't trust bargains, so they expect to be gouged. I know my Richie-riches." Posh grinned, looking particularly feral. She approached Lizbeth, scanning her from head to toe. "Michelle, people don't surprise me much. But you, my decidedly unbleached-blonde"— she pinched a lock of Lizbeth's light brunette hair between two fingers, examining—"and thoroughly Midwestern dog whisperer . . . I am surprised you brought back those collars." Posh strolled, her five-inch heels clicking against the slick floor. She clearly assumed Lizbeth would follow.

Lizbeth followed. "It's Lizbeth," she reminded Posh.

Posh didn't seem to hear. She trailed a long, polished nail over the top of the taller plastic fence enclosing the large dog area. She tossed handfuls of treats as if throwing grain for chickens. The wink of leather and metal from the four new collars appeared among a pack of dogs racing toward her. They scrabbled for the bright red, donut-shaped treats. When Lizbeth saw the treat colors she groaned to herself. A junk brand. Diarrhea would strike half the dogs before 3:00. Lizbeth would have to clean it.

Lizbeth opened her mouth to protest.

Posh wheeled, spoke first. "You say you've worked with dogs all your life. But you avoid them here, unless I give instructions otherwise. Why?"

Lizbeth closed her mouth.

"Don't look so worried. You're doing a great job, feeding them and cleaning up, taking care of the paperwork and errands and things. It's just strange. You told me you loved dogs in the interview, but you don't spend much time with them." Posh upended the treat bag, emptying it. The dogs boiled around the food, but Posh barely glanced down. "So what's the deal?"

With lightning-strike suddenness a dogfight broke out. Snarling from a half-dozen canine throats, yips of pain, and one mournful howl that sounded so familiar to Lizbeth it rooted her to the spot.

Posh cursed, ran to her office, and returned. Before Lizbeth could protest, her boss cracked a bullwhip over the heads of the fighting dogs. "Stop that!" she commanded.

The fight stopped as if by magic. Wrestling dogs separated. Winners and losers both looked shamefaced. A greyhound favored his leg for a moment, but the limp disappeared after a few elegant steps. His new collar seemed bulky on his graceful neck. Lizbeth could have sworn he licked the air in Posh's direction with something like adoration.

Posh glared at one dog in particular. "The Labrador started it. I saw him bite the Australian shepherd."

Lizbeth stared at the perpetrator. "Charlie started it? But he's . . ."

"The overly friendly one. Drools on your khakis. Wags his tail and follows you around when you scoop poop. Yes, him. Put him in solitary to cool off."

"Do you have to call it solitary?" As if the single-occupancy rooms were jail cells. It smacked of cruelty. Yet Lizbeth found herself unhooking a leash at the gate. She didn't have to call Charlie to her, since he was right there wagging his tail and smiling his distinctive Labrador smile. His long, white teeth sparkled more brightly than she remembered.

"Time-out room, then. Rest room. Pick whatever euphemism suits you. God, why did I ever start this business? Are you having some kind of trouble?"

Lizbeth tried to control her shaking hands, but they trembled despite her mind's commands. She managed to clip Charlie's leash to the collar, though he lunged away with an excess of enthusiasm. He wagged his tail furiously. "No trouble at all."

"Good. I'm taking the rest of the day off. Lock up when you leave."

"But I leave at 3:00. The dogs' owners get here at 5:00."

"Would you please stay until 5:30, just for today? I'd really appreciate it. Thanks, Michelle."

At that moment, Charlie pulled forward. Lizbeth stumbled and almost fell on her chin.

As she hauled the dog back, his leash pinching the tender flesh of her palm, she noticed one of the other big dogs squat. The first of her afternoon chores streamed out.

The front door clicked shut.

"Great!" she shouted mutinously.

But Lizbeth stayed late, cleaned up, and matched the dogs with their owners when they arrived, some of whom she thought she recognized from television. She stayed past 7:00. Who else would care for the dogs, if not her?

The Hollywood types were nice enough people, but many carried an air of demanding impatience—as if they'd pigeon-holed Lizbeth on first glance as a submissive and therefore didn't need to treat her with respect.

Then again, maybe she was oversensitive about dominance and submission issues, Lizbeth thought wryly as she drove the long way home, squinting at the lingering Los Angeles sunshine.

She had no business driving to The Dungeon.

An orange quality to the light, flashing off building windows and car paint jobs and sidewalks, soothed her. The smog and heat made her somnolent, and the memory of Ro's face appeared in her mind, handsome and stern and knowing. Her flesh felt heavy and tingly with desire as she thought of Ro's touch.

She had to see him again.

Her heart began to hammer in her chest. It was wrong, it was perverse, it was dangerous. She should drive straight home.

The lure of Ro directed her steering.

She parked in front of the club.

He was outside.

Ro worked on the sidewalk, cleaning glass and staring critically up at his nightclub sign. The sight of him outside, laboring in the fading daylight like an ordinary mortal, made him less intimidating. He worked for a living, just like her.

Then he looked up and their eyes locked. No, he was anything but ordinary. He was more attractive, more graceful, more *there* than other men. His torso twisted as he set down a sponge, and his graceful stride toward her exuded power and confidence. She felt a momentary clash of desires: she wanted him, badly, but she also desperately needed to possess some of that power and confidence.

She laughed, a bit bewildered, as she climbed out of her car. Amazing how he had the ability to turn her mind into a twisted mass of contradictions, and make her body eager for his touch, just with one look.

He wore black jeans, this time, and a snug-fitting black T-shirt that showcased his strong shoulders and taut waist.

"I was just going to grab a bite to eat inside. Join me?"

"I don't mean to interrupt you . . ."

"Sure you do. You just told a lie." His eyes laughed. She sucked in her breath as memories of the night before filled her mind, her skin tingling all over as if he were touching her once more.

He stepped into her personal space as if he had a right to it. She supposed she'd given him the right last night. She sure wasn't about to revoke it. He towered over her and around her once more and she had to fight the urge to drag him into the club, back to that alcove. . . .

She concentrated. "Yes, thanks. I'd welcome some real food. The dogs ate better than I did today."

"You train them somewhere nearby?"

"Um . . ." Tell the truth, that she was a lowly peon? Images of everyone she knew, from Posh to the customers to the dogs themselves, all united in their disregard for her, speared her with anxiety. Ro might stop his unique tutelage if he suspected she was that much of a doormat. "I run a dog day care facility not far from here." She did run it. When Posh wasn't around.

"That's wonderful. You must be great with animals. And, you can relate to the problems a start-up business faces."

"Yes. It can be a challenge." Stretching the truth again. But she had owned half the breeding business in Alabama. She shifted on feet sore despite her cushy, thick-soled work shoes. Lizbeth remembered the tall, slim heels Posh wore with such ease. She'd bet Posh didn't have sore feet.

"I'm all alone for hours and hours. Until doors open tonight." He offered his arm once more. "Keep me company?"

She doubted a man like him lacked for company. Whenever he wanted it and with whomever he chose. His proximity and his words gave her a familiar breath-stealing pang of delight. She placed her hand on his arm.

She narrowed her eyes with the sensual pleasure of touching him. How nice to feel his bare skin, his lightly haired forearm warmed by the sun and his own body heat. Her hand wanted to move over it, caress it. She made herself keep still. His natural scent—a clean masculine sweat and some faint exotic cologne—intoxicated her.

Her mind leapt ahead, wondering if he'd lead her to the café she remembered from the night before . . . or to that alcove, which she remembered so much more vividly.

She blushed, appalled at herself. What kind of charisma did he possess that ran such end runs around her second thoughts?

They walked together up the steps into the vast and silent darkness of the empty club.

When the heavy door swung shut behind them the resulting echoes made it feel as if she'd stepped into a cavern rather than a club. But there was the same long bar. Its smoky mirror reflected the fading light from the front stained-glass window. And the clean-scrubbed dark wooden floor was fully revealed.

She hadn't noticed the beautiful matched sets of wooden chairs and tables in the café.

"Do you want it fast, or do you want it good?" Ro asked as she settled into a chair.

She couldn't help the thoughts that sprang to mind. "Excuse me?"

"The food."

Lizbeth's heart slowed down. "Fast. I need your expertise on something, afterward."

He nodded, noncommittal, and walked past her to the back room. Moments later he returned with a couple of saran-wrapped sandwiches and two sodas. "I keep fresh stuff in the fridge for me and the staff," he explained as he placed hers on the table.

She tried not to wolf the delicious sandwich.

He did wolf his. Gone in four bites. He grinned, lounged in his chair, his eyes resting easily on hers. His relaxed confidence failed to put her at ease. She could tell those eyes missed very little. And why couldn't she stop thinking about those danger-ous teeth nibbling their way down her body, pausing every so often to bite?

He shifted in his chair and his T-shirt stretched across his chest. She tried and failed to avoid looking at the pectorals it re-vealed. His arms looked immensely capable, too. Which they were, she remembered.

"It's not just for the dogs, is it? Your need to learn domi-nance."

Lizbeth jerked in her seat. She lowered her food to the plate. How did he know?

"Something's happened to you to make you want to change. You don't have to tell me. However, my 'expertise' might be better targeted if you do." He waited.

When she didn't speak, he nodded. "Let me tell you some-thing then, Lizbeth. Submissive people, just like animals, give off a subliminal vibe. Gestures and posture combine into a wavelength that tells me they're looking for a dominant. Someone to take control. To make them feel safe and fulfilled. There is absolutely nothing wrong with someone giving this vibe. Submissiveness is as natural as dominance, and subs wield more power than you might suspect. But you. You give off a mixed signal. I wonder why."

Should she tell him? Lizbeth agonized, picking at the remains of her sandwich. He might despise her. On the other hand, he sounded as if he might actually understand.

She mulled, then decided.

"My dog Sasquatch. He bit me." Lizbeth took a deep breath. Plunged in. "Long story short. Mom and my older sister always lectured me to stick up for myself, while bossing me around. Dad left her when I was very young—maybe that had something to do with it—but they were real control freaks. Mom was the worst." Lizbeth shrugged and smiled, but felt the thickness in her throat that presaged tears. She fought them grimly. "When I wanted honest affection and someone to listen to me, I preferred my dogs. Mom didn't mean anything bad. She just wanted me to grow up capable and strong, so I'd never be a victim. But I wasn't like Nora, and they never stopped trying to improve me. Pound me down a lot, then build me up a little. You know? Then, Ted. Single-minded, financially well-off, traditional values . . . and willing to take over from my mom in regard to controlling me."

She didn't see Ro change position, but sensed a sudden stillness in him, as an animal coming to cautious attention. "Ted let me start my own dog training and breeding business. It started small, but when I bred some pedigreed champions, my reputation grew. Then one of the local TV channels covered my training routine. Business started to boom, and Ted became a partner to help manage the money.

"Then, disaster. My Akita, Sasquatch. My gentle, humane

methods of handling and training—using clickers and treats and lots of patience—seemed to work most of the time, but not always. When Mom and Nora heard from Ted about the hourly rates I charged for training and the premium stud fees I was able to get, they got involved, too. They started micromanaging, and I started doubting myself, just like always. It all went to hell when I got in a difficult bitch to mate. Sasquatch took one sniff and growled at her! I put the bitch in the rack, but Sasquatch still wasn't interested. He ran away from me and wouldn't come when I called, even when I tried to lure him with treats. Nora and Mom kept saying I should use a stronger hand, that I wasn't assertive enough. Ted . . . he just smirked. They all said I'd never get Sasquatch to obey me unless I showed him who's boss." Lizbeth felt the self-disgust that accompanied the memory. "Part of me thought they might be right. I got an animal control loop and dragged Sasquatch toward the bitch. 'Don't you let that dog walk all over you,' Mom was yelling. And so help me, I wasn't going to. He struggled, so I threw him to the ground four or five times.

"When I let my guard down with Sasquatch, he bit me. Hard enough to draw blood. Then he ran and hid. Mom and Nora flipped out about him biting me. The next day, while I was out, Mom sold Sasquatch." Lizbeth blinked away tears. "Ted claimed he didn't know about it. I was finally able to pry the buyer's information from Mom and drove there within a couple of days, but the family she'd sold him to wouldn't sell him back. Said their youngest kid had already bonded. They let me say good-bye, though. The hardest thing I ever had to do was leave Sasquatch there. I heard him howl when I drove away."

"That must have been incredibly difficult."

Lizbeth managed a small, bitter smile. "Yes. Because it's all my fault. Oh, my mom shouldn't have sold him behind my back. But it never would have happened if I hadn't been such a doormat." Self-loathing colored her voice. "I should have been the alpha dog with Sasquatch all along. Not to mention standing up to them all along. When I finally did try to be the alpha, I did it wrong. I didn't know how."

Ro spoke in a low, encouraging voice. "And that's when you moved here and started over at the dog day care?"

"Uh-huh. Clean break from the past. Except . . ."

"Except the past followed you here."

Lizbeth started, remembering Ted's arrival. But of course Ro didn't know about that. He knew nothing but what she told him. She was determined to tell him the truth as best she could. "Yes. I wanted a fresh start. But it's like Mom and Nora are still in my head whispering that I'm not smart enough, strong enough. I can still see Ted smirking. At work, customers walk all over me. Everywhere, I have trouble sticking up for myself."

Lizbeth lowered her gaze, feeling her face heat with the shameful admission. Now was when he'd make some excuse and throw her out, if he was going to.

She felt his large, warm fingers gently tilt her chin up. His lips curved slightly in an understanding smile, and his eyes were compassionate. "Thank you for trusting me. It means more to me than you realize."

Lizbeth felt her insides swirl pleasantly.

"I think I see," he continued, gazing at her with speculation. "And now, here you are. Where you think you can learn assertiveness. From me."

The way he was looking at her made her nervous, but it wasn't the kind of nervous that made her want to pinch her arm for relief. Instead, her heart beat a little faster with anticipation, and she felt warm all over.

"Isn't that right?" He waited for her to nod. "Then, let's practice taking what you want. Come with me."

"Now? Here?"

"Now. Here." He smiled at her reluctance, unfazed. "Trust me."

She felt a smile tug at her lips. The odd thing was, she did trust him. Her instincts informed her he wasn't a sadistic killer. Sadistic, perhaps. He might torture her. Just not to death.

She stood. "Lead on."

He did. When he reached a thick wooden door, he stopped. It was the Cage Room she remembered seeing last time.

Ro made a long, old-fashioned bronze skeleton key appear in his hand. "This room—this key—is special. It's awarded as a judgment during The Dungeon's Saturday night Crime and Punishment Party." He handed her the key.

Feeling a return of the sensual exhilaration that he brought out in her, she inserted the key into the lock.

4

Ro watched Lizbeth push open the thick wooden door.

When she saw what lay inside, her sweet little mouth parted with astonishment. She stood as if rooted.

He smiled at her reaction, savoring the avaricious look that stole over her face. It was a special look he'd come to recognize, one that reflected the desire any submissive felt upon gazing at BDSM tools and furniture.

And Lizbeth was a submissive. She didn't know it yet, and wouldn't like it when she found out, considering her stated goal to be dominant. But there was no doubt in Ro's mind, not after the way she'd responded to him.

She slowly circled the room.

Compared to the main nightclub, this more private room contained a larger ratio of imaginatively designed equipment. He gazed with pride at his enormous St. Andrew's Cross against the opposite wall, the enormous X of sturdy, solid wood with D-rings bolted at each corner. Would she stop at that one? No, she kept going after only one curious touch. The padded wall rack barely won a glance. She lingered over the altar-style bondage bed, the hardwood centerpiece to the room with its leather straps and steel rings. Supported by four thick legs and varnished to a warm satin glow, it would have made a delightful choice, to him. But aside from testing its upholstered surface and trailing fingertips over its attachment points, she gave it no more attention than the rest.

She stroked a wooden wheel, taller than she was, and fondled the four restraints jutting out. He couldn't help being charmed by the tentative way she touched the assorted sizes of Ben Wa balls, then picked them up to squeeze them, clearly baffled as to their purpose, before moving on to examine a black alloy spreader bar with adjustable cotter pins.

He watched, increasingly aroused, as Lizbeth gazed a long time at his pride and joy, a functionally modified iron maiden, set tall and imposing in the far corner. What sublime heights he could take her to, if he could strap her inside that monster, helplessly waiting to be pierced.

Lizbeth reached the rocking horse with its pleasure saddle. As she ran her hands over the saddle's erect and waiting double dildos a small surprised sound jerked out of her. Ro felt a twinge of desire that narrowed his eyes. Lizbeth impaled and begging, but forced to keep the horse rocking: the erotic fantasy made him rock hard.

He couldn't help it. Part of him thrilled to a woman being tied up, straining at the bonds while he teased and pleasured her. Flesh pinkening under his ministrations. Gasps of pain, tears of frustration, screams of ecstasy. He adored it. It was reason enough to open a place like his Dungeon, he supposed, but of course not the only reason.

It was time to teach Lizbeth her true nature. His voice came out rough. "We're going to play a small game. The name of this game is Take What You Want. Pick a toy, a piece of furniture, a bondage tool. Use what you wish, as you wish."

She flashed him a playful smile that surprised him. "Anything? You mean I have to choose?" She stroked one of the dildos. It set his cock on fire.

"You want to learn dominance. If that's truly what you want, then be dominant. Be aggressive." Ro held out his arms, offering his bare wrists. "I won't resist. My safe word is . . . 'butterfly.'"

"'Butterfly'?"

He saw her skepticism. He hid his smile. He'd picked the gentlest, most innocuous little safe word he could think of. He wanted to be totally unthreatening to her. "I don't plan on saying it," he taunted her. Deliberately goading, he added, "You couldn't get me to say it, believe me."

Her eyebrows shot up. "A challenge. But, I thought you said I had to learn to 'bottom' before I could 'top.'"

Was that a note of longing in her voice? Ro hid another smile.

"Originally, yes. But now I understand your desperate desire to become dominant. Dominate me."

"Okay. Um . . . would you please go to the back corner, by that tall sarcophagus thing?"

He liked that she'd picked the iron maiden. But he didn't move. "Really? That polite little request is your idea of dominance?"

"Should I just grab a whip and start hitting you?"

She was becoming frustrated.

Good.

"Is that the best you can do?" he chided. He sauntered, slow enough to show his disregard. Away from the iron maiden.

A loud crack in the enclosed room halted him. He turned in time to see her holding a bullwhip away from her with a look of shock on her face. "It's louder than I thought." She flicked it again, cracking it closer to him. The sound was like a pistol shot.

He took a hasty step back. "Maybe you should—"

Crack. Her intent look of concentration would have seemed pained, if it weren't for the sadistic glint that suddenly flashed in her eyes. That was as he'd expected. She felt the sense of power, but didn't inhabit the role naturally. It was work.

He played along. "What if you slowed it down a bit—"

"Quiet, worm!" Another crack of the whip. "Get over there."

Ro complied. Very soon now, she'd remember how much she'd enjoyed being bound and dominated. She'd accept her nature. Any minute.

She pointed the whip. "Get inside."

Ro inched into the iron maiden, the vertical casket with its chains and restraints, and its forest of spikes. The spikes were made of pointed rubber. Far gentler than the rusty metal spikes in authentic iron maidens, designed to impale the victim when the casket closed. But the rubber ones gave an attention-getting poking if one weren't careful.

Anticipation about what she'd do next zinged through him. How long had it been since he'd let someone dominate him? Even with Lizbeth a raw novice, he couldn't deny it was exciting. Not nearly as exciting as mastering her body again, but fun.

How long would it take her to figure out that only submitting to him could truly delight her? He settled in, determined to wait her out.

From his position inside the iron maiden he watched her peruse his Cage Room. She approached the wall where the accessories were kept. Slapper bats on their hooks with the other tools: leather and fleece rods, braided and knotted riding crops, even metal-studded paddles and gloves. She glanced at the other, less-common accessories. He doubted she'd use the balls, bars, gags, clamps, cages, or spreaders. But that blindfold . . . ah, she lifted it off its hook. She stroked the softness of its leather. Contoured, with an elastic back.

She approached, letting the blindfold dangle between two fingers. "Put this on."

Ro eased it over his head. He could feel the leather dent his hair. His vision departed, replaced by blackness.

Doubt suddenly assailed him. What if he was wrong about Lizbeth?

Pressing his lips tightly together, his hands by his side, he made a granite block of his chin, holding himself as immobile as he could.

She touched one of his arms, and it took all his control not to react. Next to his hip there was a padded leather manacle. She closed it around his wrist. The delicate, warm touch of her fingers threading the buckle stirred him. She did the same to his other wrist. Interesting sensation of vulnerability, being blindfolded and buckled.

Then, nothing. No sound of her movement. Possibly she was stumped. Perhaps she was wondering why she didn't feel the same titillation about locking him up as she did about being manacled. It was the nature of the beast.

He was about to tell her so, when she kissed him.

Silent, hot, and ravenous, her lips met his. Startled, he jerked, then hissed as the rubber spikes poked him in the back. Every one of his nerves seemed to be extra receptive, and though pain-pricks didn't pierce flesh, it did get his full attention. Very interesting.

"Steady there, big fella," Lizbeth said, her own voice mirroring his earlier mocking tone. "I'd hate for you to damage this body." She ran her hand over his chest, up to his chin, and over his lips. She replaced her fingers with lips again, and he could feel her heat radiating from her mouth. Her chest pressed against his. Very bold.

She wouldn't get any more reactions out of him, he determined.

He heard her rummaging. "Hmm, what's this?" From the

buzzing, she'd discovered some of the battery-operated toys. Then, rattle of metal. *Handcuffs.* Clinking. *Anal beads.* Clicks and clanks and snips and thuds. *Metal-studded cat-o'-nine tails, chain sets, nipple clamps, ball gags.*

Was she trying to intimidate him with their various sounds? He smiled even as his breath sped up. She was so cute.

When he could feel her in front of him again, he slowly arched one eyebrow over his blindfold. He gave a small, mocking smile. He'd bet anything she was blushing like an embarrassed schoolgirl caught playing dress up.

Suddenly, he felt her small warm hands moving over his chest in little circles, as if savoring the feel of the broad expanse of his chest through his shirt. He tried not to enjoy her surprisingly aggressive touch, especially when she grazed his nipples. He noticed the way her breath quickened.

She let her hands wander up to his shoulders and down one arm, lingering on his bicep—he felt a moment's vain satisfaction that he'd never stopped working out—and down farther, caressing cord and sinew on his lower arm before the leather of the manacle interrupted her exploration. Fingertips trailed sensuously against his half-open palm on the other side. He couldn't completely keep his hand from twitching slightly, which irritated him.

He wished she would step against him to feel the length of his body pressed against the length of hers. He would have done that.

She did ease closer. He could smell her heat, and the scent of fabric softener under the musk of the dogs she'd worked with all day. Good, earthy smells.

He thought rapidly, trying to distract himself. He wondered at her experience training dogs, at her need to dominate them. To become a more dominant person. She failed to realize she didn't need force and intimidation to control dogs, or to stand up for herself with people. She didn't need to become an aggressive, leader-of-the-pack type. She simply needed to sense her own gentle authority.

He hoped their play session helped her sense it. Soon.

Ro felt the air warm as the space between them shrank. All thoughts of pack dynamics evaporated. Her body met his like a homecoming, her heat mingling with his own. She turned her head, rubbing her cheek sensuously against the soft material of his shirt. Her low sound of satisfaction had him twitching again, with increasing discomfort from the ache in his cock.

He felt little tugs as she nipped at the material of his shirt. "Good enough to eat," she said.

Ro cleared his throat. "Okay. I think we might want to switch things around. . . ."

Her only response was to nibble at his chest and then his belly, causing a warm flurry of desire to cascade through his body. He tried desperately to remain impervious.

When she exchanged nipping for licking, he knew he was in trouble. Warm moist heat followed the point of her tongue. A sudden gust of cool wind told him she'd lifted up his shirt. He flinched at the sensual assault of her hand sliding underneath to caress his stomach. She followed the trail with her lips. Around, up, down his taut belly. She stuffed his shirt up under his pinned arms.

Pleasure spiked through him as she ran her hands down over his waistline, then traced the juncture of pants and flesh. He noticed his mouth had fallen slightly open only when he shut it so hard his teeth clicked together. She wouldn't dare. Would she?

"You don't think I'll do it, do you?" She didn't need to explain what "it" was, not while her fingers investigated just under the rim of his pants.

Ro was worried. One could only withstand so much.

When he felt her kneel, his breath caught in his throat. There were her hands again. Stroking his legs, exploring slowly up the back, as if she enjoyed discovering him inch by inch. Her hand brushed across the front of his crotch. His entire body vibrated. He felt a twinge of pain and realized his wrists had strained against his bonds to the point of pinching. "Let me out."

"What's the magic word?" Her voice was a singsong. She was enjoying this? When he had her at his mercy, he was going to take diabolic revenge.

He determined anew to reveal nothing further. Made his voice bored. "I thought you'd finished playing. When you're ready to learn how it's done, let me know."

"You'll know when I'm done."

The sensual promise made his stomach sink pleasurably with sudden fierce desire.

He heard something that made his blood stop, then surge hotly. The whisper of material as she pulled her clothes off. He imagined her lifting her shirt over her head, and the mental image teased him like a feather tickling the inside of his brain. He could almost see it. He could feel it and smell it: Lizbeth held the shirt to his cheek, rubbing it against the rough shadow-growth on his jaw, gliding it under his nose before letting it drop down next to their feet. There was a muted snap; her bra being unhooked. Confirmation came when she treated him to a face rub with those lacy cups, as well. He felt it slither from her fingers to join her shirt at their feet.

He swallowed audibly.

The peaks of her breasts were pebble hard when she stepped against him. "Nice," she crooned in a breathless voice, rubbing herself against him. Shameless and teasing. A bitch in heat. He certainly felt like a stud ready to mount her, rut with her. He could think of little else.

She slid her hands around his body, to rest on his back. Just when he started to relax, she raked her nails forward, modifying the pressure so that it didn't break the skin. At the same time she kissed one of his exposed nipples, swirling her tongue around the edges where the thinnest hair grew.

He hissed with surprise. It made her tilt her nails up and reverse direction so that her fingertips caressed the path she'd taken around his side, soothing him, then reversed again until she could run her fingers up his front with gentleness. "Sure you don't want to say your word?" she asked. He could only press his lips together as she kissed the nipple, and then just below it. And then lower. His stomach again. Flicking her tongue.

He knew where she was going; she'd given him enough clues. His restraints rattled as he made a reflexive move backward, then he cursed softly as the rubber spikes reminded him backward wasn't an option. His hands fisted.

Her hands rested on the belt of his jeans. She wiggled the leather end, slapping it playfully back down against him. "What was that word again?"

He could feel the dampness of perspiration on his forehead. With a supreme effort he kept his voice steady. "A pretty, flying insect."

Giving an especially forceful slap with the belt, she traced after the path of her slapping with her fingers. Stinging pain, caressing pleasure. Then she began unthreading his belt. He knew the evidence of his arousal bulged against the seam of his pants, but there was nothing he could do about it. He would be lucky not to embarrass himself.

She laughed. The throaty, womanly sound of it was a delight to him, even as it drove him to previously unknown heights of arousal. How he wanted to punish her for her presumption. How he wanted her to continue.

Unzipping the front of his pants, she revealed inch after inch of what made his pants bulge. His soft briefs slid down as she opened his pants.

"Oh lord," she breathed. She touched him experimentally. He felt his cock jump against her palm. She stroked once, reflexively.

He made a choking sound in his throat.

She moved her hand.

He had to hold out. Ro desperately shifted away from her bewitching touch, but she chased him, grasped him. Stroked again.

When she took him into her mouth he lunged against the spikes. A curse jerked from him.

Lizbeth paused long enough to say, primly, "That does not sound like a pretty, flying insect."

She stroked the length of him down to his dark nest of hair, and then slowly back up. It was what he remembered doing to her: slow torture. She used her tongue on him the way he'd used his fingers on her. Leisurely, as if she had all the time in the world. From his perspective, fighting the waves of pleasure assaulting him, time dragged painfully.

She had to figure it out on her own, he reminded himself desperately.

He wasn't sure he could last that long.

He trembled, stilled, trembled again. She cupped him where he was soft and let her warm breath whisper against his flesh. Then she dove down with her mouth once more, wrapping her hand around his root and moving up with the rhythm that her mouth established.

Ro wished he could detach himself from his traitorous organ. Just for a little while.

Then the miracle happened.

First she made a small sound of frustration that he felt through his cock. Then she stopped. Cool air didn't chill his lust. Especially now, with what he suspected was about to occur.

He smiled, imagining her state. She'd felt the friction of her jeans against her mound as she'd moved with the rhythm, and the tightness of her nipples had to be nearly painful with nothing touching them, nobody stroking them, pinching them and caressing them. She craved his touch. But how could he touch her? He was locked up. Now she'd be realizing, with a gasping sort of pleasure, that she wanted nothing more than to give him control, so he could give her what she needed. She wanted him in the most expeditious and forceful way possible.

But that couldn't happen while he was confined, could it? Of course not.

"Tsk, tsk," he said. "An unfinished job. What are we going to do about this?"

She stood, and it was all he could do not to lunge toward her. He was as ready as she was. Obviously.

But what was this? She stepped close, tilting her head to kiss his jawline, her breath ragged with frustration. Didn't she know she was supposed to release him, not toy with him further? She gave more teasing little kisses.

Enough. He bent his head to savagely possess her mouth with his own. His lips demanded that she return the pressure, and she did, and they commanded that she open her mouth to him, and she did that too. All his senses tingled. He knew hers did too by the way her body shivered and melted against his. When his tongue slipped in to play with hers the sensations heightened until his entire body ached for her. He pulled away only with the greatest of effort.

Now. Now she had to realize that trying to torture him was torturing her more. She wanted his hands caressing her, his lips on her body. She wanted confident and punishing handling. If that wasn't exactly the raw, aching need raging across her body at this point, he'd close the place down and become a boring lawyer.

"Ro, honey?" Her voice was velvet and molasses, husky with need.

"Yes?"

"You said the name of this game is Take What You Want. I'm going to free your hands because I want them on my body. God how I want them, and you inside me, right now."

He closed his eyes with relief as she lifted the blindfold from his head.

She unbuckled his wrists, one hand after another, and stepped back. He didn't try to hide the passion burning inside him as he opened his eyes.

He observed her moment of apprehension as he rubbed his wrists against each other, absently soothing his self-inflicted abrasions. Stepped out of the pooled material of his pants without the slightest self-consciousness. Taking his time. He stoked her fear and lust by just staring at her, sure his eyes threw flame as they roved over her body. "You are going to be sore tomorrow."

He didn't miss the way her breath caught, hearing it. Or the way her nipples stayed nice and hard.

With one rough move he grabbed her, dragging her against him, locking her in the vise of his arms. His mouth came down on hers, bruising in its intensity. Her small cry of helpless need rolled through him like the most potent aphrodisiac in the world. This was what they both needed. Crushed against his cock, she was causing him pain as well as pleasure, but he didn't mind.

He was about to return the favor.

Her arms wrapped around his neck as she offered herself up to him. Her lips, parted and swollen in the fiery aftermath of his possession, looked wetly ripe.

Gazing down at her, he felt an unexpected surge of affection. "Go lie face down on the spanking bench." Without waiting for her to obey, he shoved her in the desired direction.

Stumbling, but clearly still high on sensuality, Lizbeth looked at him with pleading eyes. Submissive eyes. It was all he could do not to rip her clothes off and take her immediately. She slowly went.

Not fast enough. "Now!" he barked, landing a blow with his cupped palm on her ass. Her clothes would blunt the sting, but not the shock of his hitting her, however gently. Her eyes widened. This would be the test of it, he knew.

"Ro. I . . . you're not supposed to . . ." Lizbeth panted for breath, obviously still wanting him. And wanting she knew not what.

Ro smiled. He knew what she wanted, even if she didn't. "Do you remember your safe word?"

Her hands floated to her neck. She nodded, understanding. Without another word, she turned and went to the padded bench. She crawled onto it, positioning her knees on the spread pads. After a moment, she grasped the handholds.

His heart swelled with gratitude for her trust. "Well done. Except for one thing." He strode to the bench, felt her twitch as he grasped around to the front of her pants, unfastened them quickly, and pulled them, along with her panties, to mid-thigh. The smooth pale globes of her ass looked as inviting as anything he'd ever seen. "Better," he breathed, his hand tingling with anticipation.

Nothing could have kept him from running his hands over her bare cheeks. "You know what's going to happen now, don't you." She trembled. He waited for her to nod awkwardly, her forehead down against the bench pad.

He positioned himself by her side, not yet letting any part of his body make contact with hers. The bench raised her to the perfect height. His hands were large and sensitive, the fingers thick and long. Cupping his hand slightly, he let it settle on her sweet spot, the lower area of her ass that would be creased if she were standing rather than bent over before him. Her small sound of distress made him smile.

Then he raised his arm, palm still cupped, and swung it

down to make sharp contact. The force of it made her lunge forward slightly. She gasped, then stilled when she felt his hand still on her, transmitting its heat and his domination directly into her body. She whimpered, and he narrowed his eyes with pleasure.

He raised his arm again, and brought it down once more. Another lunge and gasp, but this time her trembling continued. Not waiting this time, he raised his arm and brought his hand down on her sweet spot repeatedly, making it considerably warmer and drawing louder gasps from Lizbeth.

When he judged the time was right, he flattened his hand. With the harder, sharper feel of his flat hand he slapped first one rounded cheek, then the other, until both turned bright pink. The sight of his hand's imprint moved him. The feel of her heated skin, the sound of her lunging against the bench with her little grunts of distress, the sight of her exposed and vulnerable position, all stirred him emotionally.

There was a thickness in his throat that he sometimes felt during an exceptionally hot session.

He paused, stroking her back, and checked in with her. "Are you okay?"

No answer.

"Lizbeth." He said it gently. After a moment, he said her name again, and lifted her chin so he could see her face.

Her eyes were dreamy, unseeing.

Ro laughed, delighted.

He gently pressed his lips against her neck, nibbling, knowing it left hot trails of tingling sensation up and down. He alternated, bringing his hands into play, giving delicate, tantalizing touches as he bent to where her breasts had been pressed to either side of the spanking bench. He enjoyed her shivers of delight almost as much as her fearful cry earlier, as he plucked at her taut nipples.

Then his hands moved gently down her sides, up over her

back. Soothing her. "You've done very, very well," he praised her.

She trembled. Her ass moved in a slow, grinding circle against the bench. Then: "*More.*"

He heard a tormented groan, and realized it was his own. She was astonishing. He couldn't keep going like this. His cock had endured enough.

She ground against the bench again. He cursed, then yanked her pants farther down her legs. She helped, panting and eager, as they both tried to remove her clothes, getting in each other's way with their urgency.

When she lay totally exposed, her cheeks pinkened and positioned just right for him, Ro stood behind her. He'd selected one of the thinnest, full-sensation condoms and as he rolled it over himself he spoke to her. "You said you want my hands. And you want me inside you."

His cock nudged at her inner thigh. He probed with his fingers, using them to spread her. He let his thumb and forefinger twirl her clit, yanking a cry of pleasure from her. As the cry peaked, he shoved himself inside her, deliberately rough. The cry changed to one of alarm.

He shoved harder, bending over to whisper in her ear. "You asked, and I'm giving it to you. I know it hurts.

"Take it."

He thrust into her again. He could feel her rapture in the way she stopped fighting it, meeting his thrusts with trembling eagerness.

Desire snaked to the pit of his stomach, rose to his heart. It was perfect. She was perfect. He was going to come like he never had before.

Suddenly, a loud crash came from the main room.

5

Ro's reaction—cursing, withdrawing—yanked her right out of the exquisite sensation of their coupling.

Stunned, she froze for a long moment, as if her tight grip on the handholds would make the interruption go away. By the time she pushed herself to her knees, and then up to her feet, Ro was zipping his zipper and rushing out of the Cage Room.

Lizbeth could still feel his heat on her body. Her lips tingled as she exhaled into the suddenly empty room. The magic he'd made her feel still fuzzed her brain and made her legs wobbly and uncertain.

Belatedly, reality set in and made her dive for her clothes, yanking them on. Was it a robber? A gang? Was someone still out there, and did they have a gun?

She whirled around, looking for a weapon. She wouldn't rush out behind Ro only to end up like those root-tripping girls in Hollywood horror films, meat for the butcher. Neither would she huddle in the back room while her man was mugged and beaten. Her eyes fell on the line of whips. She picked up the largest and raced toward the door.

She met Ro racing back in. He was backlit by the club lights he'd turned on in the main room. Between those and the dim lighting of the Cage Room she could see his agitation. He held something in his hand.

He blinked when he saw her brandishing the whip. Plucking it deftly from her grip, he said, "You were worried for me. Thank you." He touched her cheek. "I'm not used to people worrying about me."

She imagined he wasn't. He looked capable of handling anything.

He hefted a chunk of cement cinderblock, held it sideways so she could clearly read the spray-painted words. "Someone threw this through the stained-glass window."

" 'Pornographer' . . . ?"

He turned it until the offending word faced the floor. He said nothing.

"Who did this?"

Ro shrugged. "Good question."

"Someone who doesn't approve of your business. . . ."

"Yes."

". . . and someone who thinks you're a pornographer." A horrible thought occurred to her.

Tracking it, he frowned. "No. I'm not a pornographer."

Lizbeth felt chastened by the disappointment in his voice.

He continued with dignity. "I run a fetish nightclub. A well-organized, clean, and highly supervised club for consenting adults."

"Of course you do. I know that." She stared at the hunk of cement. "Aren't you going to call the police?"

Ro laughed, a cynical sound. "Not this time. I did a few weeks ago. I asked them to clear some noisy transients from the alley—you know, next to the sidewalk where the line forms. When the cops showed up and saw some people in bondage gear, they didn't bother. They called The Dungeon a titty bar to my face. Said it attracts trash." A small facial tic twitched next to Ro's eye. "They didn't clear the transients. I doubt they'd try real hard to find the vandal, seeing as how they share his sentiments."

"They can't just—"

"They can. They have. It baffles me how ignorance can flourish to the point where peace officers don't do their jobs. I could pursue it—it wouldn't be difficult to bring a lawsuit—but that's not my bag anymore. This stupid vandalism, it's not what's important."

Ro set the cement down. "I haven't given you anything close to proper aftercare." He enfolded her in a comforting bear hug. "Mostly because I hadn't planned on ending the scene quite so abruptly."

Lizbeth enjoyed the bass vibration of his voice. She felt enclosed and safe in his arms, which seemed contradictory: he'd been the one hitting her. And then having sex with her. Emotions swirled through her: deep shame, undampened lust, vulnerability, fascination. The pain hadn't really hurt. Well, it had, but it had gone deeper than that. Deeper and sweeter. She'd felt so wonderful, euphoric and floaty, and then it had all crashed. Literally. "Aftercare," she murmured, snuggling into him, needing the comfort. She felt his warm exhalation against her hair. "I like aftercare."

"Most submissives do."

She stiffened against him. His words had been like icy water poured over her. "I'm not submissive." She stepped away.

Ro looked pained. "You're magnificent. Brave. Assertive." He reached for her, but she dodged his grasp. His eyes telegraphed his disapproval. His disappointment. And . . . his hurt?

She hated hurting him. It surprised her, how much she hated it. But she hated what he'd said more. "You called me submissive."

"Lizbeth. You are an amazing woman. Responsive and sensual." He made a small movement of his shoulders that was almost a shrug. "You took what you wanted, didn't you?"

"Yes . . ."

"You don't feel regrets?"

"No. But you called me—"

"I call you my fantasy come to life." He was looking into her eyes when he said it. She could see the truth of his words. Her heart fluttered pleasurably. "Am I? That's nice."

Ro's lips quirked into a small smile. "Nice? I practically call you a goddess, and you say I'm 'nice.' Wonderful."

They gazed at each other. She felt the pull of him. Resisted. "Ro. I hope you won't take this wrong, but I'd like to go process all this."

He was nodding before she even finished. "I understand. You'll be back? You'll be in touch?"

She eased away. "Certainly." It would be foolish to leap into a relationship with Ro, the way her heart and her body wanted. Too crazy and too soon. Even if he was the most intense thing she'd ever experienced. The pile of doggy-doo that was her old life was still being scooped. Ted living in her apartment made things extra messy. How could she explain him to Ro? She'd have to confess her lack of spine in kicking Ted out, and that would just confirm his diagnosis of "submissive."

She had to get rid of Ted. She swallowed. "Ro, I really should go."

He gazed at her. "Okay. At least promise me you'll come back on Friday. It's The Dungeon's first Crime and Punishment Party. Should be lots of fun." His eyes sparkled as he offered her a small, wicked smile. "No participation required."

Lizbeth was already nodding. "Definitely!" Then, because she couldn't resist the cruel curve of his lips, she stepped against him and planted a good-bye kiss before leaving to deal with her unwanted roommate.

*   *   *

Days later, she was still trying to get rid of Ted.

"This is so great," he enthused as they passed through another savory cloud of aroma outside another popular Santa Monica promenade restaurant. "I'll miss this when we go back home. Let's read the menu." He pulled her, too hard, to another plastic-laminated menu just off the restaurant's patio seating area. Giorgiana's Italian Cottage, was this one. Smallish and crowded with beautifully dressed, exquisitely tanned men and women. Most everyone looked thin, healthy, and suspiciously blond.

"Quaint," Ted observed. The touch of his finger to his lip was an affectation he'd developed seemingly overnight, as was the precise walk, so different from the head-down stride he'd had in Alabama. Los Angeles was bringing out a strange side of him. It was as if he'd absorbed the week's bright sunshine into himself, only to emit its glow during the city nights. Or maybe his exuberance was pride in his new clothes. He'd always lived in loose jeans or khakis with a knit shirt in a neutral shade. The purple shirt he wore kept shocking her with its splash of vibrant color, and his new black jeans fit snugly over Doc Marten boots.

She felt her legs swish against the medium-length black silk skirt she'd chosen. Tonight was a special occasion.

She planned to instruct Ted to go back home. Alone. Immediately.

She wasn't sure why it was so hard to unload him. It had something to do with his inoffensive fondness of her, expressed in countless small ways that would've had her delirious with joy, back in Alabama. And it had something to do with his enthusiasm for Los Angeles and all the exciting activities it offered—an enthusiasm she definitely shared.

But mostly it had to do with her lack of spine. Tonight, finally, that would change, she swore to herself.

He was humming a new Kylie Minogue song and smiling at

a group of men behind them in the line to check in with the restaurant host, who was yet another handsome man. Though not, of course, as attractive as Ro.

She missed Ro. The nights away from him were torture. The only thing that cooled her ardor was his pronouncement that she was submissive. That still rankled.

All the more reason to redouble her efforts at becoming more dominant. No way was she going to stay a victimized little dog, not here in what was supposed to be her big-city fresh start, her new life.

Seated at their intimate round table, next to the sidewalk and near enough to a heat lamp to remind her of Ro once more, Lizbeth silently rehearsed her eviction speech.

A scrape of Ted's chair drew her attention, and she felt her first misgiving when Ted scooted so close their arms bumped.

She should have just tossed his luggage out when he'd gone shopping. Changed the locks.

Exasperated, she patted his arm, twice—pat-pat—before surreptitiously edging away and turning her attention to the bustling promenade.

People strolled the sidewalk, on their way to other restaurants, shops, and movies, going in twos and threes and individually, too. Did any of them have the same kind of issues, she wondered? Was there anyone out there balancing an unsavory task with painful personal growth? Would someone be able to offer her advice?

Ro's handsome visage flashed in her memory. She blinked, dissolving it. *Not yet.*

She glanced at Ted and felt a spike of horror. He stared seductively at her; there was no other way to describe it. Her heart sank. He was wooing her.

He had no clue that the time for wooing was in the past. If it had ever existed.

Any other woman, she mused. Anyone else would be gobbling up such attention. He was handsome, in his own way. Dressed neatly. Had plenty in the finances department, with an upwardly trending portfolio. Enjoyed good food.

She had to cut him off before it got worse.

"Wine? Yes. Two bottles of your best Chianti," Ted told their waiter.

"No," she objected.

He waved away her words like so much wind.

Ted always had been bossy. But not dominant. He was no Ro.

The wine came. Ted tried it, gave the waiter the go-ahead to pour. He lifted his glass and said, "To us. To love. To us, my love," and gulped it down.

She shook her head and sipped a tiny amount.

Encouraged, he took her hand. "I know things haven't been perfect between us, but that's all going to change now." He gazed at her with a desperate sort of determination. He drank the rest of his wine.

Before they received their appetizers, he flagged the strolling flower girl and ordered two dozen long-stemmed red roses delivered to their table. Again Lizbeth's objections were nullified, so the blossoms bristled next to her empty plate, a thornless offering. But when Ted signaled the three strolling violinists to plant themselves at their table and play one love song after another, hot embarrassment rose to her cheeks—for him, and for herself. The servers had to bend themselves around the entourage to plant the entrees. Ted raised his glass again. "To meals shared with loved ones." He drank.

And drank.

Liquid courage? Drowning his misgivings?

She closed her eyes.

Then opened them. She was being submissive! Just like Ro said.

"Ted, I asked you to dinner tonight for a reason. We've known each other a long time—"

"To know you is to love you. 'How do I love thee? Let me count the ways. I love thee to the—' "

"You've got to stop this. I know it's just the wine . . ."

"I'm glad y'like it," he said, his eyes glassy and heavy lidded. "I thought you didn't love me, but you do, don' you? We're a pair. We got to hold it together."

She blushed, but didn't lower her eyes. "Ted, we need to talk. I've recently discovered some things about myself. Los Angeles is so different from Alabama. . . ."

He pushed his chair back, shaking his head. She had her eyes trained on his. She saw his panic.

"No. I do not accept that." He pronounced his words with deliberate precision. "Band!" He summoned them closer with big arm-swings, knocking over his glass of water. He didn't notice. He stood, his head cocked at the three violinists.

"Play 'That's Amore.' "

"Ted, sit down. Please?" He listened to her as well as the dogs did when she had no treats. Swallowing, she felt the first stirring of irritation. She remembered the power she'd had over Ro, the feel of the bullwhip in her hand. She wasn't submissive! "Enough!"

Ted didn't sit down, but he cleared his throat and extended one arm toward her, palm up. "Yes, enough delay! This is the woman I love! Do you hear me?"

Everyone on the patio heard him. Everyone walking by also heard him. The entire restaurant and all passersby stopped to stare.

Not noticing how she'd shrunk down in her seat, Ted continued, "The most beautiful woman, the most desirable woman, the most *woman* woman, anywhere in the country. In th' world!"

He was enjoying himself far too much in his boozy state, she saw, humming along with the violin with tears standing in his eyes. She grabbed her purse to leave.

He sank to one knee. "Michelle . . . will you marry me?"

"Oh, no." Her purse fell from nerveless fingers. She retrieved it, trembling. "Let's talk about this later."

"I'm happyyyy and you're the woman of my dreams! I shoulda proposed in Alabama. The wedding'll be there."

"Not here. Not now. Let's just go." Embarrassment immobilized her.

"We'll go together, safe and sound. Say yes." He stood, truculent, as if nothing would move him but her assent.

"Yes. Anything. If we can just . . ."

"She said yes!" Ted whooped, and everyone began to applaud.

There was no way to prevent what happened next. Pinned by the table on one side and the sidewalk rail on the other, she had nowhere to dodge when Ted swooped, emotion brimming over, his arms wide and his legs propelling him not so much to her as at her. He crushed her in an embrace, smashing his wet lips against hers. She could only squeak in protest.

He spun her around as he planted another sloppy kiss on her mouth and she felt him stumble. She bracketed him with her arms, bolstering, trying to keep him from falling down.

When he pulled away she faced the promenade. There wasn't even an opportunity to wipe her mouth. Ro stood scant yards away, watching.

Had he seen Ted kissing her? How much had he heard? Had she really said yes to Ted's proposal? She hung her head, trying to gather her thoughts.

When she opened them, Ro was gone.

A crash made her turn around. Ted had backed up over his own chair, lost his balance, and fallen down. He'd pulled at the tablecloth in an effort to correct it, which brought with him most of their plates and glasses.

He groaned once, then didn't move. Passed out.

She looked down at Ted in the middle of the mess. Then back to the sidewalk. Ro was nowhere to be seen.

The waiter wasn't having any success in rousing Ted. Maybe he'd hit his head.

She forced back uncharitable thoughts.

But she did help the waiters wake Ted, slapping him a little harder and more rapidly than completely necessary.

Morning light flickered across Ted's eyelids, but when he moved to drag the blanket over his eyes, a lightning strike of pain seemed to split his head open. Nausea rose, then fell.

Then rose again as he remembered.

Not the failure of his marriage proposal to Michelle—he wasn't going to call her Lizbeth, that was ridiculous—and not the property damage he recalled causing at the restaurant.

No. Those were bad—Ted slit his eyes against the pain long enough to confirm he still miraculously resided at Michelle's apartment, then closed them again—very bad, friendship-ending bad, perhaps. But as bad as those things were, worse existed.

Nausea rose higher in him and he crawled to his feet. His head shrieked protest and his eyes watered as he staggered through a beam of entirely too bright Southern California sunshine. The awful glare was only one of the many things wrong with the place. Los Angeles, especially its alternate lifestyles, frightened him.

It made him lust for things he had no business lusting for.

It was an unnatural place. A perverse place.

A seductive place.

He barely made it to the bathroom before he gagged, kneeling before the toilet.

* * *

He felt slightly more human later in the day. His grip on the plush dog toy, an Akita to remind Michelle of her old dog Sasquatch, tightened as Ted parked. He'd wasted the trip. Her car was missing from the small lot in front of the dog day care where she worked. So much for his gesture of apology.

Maybe he could leave it in her office. Did she even have an office? Ted was curious. Time he found out.

The door opened smoothly to the sound of dogs barking. A good-looking man stepped aside to let him pass, and Ted felt a surge of pleasure course through his body as they checked each other out.

Oh no. Not again.

The man brushed by him with a wink and the scent of musk. Ted felt clubbed.

It was the hangover, he told himself desperately. And the city. The festering, contagiously hedonistic vibe of Los Angeles.

Ted exhaled through his nose as he entered the facility, exasperated at the unpleasant odor of ammonia after the good musk. Michelle could live on easy street if she'd just agree to move back with him to Alabama. They would buy a huge house. They would have kids.

She hadn't accepted his proposal. Michelle would rather disinfect dog-soiled surfaces. She'd rather stay in this infected city.

"Most people bring in a real dog."

Ted flinched when he saw the imposing woman who strode to him. She fondled a leash. Ted had the bizarre thought that she would attach it to him. A residual headache thudded still, and he squinted against it. "You must be Posh."

"Aren't you in bad shape. Rough night?" Posh nodded to herself, circling him. "Let me guess. Pasty white under a brand new sunburn, wrinkled sweatshirt with an Alabama college drama club logo, hangover from hell. Michelle has a visiting boyfriend." Her gaze sharpened suddenly, glancing at the entrance, then back to Ted. "Or does she?" Her eyes raked him up and down.

"Michelle warned me about you. A ball-buster." Ted considered. "Those weren't her exact words."

"Mmm, no, but they're yours, though, aren't they. What an interesting choice of words."

Their eyes locked, and Ted felt naked, but in a strangely nonsexual way. He couldn't fathom why Michelle didn't like Posh. He immediately felt comfortable with her.

"I brought this"—Ted made the dog toy dance—"for her. I was sort of a jerk last night. Desperation will make a person do crazy things." He sighed, rubbed gently at his temples. "Where's Michelle anyway? I expected her to be scrubbing on her hands and knees, maybe bruised from being kicked while she was down, the way she talks about you."

"Really?" Posh looked proud. She fluffed her hair with quick, efficient fingertips. "She wants to be called Lizbeth now, you know."

"Yeah, well. We don't always get what we want," Ted growled. "And maybe that's for the best in some cases."

"Mmm. Interesting. I sent her on an errand. She's the best employee I have." Posh tilted her head, thinking. "She's the only employee I have. Why are you desperate?"

Ted tried to avoid the question. "Nice place you have here."

"I hate it. Why are you desperate?"

"It's a long story."

Posh took him by the arm. "Let's go to West Hollywood. I know a great place; it has a bulletproof hangover remedy. You'll tell me your long story. And you'll like the clientele."

"Why will I like the clientele?"

"I've been a fruit fly pretty much all my life, so don't bother with the dissembling. Besides, this is as good an excuse as any to get out of this crap pit," she added, dragging him toward the exit.

"Fruit fly?" Ted let himself be dragged. "Crap pit. But Michelle—"

"... will take care of the dogs when she gets back. She's good at it."

"Yes, she is. But I'm not dressed for meeting people," Ted protested, plucking at his wrinkled shirt.

"You look adorably rumpled and corn fed; you'll be a hit, trust me."

Oddly, Ted did.

6

Ro went through the motions of directing the Slave Auction. His thoughts strayed. Even as he accepted the winning bid for an impressively endowed, double-jointed submissive who demonstrated she could individually control all the muscles of her right and left butt cheeks, part of him remained sunk in despondency.

It was slightly obscene, what he was doing. But was it pornography? Was this something he could look back on at the end of his life with pride? Titillating the masses? Deliberately, he juxtaposed his original concept for The Dungeon—creating a safe haven of fun, honesty, and freedom—with the current activity of Butt Cheeks being happily led from the stage by her new "owner."

It was superficial. Even tacky, perhaps. But hardly pornographic.

He'd hoped that Lizbeth would arrive at the realization she was a born submissive, and come to him on those terms. He'd never seen someone drop down into subspace so quickly and completely. Her shudders of pleasure, her glazed eyes, were all clues to how the endorphins had suffused her sweet, submissive little body.

But instead, she'd accepted a marriage proposal from some drunken, effete-looking guy. Maybe because she thought Ro was a pornographer?

Without joy, Ro replaced the signs in preparation for his next show. His employees cleared the stage of Slave Auction accoutrements. He felt a flash of anger when Vivian finally strolled onstage to help, pulling on the studded hood that gave her eyes such a menacing, shadowed look. "Where have you been?" He glanced at the caged clock over the café. "For two hours?"

She unhooked the plastic VIRGIN SLAVES FOR SALE sign, rolled it up tight with more efficiency than he'd yet managed. "I've been meeting with a special friend of Lizbeth's. Took him to WeHo where we had ourselves a *very* interesting afternoon and evening. Didn't like that sign?"

Ro looked down at the stretched-out, totally destroyed sign in his hands. He threw it aside in disgust. Breathing slowly, he reclaimed control over himself.

Jealousy? He hadn't realized how much Lizbeth had bewitched him. Not that it mattered. They might have had something special together. Now she was engaged. He'd probably never see her again.

"Take over while I change clothes. Keep an eye on the place."

Ro waited until Vivian nodded, then went to change into his costume, an English judge's uniform. Vivian, as herself, would be bailiff. The rest of the employees knew to be guards.

Just as Ro was adjusting his powdered wig, Vivian rushed in. "Got a problem. Chico was busted for letting in a couple of underage girls in exchange for sex. He used his call from the police station to give us the heads up that some plainclothes cops are already here and news crews'll be showing up shortly."

Ro stared. "Get on door duty. No one else comes in," he instructed, and for a wonder, she actually obeyed immediately.

He strode in the opposite direction, his eagle eye taking in everything. He spared a brief moment to curse Chico in his mind for getting into trouble. But at least he'd called. News crews. What did they think they'd be filming? His instinct told him something was wrong. The club was packed, for a change—Crime and Punishment seemed to be a popular night—but that wasn't newsworthy. And only a total shutdown of the club would gain their cameras access, if he didn't want them inside.

What would shut down the club? He scanned, looking for an anomaly . . . and saw it. A paper screen covered one of the alcoves. But Ro's Dungeon had no screens, permitted no screens. A small throng of onlookers bracketed it on either side, peering through the small openings to watch. A bright glow illuminated the screen, and suddenly Ro knew what was happening.

When he hurled the screen aside, the brightness of floodlights made him blink. "Get out," he told the cameramen and the two naked, greased-up actors on the mattress. Ro kicked the mattress. He toppled a backdrop. "This is yours, too, take it with you. All of you, out. Now." He batted at the cameras, menacing, until the floodlights were extinguished and the camera eyes covered.

"Oh, let them finish." The speaker's plain, buttoned-up shirt and khaki pants would've identified the policeman, even if he hadn't been the very same officer who'd once called Ro's Dungeon a titty bar.

Ro ensured that the offending cameramen and actors and all the equipment was headed to the exit. Then he turned his attention to the cop. "Did you arrange this?" Ro approached him, throttling back his rage.

The man fingered his cell phone. "What's a little porn shoot to someone like you?"

"This club does not allow pornography. It does not allow filming. It respects the privacy of—"

"Oh, stick a sock in it, ya damn pimp."

Pimp? Ro stared at the man. Mustached and belligerent and sporting the squinty, yellowed eyes and reddened nose of an alcoholic-to-be. Yet he exuded self-righteousness. He wouldn't hear anything Ro had to say, and certainly wouldn't believe him, not if Ro lived to be a thousand. "Please leave," he told the cop with calm dignity, even as he beckoned to two of his largest, meanest employees in case the additional muscle proved to be necessary.

With only another contemptuous glance at Ro, the cop moved toward the front door, already dialing his cell phone. Canceling the raid, Ro was sure.

He grit his teeth. Harassment of this kind was illegal, if he could prove it. And if he wanted to bother filing a lawsuit. Which he didn't. He'd left lawyering, despite his father's wishes, and he wasn't going to be dragged back into it.

He took a deep breath.

The show must go on.

He strode onto the stage, pitching his voice to carry: "And now, what you've all been waiting for! The Crime and—"

Lizbeth walked in.

She wore her black latex playclothes. Very unlike her sedate ensemble of a few days before. She'd gotten engaged, and now she was clearly here, at his invitation, to play some more. "—Punishment Party," he finished in a deeper, ominous voice that served the announcement well. Cheering and applause rumbled through the packed club.

He couldn't take his eyes off her. She was dressed like a dominatrix. She still didn't get it, he thought, even as the cheering died down. Vivian tugged on his black robe. She was trying to tell him something, but Ro shook her off. He took his place at the judge's bench.

Ro ran through his rehearsed speech. "Here's how to play. Register at the café by stating your crime: bad boy, bad girl, disobedient slave, etc. You will be called before the judge for a public hearing. A jury of your peers will hand down judgment. If the verdict is guilty, the judge will pass the sentence. Possible sentences include, but are not limited to, public humiliation, hand spanking, paddling, restrictive bondage, and/or more additional punishment, at the discretion of the judge."

He smiled without humor. "You will address me as Your Honor. I will tolerate no contempt. And, to give fair warning, you may expect little in the way of leniency. Proceed."

The self-indicted criminals appeared before him, one after another. Vivian announced each crime in her loud, sure voice. Ro wrung the details from these self-accused, then asked the audience, the "peers," to hand down judgment. Gleeful shouts of "guilty!" always thundered back, and Ro passed sentences of public hand spanking and paddling and, once, for an unrepentant escaped slave, a full-suspension rope bondage, administered by a pro dom that Ro had hired especially for his intricate knotwork. Other doms helped with the spankings and paddlings. Ro had almost forgotten about Lizbeth when Vivian's voice cut through the murmurs of conversation.

"This criminal is Lizbeth! Her crime is . . . lying to a master." A hush descended on the audience. It was a grievous crime.

But Vivian wasn't finished. "There's more!" She kept reading. "Her additional crimes are leaving a master unsatisfied, letting a master think she preferred another partner, and insisting on topping before she'd learned how to bottom." At this, Vivian made a strange sound that might have been a laugh, but the outraged roar of the crowd drowned her out.

The roar spoke Ro's feelings for him. Though at first surprised at her stunt, he wasn't the tiniest bit pacified. Still wound up from the earlier confrontation, and still frustrated with Lizbeth's acceptance of that dweeb's proposal, this insinuation of herself into his life only stoked his ire. She thought to use his club against him, did she? To manipulate him into another session where she'd lock him up again, from the way she was dressed. Well, it wouldn't go her way.

She still had a lot to learn.

He would be delighted to punish her, if the jury of her peers handed down a guilty judgment.

They were doing more than handing it down. They were yelling at her, cursing her with an inventiveness that pleased him.

They demanded her torture.

Ro's mouth quirked into a half grin. He felt affection for them, his created family. Sadism and masochism were coming together in a feeding frenzy, with Lizbeth the stoic self-sacrifice. He had to admire the way she stood still for it, her bearing aloof, her stance slightly apart and her wrists handcuffed behind at the small of her back. He wished the swells of her upthrust breasts, and that eye-catching peek of that red lace bra, weren't so distracting. He wondered if she wore panties.

He decided he wouldn't wonder for long.

In his judge's voice, Ro intoned, "Lizbeth. The severity of your crimes merits the harshest possible sentence. I'm pleased the jury recognizes this." He grinned at her, and was even more pleased to see her flinch.

The audience had hushed. Only the background beat of music accompanied his next words.

"In response to the jury's guilty verdict, your sentence is to be public humiliation, paddling, torture . . . the works."

Lizbeth felt the strength go out of her legs. She sagged, supported by two "guards" as if she truly were a criminal given some terrible sentence. Public humiliation? She'd envisioned a brief token paddling as the price for a much-needed private talk.

Almost in reflex she began to struggle, trying to free herself. "I don't think—"

"Relax. It'll be over with soon."

Lizbeth met the sadistic gaze of the guard on her right, and swallowed. His smile reminded her of Ro's. She struggled harder.

"You'd better stop that."

Ro questioned the guard in a silky voice. "Is the convict giving you trouble?" He'd taken off his wig, she noticed. His dark hair was cut short enough not to look too rumpled, but the uncombed spikes of it made him look even more dangerous.

Feeling panic that sent a surge of adrenaline to her limbs, Lizbeth stomped on the guard's foot and lunged from him. If her center of gravity weren't shifted by her hands being locked behind her back she would have made it, but he just clutched her more tightly, cursing.

"For that escape attempt, I am adding a whipping to your sentence." Ro stared down at her, frightening yet compelling in his dark robes.

"You can't do that. I came here to explain—"

"Enough!" Ro stood. "You've been found guilty. Until your punishment is complete, you will say nothing, unless it is your safe word. 'Collar,' I believe it was? Nod if this is accurate."

Lizbeth glared at him, but nodded.

"All you have to do is utter that word and you are free to leave. Alternatively, you can accept the punishment I wish you to endure. Stay, and you must do as you're told, and keep silent. Nod if you understand."

Oh, she understood. Ro was on a power trip. But the crazy part of it was that she was responding to his scornful treatment. She felt a sinking sort of desire propelling her toward the deeply sensual zone she'd experienced only with him. She laughed, strangling it in her throat before he could hear it and hand out further punishments. She'd been split into two people. One was terrified at being surrounded by individuals who wished her harm. That person wondered what the hell was keeping her from shouting her safe word at the top of her lungs. Not to mention keeping her from accepting Ted's proposal and getting herself back to Alabama where she belonged.

But the other person was growing stronger by the second. It stirred to life and stretched like a satisfied kitten under the heat of his glare. It gloried in being roughly controlled, and hoped for more of the same.

"Nod if you understand!"

Lizbeth felt tears spring into her eyes. How could she be enjoying this? Ro's anger was real. The torture would be too.

She shivered, anticipating. Her nipples were rock hard. She nodded.

"Put her in the stocks!"

"To the stocks!" the guards echoed, frog-marching her toward the large, hinged wooden boards in the middle of the stage.

The masked dominatrix suddenly replaced one of her guards. Lizbeth felt nails dig into her arm, and looked up into the dark pools of shadow where her eyes were shrouded. "You don't have to do this," the dom whispered in her ear. "Don't do anything you don't want to." She contrived a delay, holding Lizbeth back, making the sadistic guard huff with impatience. She waited for Lizbeth's reply.

"I know," Lizbeth said. "I . . . I want to."

She squeezed Lizbeth's arm hard enough to leave imprints, but even as Lizbeth winced, the woman whispered, "You are superb. Go get him." She backed two graceful steps.

She felt her sexual buzz increase as the guards lay rough hands on her. As they positioned her between the boards, a familiar masculine hand suddenly reached between them, pinched her nipples viciously, and pushed aside the cups of her red bra with two quick scratches of lace.

She was uncovered! "Hey!" she protested.

"Last warning," Ro intoned. "Another word out of you and I'm going to place a gag in your mouth. You can give your safe word by giving a thumbs-down instead. I think I'd like to gag you. Say something else."

Lizbeth looked at him stubbornly.

Ro shrugged. "Too bad. Your mouth would look good all stretched around . . . a gag.

"Back in the Cage Room, anything goes. With an audience, if I wish. Interested?"

She shook her head, feeling her breasts bounce. The cool, unfamiliar air on their tips brought moisture between her legs. They'd folded her in half, her ankles placed by the guards on the half circle. Ro gently brought her wrists forward to place them next to her ankles and a few inches to the outside. Then he lowered the top board, enclosing all four limbs. She was trapped.

The awkward position was a new one to her body, and her muscles already complained. She'd never seen quite this cruel, efficient side of Ro. But he wouldn't actually hurt her, would he? Not really. Even with his frightening anger, probably thinking she'd made out with another guy and accepted a marriage proposal mere days after their session in the Cage Room, Ro wouldn't hurt her.

Impersonal hands removed her black high heels, exposing her bare feet. The nerve endings on the bottoms of her arches flickered to life as a finger drew slowly down it. Tickling. She flapped her feet in reflex, but the boards prevented further movement. She was shocked at how sensitive her feet were. Ro flicked at her heel, looking satisfied, then stepped to one side.

She was to be presented to *everyone?* She stared up at him, mutinous. In her bent-over position her cleavage was presented to passersby and her nipples pointed at a patch of floor a yard in front of her. It was humiliating.

As he'd intended. She watched the cool smile that touched his lips, and knew he could sense the direction of her thoughts.

People trailed by. Strange fingers touched her toes, stroked her arches, tickled her mercilessly. They laughed when she squirmed, so she tried not to, but she couldn't help it. How had she never known the vulnerability of her own feet? Worse, as she shifted around, her dress rode up. Everyone could see the color of her underwear.

She gave silent, heartfelt thanks for her decision to wear silky black bikini briefs instead of a thong.

Even as her embarrassment increased with each torturer playing with her, she felt a jolt of pure lust engulf her body, as if there were a direct line from her feet to her sex. Every time Ro allowed another stranger to tease her feet, to tickle her without relief, she felt a greater measure of desire.

Ro wasn't even participating. He only watched with an aloof expression that denied any personal connection.

That diminished her as much as her shameful response, until she had to hang her head in humiliation.

Ro immediately stepped forward. "Next punishment. Paddling, and whipping." The guards raised the board encasing her wrists and ankles, and Lizbeth flinched as they touched her feet to help her out of the stocks. She rubbed her wrists.

Before she'd reclaimed her body sufficiently, Ro barked an order. "Stand up!"

She did, wobbling on feet that still felt too sensitive. She ground them against the wood floor and tugged the hem of her dress down as far as it would go. The eyes of dozens of strangers drilled into her. Part of her felt bashful. Another part felt exhilarated by their scrutiny. She even smiled. The guards rotated her gently in a half circle, as if turning precious artwork around for the audience's viewing pleasure. It really wasn't so bad.

"Bend over and grab your ankles."

Lizbeth stiffened. She faced the back of the stage. That meant . . .

"Yes, your ass is going to be on display. While I paddle it. Bend over and grab your ankles. Now."

Shame replaced her shaky confidence, but she knew she'd like less the consequences of defying Ro's order.

She bent. Her dress hiked up again. Her hair hung down.

Ro's tender touch on her neck made her flinch. He trailed his fingers sensuously around the base of her head, massaging her. "Good girl."

A moment of pleasure, a moment of outrage. He'd spoken to her as if she were a dog! The crowd murmured its approval.

"I'm going to give you twenty-five strikes. If you move from this position, I will start again at one. Ready?" He was asking the audience, not her. They shouted assent.

"It's a naughty bottom, isn't it?" Ro caressed her ass cheeks with casual ownership. Lizbeth felt her face heat with mortification. The worst of it was that part of her leapt to his touch, reveled in the sweet warmth of his palm gliding over her silky, too-brief panties. She gulped as his hand delved slightly between her cheeks, brushed the softer mound between her legs. The sound of her breathing was loud to her, trapped inside the curtain of her hair. She thought of all the people watching what he did. Thank god she was wearing underwear.

"I think these panties should go, don't you?"

She made an outraged sound and tried to wriggle away from him, but he'd anticipated her. One arm snaked down, whip quick, pinioning her to her original position. The other hand peeled her panties down, exactly as low as last time: enough to reveal her cheeks but not so much to show what lay between them. There was that, at least; her legs were together.

For the moment. She whimpered, afraid of the consequences of using language, or moving too much, beginning to feel like the dog he addressed. "Down, girl. Settle down. That's right, you're fine, this is what you want. Isn't it, Lizbeth?"

Yes. It is. Part of her did. And in response to his affectionate, knowing, honeyed voice, all she wanted to do was to please him. Then they could talk. Then they could straighten—

Whack. "One!" The crowd counted.

The stinging pain was immediate.

Whack. "Two!" The sound was harsh on her ears, the leather-covered paddle slapping bare flesh high and sharp and very personal.

"Three! Four! Five!" Her bottom began to feel hot. Then itchy, cool, then hotter. He increased the tempo. And strength. She couldn't help moving. She wriggled away from the fiery hurt, moving her hands from her ankles for a moment, uncomfortable.

"Tsk, tsk. Have to start again at one."

Whack. "One!"

As the blows rained down, her bottom heated further. She tried to lessen the sting, but knew that within her limited position the movement only made her ass wiggle as if she craved more. She was on fire. She felt another crush of mortification as cool air caressed her ass and her mound. Ro had paused, reminding her how she was in full, air-circulated view of the public. Then the paddle fell on her right thigh, then her left, then higher. And on the other side. Then five strikes quick and hard, not giving her a chance to recover. It was unbearable.

She became aware of the sound of her moaning only when he stopped. "Very good. You may stand. For the moment."

Hearing the rough passion in his voice, she felt a spike of lust. Her bottom and upper thighs felt as if she'd had a bad sunburn, and tinglingly alive when she pulled her panties back up.

"You've been very bad," Ro said. Was that a lustful edge in his voice? Was he as inflamed inflicting this violence as she was receiving it? If so, it was not in evidence by the time he spoke again. "And you will endure the remainder of your punishment without your panties. Take them off now."

Lizbeth opened her mouth to refuse.

Ro raised a bored eyebrow, as if her refusal would be utterly predictable. His lips curved upward in a tight smile.

She closed her mouth. Though she wasn't sure how on earth she could bring herself to "take them off," as he'd ordered. All she knew was that she didn't want to leave before she'd had a chance to talk with him. But take off her underwear? She looked her quandary at him.

"You can," he answered her, moving only his mouth. "You will."

Then, "Or, I will. You won't like the way I do it, though."

She gave him a poisonous look. Then, trying to ignore the audience, and keeping her dress pulled firmly down with one hand, she wriggled her panties off. Then kicked them to him. Ro scooped them up with one graceful lunge and steered her toward another part of the stage. She moved as if in a trance, the familiar warmth of his hand on her a link to their previous intimacy. Didn't he remember? Wasn't their connection still there?

"Good, they've prepared the bench."

Lizbeth halted immediately, but he was prepared and scooped her up much the same way he had her panties.

The feel of being held against his warm broad chest evoked more memories. She hid her face against him, breathing in his now-familiar scent. This was like her worst nightmare and her best fantasy combined. The only thing that could make it better was if Ro cared about her in a meaningful way. That was what she needed to talk to him about. She needed to get this "submissive" business out of the way, and then confess her growing feelings for him. They could have something really special, she knew. All that remained was to find out whether he felt the same way.

He was actually going to put her over a bench again? Would he mount her again, too? She laughed silently, feeling a little hysterical. He felt her movement.

"This amuses you?" He dropped her feet, setting her down with a jolt. "We'll see how amused you are when you're wiggling on all fours locked to the bitch hitch. That's what we call it here. You can see why."

She could. Though she'd expected something like it, this device he meant for her had tie points. She'd be locked to it. She shook her head, tried to back away.

"Oh no, you don't." Ro signaled the guards, and in a short time she was on all fours, her midsection supported by foam-covered straps, her wrists affixed together and dangling similarly from a steel crosspipe above, and her knees forced apart with a spreader bar. She tried to close her legs and failed. A sense of ultimate vulnerability cascaded over her, titillating and frightening. Humiliating. Delightful. She could only give small thanks that Ro's bitch hitch faced the side wall rather than the audience, and that only he could see her spread crotch.

"We can't forget the muzzle." She jerked away from the vinyl muzzle that dropped down in front of her face like a gas mask. But the grinning guard tilted her head up with one hand

and placed it over her head, inserted the anatomically correct protruding gag into her mouth, then tightened the straps.

"I assume you remember how to give your safe word when your mouth is occupied? Why don't you show me."

Lizbeth lifted one finger at him. It wasn't her thumb.

The audience gasped.

Ro touched her face with gentle respect. She could swear she saw humor and affection in his eyes, but when he spoke his voice was cold as doom. "This criminal wants a thorough, vigorous, severe punishment." He lifted a long, thin crop from where it nestled in its own crevice on the rack, sinking down to a working position on his knees, leaving Lizbeth and the rack in profile view of the audience.

Silence reigned.

Lizbeth held her breath. Her whole body clenched, dread and exhilaration a whirlpool threatening to engulf her.

A hiss split the air and a line of fire exploded on her cheeks. Her body tried to jump to safety, but the restraints caught her, swung her back to him. He whipped her again. And again. Sweet sharp pain licked at tender flesh already heated by the paddle. This time the audience merely watched. Their deep quiet struck her as fascinated, almost respectful.

Suddenly she felt a large hand on her thigh, the side hidden from viewers. Ro's free hand. It encased her leg in a rough grip, holding her still. His fingertips wormed up her thigh, burrowed between her cleft. He stroked her where she was most sensitive. As the whip rained down on her and her body lunged, his hand pressed her back into position as his fingers worked cleverly between her legs. Despite the blows that threatened to split her skin, all her awareness went to his fingers.

He moved the whip's attentions to the right cheek alone, beating there until she whimpered. Then he chastised the left, the dual action of his flicking finger ripping moans out of her.

By the time he marked her lower cheeks with a skillful pattern, making sure every inch was well attended to, she nearly vibrated with the peaks she almost reached. Pleasure alternating with pain had her feeling floaty, sustained at the moment before orgasm, indefinitely. Every time the whip touched already torched flesh she cried out wordlessly around her gag. The combination of sensations was too intense to endure, and tears sprung into her eyes. She had to be bleeding, with the brutal whipping he gave. But with his fingers positioned as they were, she didn't want him to stop. But he had to stop.

A kind of fever threatened to incinerate her. She screamed around the gag, at the limit of her endurance.

Ro stopped. He flipped the quick-release of the spreader bar and the restraints. She heard him breathing too quickly as he stuffed the whip back into its holder.

When her hands were free and her knees bent more modestly, he finally removed the gag from her mouth. She looked up at him, feeling the coolness on her face from the tears. She held herself immobile, silent and waiting.

"This is too intense for your level of experience." Wherever his gaze touched her, it seared her as surely as the whip. Entranced by the look in his eyes, she wanted him so badly she shook.

"Her punishment is complete," Ro announced. Applause thundered. She wondered if anyone else heard the unsteadiness in his voice.

Then his words penetrated and she wondered whether he was joking.

"You're just . . . that's it?" That couldn't be it. Not when all she wanted was to wrap her legs around him and fill herself with him again. He had to satisfy her this time. He had to finish. She arched back against him. He gripped her, stilled her.

"Not now. I can't. I have to . . . I have work to do."

"I *am* your work."

"You're not." His voice was like a whip crack. "If you were my work, that would make me a pornographer, wouldn't it? Or maybe a pimp."

She recoiled, hurt. She hid it from Ro. "Only if you do it for commerce instead of love." She yanked free of him. "I guess you've chosen."

Then, to make her point, she stabbed back at him with one pointed finger to his chest. "I don't know what I was thinking to come here tonight. I should just let Ted take me—"

Back to Alabama, she was going to say, but Ro turned his back on her. He was gesturing to the two guards who'd held her, over by the other convicts waiting to be judged. He was having her thrown out? Her heart sank. Maybe she'd been too aggressive.

He was speaking to the masked female dom. One of his actions suddenly seized her full attention. He was handing the dom his judge robes! Lizbeth heard his clipped words. "Take over. I have urgent business."

"Uh-huh. I saw her poking you." She turned her masked face to Lizbeth, and seemed sincerely concerned. "Girl, are you insane?"

Lizbeth remembered her earlier kindness. She managed a smile for the dominatrix and a shrug of her stiff shoulders. "Just trying to get his attention."

"I'd say you got it. And now you're going to get more. Maybe more than you can handle." Her voice and mannerisms seemed familiar to Lizbeth.

"One can only hope," Lizbeth quipped. She was going to get more! In truth, she felt her body coming more alive than ever, her mind seeming to float above it somewhere in a sensual cloud of anticipation. Maybe he'd punish her again.

The dominatrix laughed.

Ro nodded his dismissal. His face a mask of disapproval, he directed the guards to Lizbeth. "She raised her hand against me."

The guards looked at her in disbelief, but immediately clamped her upper arms in identical, almost painfully firm grips.

"The Cage Room."

Lizbeth felt a touch of unease as they marched her back. People stared, but there was sympathy mixed with their curiosity now. Others watched with sadistic excitement. Evidently the Cage Room was a big deal.

She felt a frisson of excitement skitter up and down her spine.

She heard Vivian's husky voice beginning to read the next criminal's offenses as the heavy wood door closed, sealing the four of them off from all but the low bass thump of the nightclub's music.

Lizbeth moved slightly, testing. She felt the two guards grip her more tightly. Otherwise they stood as silent and still as statues, obedient to Ro.

"I was mistaken about your tolerances, wasn't I? You want more. If I'm wrong, all you have to do is say your safe word."

His expression was drawn, ascetic. His mouth was a hard, cruel line. "Lay her down. No, not on the carpeted area, on the mat. That's all she deserves."

The guards kicked her feet out from under her and lay her on the black, rubber-matted floor. She could feel the nightclub bass directly in her spine. Fear bloomed in her, with the suspicion of what he intended. With others there, watching?

She struggled. The two men spread her arms apart, though, holding her upper body down.

Ro wouldn't.

An impossible surge of desire chased the fear around inside

her body, and then was chased in turn, like a couple of dogs playing dominance games. Sensuality warring with sensibility. Submissive versus rebellious. And wasn't that all it was? Dominance games? Was everything just a game? She wasn't sure anymore where fantasy ended and reality began. She tested the guards' grip again, making a small desperate sound.

Ro smiled, and she couldn't miss the heat in his eyes. "You have my permission to struggle. To fight. To scream. No one will hear you."

As if part of her was waiting for his permission, she kicked out with her legs.

Ro caught one, placed it forcefully back down. "Naughty," he breathed. He shoved his other hand up under her skirt.

"No," she protested.

But his hands worked their magic. They reminded her how his fingers felt, of the sensuality they could evoke with the lightest touch.

He wasn't touching her lightly anymore. Back between her legs they went, doing things that made her scream in denial of what he was making her feel. He thumbed her expertly, and she twisted, whimpering, humiliated that others witnessed the things Ro was doing to her.

And her response to it.

She wriggled away from him, her lower body rising half off the mat and twisting desperately, but he slammed her back down. "Hold her tight. She won't mind some Indian burns on the wrist. Will you, Lizbeth?"

His eyes had darkened to black. His lips curled in an unconscious snarl. "Maybe she wouldn't mind if you had a piece of her, too."

Her muscles strained, trying to close her legs, but he forced them apart. Would he really let them have her? Her mind shrieked protest even as her psyche reveled in his thorough dominance of her. She wanted no one but him. She could always say her safe word, she knew, and clung to the idea until his next touch obliterated thought.

A whisper of sticky latex, and her dress was shoved upward. Through blurred vision she saw Ro's cock standing erect, thick and long as a stallion's. Before she could object, he placed it at her opening and shoved into her with a grunt.

She screamed, in relief as much as shock at what he'd done. Her cheeks ground against the rubber, the pain from his earlier paddling and whipping blazing to life. The pleasure of finally being filled by him, pounded so ruthlessly on the ground while she struggled against the assault . . . pain and pleasure and the incomparable degradation of it . . . It was exquisite!

Ro used her brutally, and she reveled in the combined sensations. Waves of ecstasy throbbed through her as she orgasmed again and again.

Desperate cries for him to stop broke from her lips. "I can't . . . this is too . . . please stop!"

He gave those same lips a bruising kiss before whispering in her ear, "Not unless you use your safe word. But you don't want to do that, do you?" She met his eyes, and she couldn't lie. She shook her head, the blazing pleasure spiking her with each thrust he made. She surrendered to it, feeling diminished and transported at the same time. She endured the shameful pleasure he gave her.

Almost immediately, another orgasm ripped through her with an intensity that had her lunging mindlessly against the restraining hands.

He reached his in the next moment, his lips curved into a snarl. She half expected him to bite her, and just the thought of it sent another ripple of ecstasy all through her body.

She lay, limp and uncaring in the afterglow. She closed her eyes.

Ro tugged her dress down. "Good job. Now, please leave,"

he told the guards. She felt hands release her wrists, leaving behind a tingling soreness that she knew would become bruises. She smiled.

"You got what you wanted," Ro observed. She opened her eyes. Clothed, it was almost as if he hadn't just forced her. They could be back at the beginning, when she was asking him for lessons. God, he was handsome, with that satisfied, cruel look of his.

"I did," she drawled. "And so did you."

"Yes." A pause. "How will your fiancé feel about all this?"

Lizbeth closed her eyes again, smiling. "I tried to tell you. He's not. He's just an ex who wants me back."

Ro was silent for another long moment. "And do you want him too?"

"No. He seems to have a problem with my learning how to be dominant."

"Umm." Ro was uncharacteristically quiet. She opened her eyes, met his evaluating stare. "I worked you over pretty good."

Was that pride in his voice? Lizbeth grinned. "I could try to return the favor. Didn't you say this is how a bottom learns the ropes?"

"Yes. That." Ro's smile faded slightly though. "I'll always be up for playing games with you. Exclusive dating. Anything you want, really. But . . . you should know, your inclinations are pretty obvious. I've never seen anyone respond to a chastisement quite like you." He stroked her hand, a respectful caress. He picked it up. Kissed it. "You have no idea what you do to me."

"I know. You do the same thing to me." Lizbeth leaned into his caress. Then frowned. "I liked it a little too much."

"No such thing."

"There is, though," she said, her history of submission playing out in her mind. She'd come so far, only to find herself flat on her back. Literally. A tight ball of sadness quickly grew and prickled in her throat as she thought of her failed attempt to become stronger than she'd been.

Ro looked as if he wanted to say something.

She spoke first. "I could still learn." She could give others such sensations too. She climbed to her feet, looked around, selected a multiple-strand whip, swished it back and forth experimentally.

But instead of empowered, she felt a little silly. Maybe she should display a little more aggression, strut around, get into the role.

She strode to him, hoping the curl of her lips looked as vicious as his did. She whacked the whip into her palm. Winced. Gamely, she stared up at him, wishing she still wore her heels. "You seem uncomfortable with a woman holding authority," she drawled, waving the whip threateningly.

"Actually, Vivian is my best dominatrix and I respect her tremendously."

Her heart plunged. That didn't fit the script. What was she supposed to do with that? Jealousy tugged at her. Did he want Vivian? Suddenly she truly did feel like hitting him with the whip. Why wasn't he helping? Why wasn't he letting her become something more than a doormat?

"Lizbeth." Ro plucked the whip from her, an adult taking a dangerous weapon from a child. His voice was laughter and truth. "You don't want this. You can't hide your innermost desires from me. Stop pretending to be something you're not."

No fantasy. Cold reality. She would never be strong. She could never be the dominant one in any relationship, human or canine. Never hold authority. He'd diminished her, but instead of the first step it was supposed to be, it was the last.

Was that pity in his eyes?

She had to get out of there and never come back.

Even as she thought it she acted on it, fleeing the Cage

Room and dashing across the nightclub, nimbly avoiding the press of bodies. She exploded out the entrance. She heard Ro calling. She ran faster, her shoeless feet slapping against sidewalk, speeding her to her car and flooring the gas pedal to escape the inescapable truth.

She fought back tears. She headed home until she remembered Ted would be there. One look at her and he'd ask questions she couldn't possibly answer, especially after his failed proposal. That complication she didn't need.

Changing direction, she headed toward the dog day care instead. To be surrounded by dogs would be a comfort.

8

Ro pushed through the crowd with more aggression than seemly. He cursed when people took too long getting out of his way.

By the time he shoved, apologized, and dodged his way out the front door, all he saw of Lizbeth were the taillights of her car.

"Spare some change?"

Ro glanced down. Sitting against the wall—the same wall his patrons lined up against to wait to get inside the club—was a group of poorly dressed, foul-smelling transients. Newspapers surrounded them, and stinking trash. He even saw a discarded syringe. One degraded individual slumped sideways, swigged from a bottle of Glenlivet whisky. "You look like you could spare a dollar, mister." He went to swig again, but something in Ro's eyes froze his arm halfway up. "What?" the man finally asked. "See somethin' green?" His arm continued its upward movement.

Liquor sprayed from his mouth when Ro lifted him off his

feet and slammed him against the wall. "I do see something green. How much did he pay you?"

"I dunno what you're talking about." Smug and surly.

Slam. "Bums don't drink Glenlivet."

"I dunno what you're talking about."

Slam. "Who paid you? Who paid your friends? Give me a name." But it wasn't doing any good. Of course it was his father. Paying these people to camp outside his club. Paying the porn stars to film inside his club. Maybe paying the cops to harass him. Probably. His own father, the elder Kaliph attorney who always won. One way or another.

Ro had emerged from the club angry. Now he was enraged.

He spoke in his coldest "master" voice. "You will tell me his name and how much he paid you, or I will bring you inside The Dungeon. Do you know what happens to bad people in there?" He allowed himself a tight smile as he watched the fear flicker across the stinking man's face. It was almost too easy to play on this one's false assumptions about BDSM clubs. "Let me tell you what will happen if you don't start talking in ten seconds or less. I'll give you to Vivian. She's a talented cock-and-balls torturer. She'll hang devices from your junk that will make you shriek for mercy. She might do piercings if she's in the mood. She'll doubtless put you in a pony suit, with a mouth bit and large, expandable butt plug with an attached horsetail. You will prance and do tricks for everyone while she whips you with a riding crop until you scream. It's her favorite thing. Unless you'd rather talk now?"

He would rather talk now.

Twenty minutes later, on the porch of the large Bel Air house, Ro confronted him.

"Hi, Dad. Just back from some nighttime grocery shopping? Buy any Glenlivet?" Ro plucked the plastic grocery bag from his father's hand. He pulled out two bottles. "Thanks, you shouldn't have. Now, don't act surprised, I'm not some gullible jury likely to fall for your courtroom theatrics."

Ro steered him away from the house, onto the wide tree-canopied sidewalk. With his arm around his father's tense shoulder, Ro spoke quietly to the smaller man. "I understand why you're doing what you're doing, but you have to stop."

Ro had to give him credit: at least he didn't dissemble. "You understand nothing. Throwing your life away on a sleazy nightclub. Hurting your reputation this way. What will it take for you to return to your true calling? You're so good at the law, son. I need you."

"Wow, that was almost the whole persuasion gamut," Ro observed. "Everything but the threats. And those you delivered by proxy." They passed the neighbor's gold Jaguar, the next neighbor's shiny BMW. He stopped next to an Aston Martin. The streetlight above made its silver paint gleam. "Let me put this bluntly, because I'm in a hurry and I want you to understand me clearly. I don't want your lifestyle. I want mine. You won't take it from me. You see, I now have credible evidence that you're harassing me, bribing transients to damage my property, distributing liquor on public walkways, and interfering with my business. Additionally, I have strong circumstantial evidence linking you to certain harassing activity involving the police. I could have you in court for a baker's dozen of charges, up to and including racketeering. Dad, I hate to use this kind of language," Ro continued, turning them back toward the house, "but if I'm forced to litigate, it'll really wreck your reputation, your relationship with peace officers, and your bank account." He finished just as they returned to the porch. He patted his father on the shoulder once, then folded his arms and waited.

"That's what I mean," his dad complained. "Killer instinct, wasted."

Ro thought of Lizbeth. Of his club, his employees, his grateful patrons. "It's not wasted."

He examined Ro. "I'm not going to convince you, am I? Or coerce. You really don't want to return to Kaliph & Son?" His voice turned wheedling. "What if you could do both? Run your little club just on weekends?"

"You never give up, do you?" Ro said with reluctant admiration. "Always trying to convince me, even though it's never going to succeed. . . ." Ro trailed off, remembering his own tactics in trying to convince Lizbeth that she didn't want to be dominant. Showing Lizbeth her true nature had frightened her. Frightened her away. But there was nothing more he could do.

She would simply have to open her eyes and see it for herself. He'd helped her all he could.

He hoped she'd figure it out soon. They'd been parted for only a short time, and he already missed her. He knew what it meant that he longed for her so strongly, so soon, but there was nothing to be done for that, either.

His dad, though. Ro looked down at the aging man with fondness. He was a stubborn individual, a sore loser, and a strong-willed creature of habit, even more so than Lizbeth. He was the one who needed Ro's help now, Ro realized with a pang. Abandoned by his only son, running the family business alone, it was small wonder he'd resorted to such ridiculous criminal measures to get Ro's attention. "Let's go to Barney's Beanery like old times," Ro suggested, and was rewarded by the fierce grin so much like his own.

"I'm not changing my mind, though," Ro warned as he climbed into the passenger seat. "If you'd only come inside The Dungeon sometime you'd see why."

"Let all the perverts at me?" Ro's father paused, considered. "Are they well heeled?"

"Oh yes," Ro said with a laugh. "The women especially. Five or six inches."

9

The dogs were mostly curled up in packs, sleeping, but there was one black Labrador in the large dog enclosure that barked, and a shih tzu in the small dog enclosure that wouldn't stop whining. Ted wondered how the other dogs could sleep so soundly on hard vinyl floors, with that constant, repetitive, annoying noise.

His hangover aches and pains had returned with a vengeance.

His worst fear, confirmed. He was gay.

He drank, trying to soothe all that felt wrong with him. The sixth beer from a six-pack of Miller Genuine Draft drained into him. Michelle would laugh at him. His dad would disown him. His drinking buddies would shun him. After they kicked his ass.

Posh had taken him to West Hollywood, and Ted had felt himself responding to the energy of the place. Even more than the rest of LA, WeHo had felt like a happy home, with the kinds of carefree people who simply didn't exist in Alabama. And the men . . . Ted shivered, his mind racing from the memory of handsome man after handsome man walking, sitting, dancing. Dancing to Erasure. He'd danced, too. . . . Others—broad-shouldered and self-assured—looked at him as they gyrated with subtle cleverness and with that devious, knowing smile that made his cock harden in his pants.

He was gay. He couldn't be gay. There had to be some kind of antidote. Posh had brainwashed him. Telling him he was gay had made him believe it.

The Labrador kept barking. The shih tzu still whined. Ted envied them their simplicity.

"Don't suppress it, you'll only give yourself a complex," Posh had advised as he sipped his hangover remedy and surreptitiously (he'd thought) checked out the occupants of The Black Cap. She'd been amused at his predicament.

And later, while they'd sipped mineral water, she'd explained more than he'd wanted to know about the gay scene. He'd learned about the gay hanky color codes. The secret gay fun palaces. She was a "fag hag," she said, and that's why he liked her so much.

He didn't like her anymore.

Ted didn't want to go home to Michelle until his head was on straight again. He'd ordered beer. He'd also picked up a six-pack of MGD. No more fruity blush wine for him.

Once he screwed a woman again, the crazy wicked thoughts would fall from him like a bad dream. When he took Michelle back to Alabama he would forget all of this.

All he needed was to have sex with Michelle. It's not like it'd be the first time for them. It wouldn't be that big of a deal.

Besides. It wasn't as if he was the only one who needed moral rescuing. From what he'd seen, he'd be doing her a favor. Get her head on straight, too. Her family would be grateful to him. They'd live happily ever after with three kids and a bunch of dogs.

Ted finished his beer and tossed the empty at a trash can. It banged against the wall and landed on the floor. The noise woke the dogs, and the sudden roar of all of them barking at once almost seemed like encouragement to him, a primal masculine noise that urged him to his feet and toward the office to grab his keys. Instinct. Kill or be killed. Fuck or be fucked. When Michelle opened her apartment door he would pounce like the healthy heterosexual beast he was.

So it took him by surprise when Michelle suddenly opened the dog day-care door and walked in.

10

Lizbeth heard the dogs barking. She threw the door open and rushed inside. "Charlie, you naughty thing, are you biting that Australian shepherd again? When I catch you . . ."

"When you catch him you'll pet him and cuddle him and make friends, no matter how bad he's been. Hi, Michelle."

"Ted!" She halted. "What are you doing here? Where's Posh? The door was unlocked."

He didn't answer. His calculated stroll toward her made her hackles rise. Something was wrong with Ted. Was he stalking her? She laughed at her paranoid thoughts. The Dungeon and its protocols had rubbed off on her. There was a good reason for Ted to be here, acting this way, and she'd find out what it was as soon as she calmed the dogs down.

"Hey, big guy," she crooned. Charlie butted his head against her hand, wriggling his body as he wagged and grinned up at her with his Labrador smile. She couldn't be stern. She knew that's what got results; just look how they reacted when Posh cracked the whip. But she couldn't.

As she'd expected, the dogs quieted down quickly under her

soothing voice and quick investigative touches. Charlie let out a happy whine and raced to the edge of the enclosure to lick her hand, then leapt away, wanting to play. "Sorry, buddy. Not now." She scratched him under the chin for a moment, then turned to Ted.

"They don't seem hurt. Did you see who started the fight?"

"*I* did." Ted stalked closer. "I threw a can. Not at them," he assured her, staring at her dress but focusing on her legs. "You look nice."

Lizbeth stared at him. "How are you feeling?" She walked to the trash and peered inside at all the crumpled aluminum beer cans.

"I'm not drunk, if that's what you're worried about."

"I'm not worried."

"Good." Ted eased into her space. She could smell the beer and sense his intensity. "We have to have a little chat, you and me."

He was going to propose again. He wanted her to come back to Alabama and wasn't taking no for an answer. Again.

For the first time, she was actually tempted. She'd never be assertive, never carve a meaningful niche where she could become someone else: a strong, effective voice of authority with dogs or people. Why not marry Ted, and move back to where the disappointments were at least small and predictable?

But something held her back.

"Ted . . . this is a really bad time."

"Fine. We won't chat. How about I just remind you of how it can be between a man and a woman? I love you, Michelle. You know that, don't you?"

He kissed her. It was as wet and unconvincing as it had been the night before. She tried to push him away. "What's wrong with you?"

"There is nothing wrong with me," Ted stated. "Nothing at

all. And that's the way I'm going to keep it." His hand found the back of her thigh, traveled upward. "Hey, you're all ready to go, aren't you?"

The manhandling had felt heavenly with Ro. But Ted's hands left her cold. "Stop it," she cried, desperate.

And was answered. An outraged roar filled her ears, and out of the corner of her eye she saw a black shape vault the large dog's wall.

Charlie tackled Ted, carrying them both to the floor. Ted screamed.

"Hold still!" Lizbeth yelled. "Ted! If you play dead, and don't move, Charlie'll back off. Hold still," she repeated, using her most soothing voice, the one that always calmed the dogs. Ted stopped flailing his arms. Only his eyes rolled to show their whites as he stared at the bared fangs inches above his face.

"I should tell him to bite your dick off," she said in the same soothing voice, amazed at both the sentiment and the sight of her favorite dog straddling Ted, ready to protect her.

"No, you shouldn't," said a familiar voice. "The liability insurance for this place would go through the roof." A whip cracked, and Charlie leapt off Ted. The dog went immediately to Lizbeth to nose her hand, sniffing, licking worriedly.

Lizbeth stared at the tall woman in the black hood. "Vivian? You followed me here?" She felt confused, then hopeful. Maybe Ro had sent this dominatrix to bring her back. Then she focused on the whip. Posh's whip.

The woman walked straight to her, ignoring Ted. The black shadows where her eyes could barely be seen seemed to suck up the light in the large facility. She still carried the whip, and her aggressive stride spoke of anger. The dominatrix ripped off her hood.

"Holy crap. Posh?"

"The one and only." Her boss fluffed her hair.

"You're Vivian?" Suddenly all the pieces fell together. "Of course." Lizbeth blushed to think of all *Vivian* had witnessed.

"Oh yeah. Someone had to keep an eye on you, vanilla. Though no longer, of course." She glanced at the marks on Lizbeth's legs with approval. "He's good, isn't he, Lizbeth?"

"She doesn't look like a Lizbeth," Ted said. Both women ignored him.

She stared at Posh's muscular body and exquisite hair. It made her aware of her own rumpled state.

Posh laughed, shook her head. Black glossy curls fell around her shoulders and down her back. "Oh yeah, he's good for you, you're good for him, Cupid's been busy. I like my men more compliant. Not quite as compliant as this, though." Posh nudged Ted with the tip of her boot. He smacked it away, a pissed-off expression replacing the bewildered one.

"Touchy. We'll have to forgive him. His emergence was traumatic."

"Emergence?"

"He's g—"

"Shut up! Shut up!" Ted leapt to his feet. Charlie growled warningly. Ted stared daggers at the dog and stopped moving. He spoke. "I'm no turd burglar. You were just messing with me. Weren't you?"

Lizbeth saw the desperate way he looked at Posh. "You're *gay?*"

"Not me, him," Posh clarified.

"I'M NOT!"

This time Charlie snarled and took a step closer to Ted. "Will you call that mutt off?"

"He's a purebred, not a mutt. Charlie, be good. That's it. Let's go have a cookie." Lizbeth led Charlie to the treat bag and fed him one.

"Reward him for attacking me. Nice."

"*You* attacked *me*."

Posh laughed softly but with abandon. "This is all so priceless. Ted . . . As I said earlier. It's easier if you embrace your attraction to men. Stop fighting it."

Lizbeth strolled with Charlie to the big dog's enclosure. She let the dogs investigate her, to show them she was unhurt. "C'mon," she murmured to them. "Give me some air." They backed away, nosing each other while keeping an eye on her.

She paced, unable to keep still.

"And that goes double for you. Michelle."

Her head snapped to Posh. "What did you call me?"

"Michelle. Lizbeth. Whatever. Stop fighting your true nature. You know exactly what I'm talking about."

"Maybe . . . It's Lizbeth . . ."

"You know better. You came alive with Ro. But you ran, and here you are pining for him while you frolic with the dogs as if you were one of them. You don't master the critters, not the way I do. Be okay with that. You love them, they love you, and so your way is just as effective. Look."

Lizbeth looked. As she'd walked, the dogs had clogged in a group behind her and followed. As her stare lingered, they all sat, one after the other. Waiting for her to lead.

Lizbeth felt delight. "Hey, I'm an alpha!"

"More of a first among equals. They feel affection for you."

Posh stepped inside the enclosure, and the dogs immediately abandoned Lizbeth, sidling toward Posh with submissive postures and licking the air. "They feel fear of me." She waved the whip and they shied away, then lowered themselves to their bellies. Posh smiled. "I'm the alpha here. Even though I don't care about them, and I seriously doubt they care about me."

Lizbeth nodded, her heart expanding with the devotion she felt for her furry friends. The dogs loved her. Sasquatch had loved her. And she'd always love them. She'd take affection over fear any day.

But then she frowned. "You really don't care about them? Why keep a dog day-care business?"

"Ro can't afford to take me on full time, at least not yet." Posh twirled a strand of her hair around the handle of the bull-whip. "It just sort of happened."

Lizbeth was nodding, staring at Posh. Specifically at Posh's hair. "I remember you telling me about the dogs you groomed, and how that blossomed into a business. But Posh. Why don't you start a people-grooming business? Be a hair stylist, I mean," she amended.

"Hey, that's a good idea!" Ted said.

Both women stared at him. "What, I don't get an opinion?"

Lizbeth almost felt sorry for Ted. But she could see that part of him enjoyed the attention. And was beginning to accept his unexpected sexual feelings.

Could she do the same?

Lizbeth longed for Ro, his mastery, his touch. But if it meant letting go of her dream of becoming assertive, could she do it? She'd suffered as a submissive person. Not the good kind of suffering, either. She ran a hand over the pinch zone on her arm, remembering all the times she'd turned her fears and anxieties inward, seeking relief by hurting herself. She'd come such a long way from that. It couldn't all be for nothing.

But she couldn't give up Ro, either.

She caught herself pinching her arm just below her elbow.

"Collar," she whispered. And stopped.

Posh swished her whip. It was probably a thoughtless gesture of hers, but Lizbeth kept an eye on the weapon just the same. "What was that?" Posh asked.

"Collar," she repeated more loudly. "It's my safe word. When I say it, all BDSM play stops. I have control." She looked at her arm wonderingly. "I have control."

"Of course you do. And?" Posh studied her nails.

"It means nobody hurts me, unless I let them. Posh, I'm going to borrow one of our new dog collars, and a leash."

"Accessories! Good girl," she approved. "Ted, fetch her a collar."

"Fetch it yourself," Ted retorted. When she waved the whip in his direction he stuck his tongue out at her.

Lizbeth got the collar herself. She kissed Charlie on his furry head and promised she'd buy him an even prettier one.

Then she went to take Ted's hand, squeezed it. "I've got to go, Ted."

"I'll take care of Ted, don't worry. Here." Posh held out a black leather cap with lettering across the front. "I had this old thing lying around. You can have it. Go get him," Posh instructed her for the second time that night, and winked.

Lizbeth went.

11

She'd been waiting for Ro for more than an hour.

Lizbeth toyed with her leash, feeling it tug on the collar she'd fastened around her neck. It smelled faintly of fur. The scent comforted her.

Strangely, so did The Dungeon's atmosphere.

She sat on a padded barstool, her gaze compulsively darting to the entrance. Ro would be back, everyone told her. He always closed up his club.

People kept approaching her, introducing themselves. There was an air of respect, even deference in some of them that confused her, until one woman expressed her admiration for Lizbeth's graceful submission under Ro's lash.

Employees and patrons alike wanted to talk with her, get to know her. Some had seen her in the Crime and Punishment show. Others sensed a kindred spirit.

It would be her pack away from home, Lizbeth determined.

Except that her alpha was missing.

Anticipation and tension swirled in the pit of her stomach, and she glanced toward the entrance once more.

He stood before her. His dark eyes seemed to scald as they took her in, head to foot. His gaze fixed on her collar and the attached leash. He reached out to nudge her black cap, stroke her hair cascading from beneath it, graze her arm, then her hand. She recognized his touch as the equivalent of a dog's investigative contact. Exhilaration rose in her when she saw the look in his eyes.

"I missed you, Lizbeth."

"My name is Michelle," she stated clearly.

"Nice to meet you, Michelle." The relief, the happiness, and the heat contained in his smile made her heart give an ecstatic leap.

"You let me get away. You know what happens to strays in this city?" She waved her leash back and forth in front of him.

Ro grabbed it. "I don't intend to ever find out." He held the leash loosely. "Are you sure this is what you want? Should I assume the message printed on your new cap"—he paused to adjust it on her head—"is meant for me?" He looped the leash around his wrist once. Then twice. Bringing her closer. "Why'd you run?"

"I was scared," she admitted. "Everything happened so fast. And then, you made me feel so many things." She tilted her chin up at him, smiled. She leaned away, drawing the leash taut, testing him. "I'm not scared anymore."

"Is your collar worn for me, then?" Ro's eyes narrowed, tracking her movement. He drew the leash another loop over his wrist, stopping her movement.

"Can't you read?" She felt playful, provoking him. Her blood raced through her veins, bringing a tingling awareness to her extremities. Her heart felt lodged in her throat, half in hope, half in excitement.

"Say it," he commanded.

"Make me."

He looped the leash again with the fierce smile that made her weak in the knees. "You've earned yourself another punishment. I hope you're happy. Now say it." He trailed his fingers sensuously down her bare arm.

She shuddered, desire and emotion colliding inside her. "I want this. I'm yours, collared and obedient."

She caught her breath at the reflection of her emotion in his eyes. She thrilled to his formal tone. "And I'm your dominant and master, though never less a servant to the heart's demands." He wrapped the final loop of leash around his wrist, drawing her against him for a kiss that exerted full rights of ownership.

Then he scooped her into his arms.

Her black cap fell from her head unnoticed. It perched, jaunty, on her abandoned stool, the lettering visible to anyone who cared to look: SLAVE TO LOVE.

FORBIDDEN HEAT

1

Nora Sabine twisted the engagement ring around her finger, still unaccustomed to its feel. "I'm sorry I told you."

After a pointed pause, Ryan answered. "You said that yesterday, too. It's not like you can take it back. I just wish, you know. That your secret fantasy was more normal. A threesome. Or the Mile High Club. Or performing a lap dance." Ryan looked wistful.

"But it is normal. Fantasies about forced sexual encounters are some of the most common—"

"I just don't get it. You're a feminist, a modern woman who's vice president of a company!"

"I love you, sweetie. But you are a clod sometimes. And I'm not vice president yet." He knew she still debated taking the lucrative position. She suspected he didn't want her to. "I probably pissed them off quite a bit, taking a four-day weekend to think about it."

Silence.

"They said they couldn't get along without me. But I took the time off anyway."

More silence.

She sighed. "Okay, you're not a clod. I'd never agree to marry a clod. Truce?"

"Sure."

At his tone, she glanced at him, but he focused entirely on his driving, peering at street signs and then skidding off the main road and onto a gravel one, sending small rocks flying.

"Once a race car driver, always a race car driver." She spoke gently, intending to bolster his ego. He was so sensitive lately. Her career success in the face of his latest race losses rankled him, she knew.

"You're very sweet, setting up this long weekend at a bed-and-breakfast." She could just see the top of Oregon's Mt. Hood through a break in the trees, its jagged peak snow-covered even in summer.

As they turned into a long, winding private drive, Ryan smiled. "I never said it was a bed-and-breakfast."

"I'm pretty sure you did. Well, you wrote it," she amended. "Something about a sumptuous B and B in the mountains, and it being a romantic four-day getaway I'll never forget." She remembered her delight that Ryan was trying so hard to make their relationship work.

Black iron gates barred them from the gravel driveway of the enormous house looming ahead. Arching above the gates, ironwork letters spelled out TWISTED WOOD B AND B with sharp-edged top details.

Nora stared. "How Gothic. It looks like the entrance to a *Rocky Horror Picture Show* mansion, not a bed-and-breakfast."

"I told you. It isn't a bed-and-breakfast."

Ryan was beginning to annoy her. "Okay, what do you think B and B stands for?"

"Bondage and breakfast. Whip me beat me make me bleed, S and M is what I need."

As she stared at him, a deep voice emanated from the black speakerbox: "Password?"

" 'Fanny welt.' " The gates began to swing open. Ryan smiled at her. It wasn't a reassuring smile.

"S and M? Bondage and breakfast? You're serious." Her arm hairs rose as he drove on up to the house. Two years of dating, and she hadn't known he was kinky. How could she not have known?

She considered herself more open minded than anyone she knew—certainly more so than her married friends who'd up and forgotten her once they started having kids. And she loved adventures. She loved sex. She loved Ryan. Usually.

She glanced uneasily up the driveway as Ryan negotiated its twists and turns. "I'm not sure this is the best thing for us."

"I am."

She looked at him.

He tried another smile. "Please?"

She was fit for a 28-year-old woman. She ran every day and lifted weights to stay firm in all the right places. Making a fist, she looked down at it and wondered whether it would help or hurt matters to hit Ryan with it. This wasn't her idea of a romantic getaway.

She was about to insist he turn around and drive her home, when she spotted the man lounging on the rough-hewn wood steps leading up to the home's enormous wraparound porch. The flat black color of his clothes soaked up the sun and gave back no reflection, but his eyes glittered like a wolf's scenting prey.

As their eyes met, she felt pinned and held. It was a mildly unnerving sensation, underscoring her urge to flee. Yet somehow she couldn't quite bring herself to speak.

The man rose gracefully to his feet, his eyes never leaving hers. Another, more slender and younger man appeared by his side.

The sound of the door shutting alerted her to Ryan's leaving the vehicle. Startled, she realized the car had stopped. She followed him quickly.

Gravel crunched underfoot as they crossed the section of circular driveway. Early afternoon sunshine flooded the courtyard, but walls of forest surrounded it. On all sides the cedar, oak, and Oregon maple trees seemed to strain inward, as if trying to get at the magnificent house. Or possibly the magnificent, black-clothed man. Nora could hardly blame them. She swallowed as they got closer.

He wasn't classically attractive, like Ryan. Darker, bigger, and rough hewn like the steps he'd been sitting on, he radiated an almost electric charisma that made it difficult to notice anything but him.

"Hello. My name is Sylvester Vincent. Welcome to Twisted Wood." The greeting, given with a proper, polite disregard, was directed at both her and Ryan. "Little Peter will bring in your things."

A bobbing curtsy succeeded in pulling her attention away from the man's cool appraisal of them both. Little Peter, a small, beardless man who appeared to be in his early twenties, wore a red and white French maid uniform, complete with ruffles, bustier, garters, lace cap, and heavy makeup. "If it pleases you," Little Peter said to the air between her and Ryan.

She looked at Ryan. Ryan looked back at her. They both turned to look at Little Peter. "Um, okay," Ryan said. "Thanks." Ryan made small talk, in his overloud voice he put on when speaking to other men. In some circles it worked well for him. Here, with these men, surrounded by acres of forest and with an elegant, Gothic mansion looming over them, it didn't.

Little Peter only responded, "My pleasure to serve." Another bobbed curtsy, and Little Peter scurried toward their car.

Sylvester didn't smile. "Mistress Kiana let me borrow him for the day. She's trained him well, though for a service submissive he's still unpolished. May I show you to your room? You can relax and unpack before meeting the others at dinner at 6:00. Then after, perhaps a tour."

She felt Ryan's gaze on her again, and when she looked back she caught a strange, apprehensive expression on his face. Second thoughts about their stay? If she wasn't mistaken, he was about to grab their luggage, make some excuse, and herd her right back down the hill.

For her part, she was intrigued. Little Peter seemed sweet and sincere, even if he was dressed like a transsexual guest at a wild Halloween party. The grounds seemed vast and pristine. The house was so magnificent from the outside, it had to be amazing indoors. And the man . . . "Sylvester Vincent."

He didn't react to his name. He didn't smile. He watched her carefully. Waiting.

Nora turned to her fiancé and spoke in a wry tone. "You picked a fascinating place for our 'romantic getaway,' honey. Let's get settled in."

Nora Sabine wasn't what Sylvester had expected.

He reviewed his impression of her after he deposited them both in the Sultan Room. He enjoyed her pleasure at the sight of the low-lit exotic room with its wall-to-wall bed, glittering erotic art, sensual pillows, strategically placed mirrors, and whisper-soft draped canopy.

An executive's polish and confidence, check. Her age, her health, both as described. But she didn't quite match her checklist.

The BDSM Play Partner Checklist he had all his guests mail along with the check to hold their reservation provided an overview of their kink involvement, identifying their interests, any medical issues, and their sexual limits. It helped him build a guest list of people who had common ground for play.

His instant attraction to her was unexpected, as well. Those huge dark hazel eyes . . . Her gaze through the car window seemed at first totally captured by his, almost fearful. Then simply interested, then eager. Fascinating. Eyes that contained depths that pulled at him, that was something he hadn't expected.

Her simple, unadorned beauty set her apart as well. Long, straight, dark brown hair that flamed to a rich amber in the sun. A finely tapered, firm young body. Expressive brows. White teeth when her mouth parted to smile the fierce smile of one who craved adventure.

Still, he couldn't think her idea of good fantasy adventure included a chase and capture, followed by a rough rape. Her checklist included that, and more. He reviewed it again, puzzled. According to Nora's list, she derived gratification from serving as an ashtray while wearing a chastity belt. She enjoyed infantilism, heavy bondage, golden showers, electric torture, and having her face slapped.

He scanned the rest of the list. Blindfolding, sexual torment, anal plugs, gags, paddlings . . . mostly garden-variety stuff.

What gave him pause were the more hardcore, advanced-level items next to which she'd checked "5" on a scale of 1 to 5, meaning the activity would be a wild turn-on for her, and she'd like it as often as possible. Not only had she marked 5 on nearly everything from breath control to pony play, she'd placed a double asterisk next to each item, meaning she was willing to do them even with casual and multiple play partners.

He'd never heard of her before in the local fetish community. People talked. He'd have been told about a gorgeous woman who enjoyed wearing diapers and horsetail butt plugs. Something was wrong.

Maybe he was wrong. Very little surprised him anymore after two years of owning and presiding over the only local fetish-scene B and B. It was his domain, his exotic fortress in the middle of twenty-one private, wooded acres, and the high demand for an incomparable interlude at Twisted Wood Estates added to his dot-com wealth.

Often it was the most buttoned-up, prudish-seeming folks—the repressed bankers, the frustrated mothers, the shy computer programmers—who harbored the wildest and woolliest fantasies. Nora might very well have such twisted fantasies they'd make even a jaded recluse like him blush.

It wasn't as if he'd never been wrong before. Grievously wrong.

He folded her checklist, opened Ryan's. Sparse. He was interested in a threesome, with women only. "Women only" was underlined five times. He liked to watch. And, oral sex. Receiving only. That was it.

He folded Ryan's checklist, put it with the others.

If Nora actually liked rough sex and every single nonpermanently damaging activity on the list, good for her. He'd do his best to facilitate her adventures.

Now if only he could rid his mind of his own fantasy: Nora fleeing her pursuers, then captured. Rebelling against taunting words, struggling against violating hands. Her arms pinned above her head. Her legs forced apart.

Sylvester's cock hardened in his pants.

He cursed himself for it, turning his mind to more productive pursuits, like supervising Kitten and Little Peter's dinner preparations, and checking in with Mistress Kiana as she put together a savory feast. Perhaps he could help.

Anything to take his mind off fantasy-raping Nora Sabine.

2

Nora admired Ryan's nude form in the mirror. The mirror's placement, tilted against the wall to show a long view of what occurred on the bed, pleased her.

Ryan, however, didn't.

She grimaced. His body was certainly blameless. His missionary positioning as he thrust away showed his strong arms, tapered hips, and muscular legs to good advantage. He looked better naked than clothed; he wore his ironed pants, tight shirts, and trendy jackets with a sly self-consciousness rather than making the clothes an expression of himself.

When he reared back, and his natural blond hair brushed the tops of his tanned shoulders, she watched in the mirror, filling her eyes with the beauty of their bodies joined together.

He made a small sound, and she glanced up in time to catch his moment: eyes screwed shut, mouth the shape of agony.

"Mmmm," she said, rubbing herself against him, longing for more. He'd been even faster than his usual two minutes. She supposed the dinner engagement prevented her from protesting, this time. Bad form.

Still, she couldn't stop herself from reaching down, touching his flaccid member. An investigatory stroke.

He pushed her hand away.

She sighed. Maybe later she'd climb on top, the only way she could claim an orgasm with him.

The silk cover felt luxurious under her hand. She let her fingers trail up the bed to the headboard with its conveniently placed eyebolts. Ryan hadn't shown the slightest interest in using them, or the leather manacles hanging discreetly next to the bed in a mirrored wall case.

Ryan had laughed when she'd suggested it. "I was kidding about the whips and chains being what I need." He'd flicked the eyebolts contemptuously. "But let's try out this huge bed. . . ."

She flipped over onto her stomach, watching him dispose of the condom and get dressed. "Why'd you want to come here, to a bondage and breakfast?"

"You'll see."

She squirmed on the bed, residual heat from their unsatisfying encounter infusing her body with energy. "Good. For my part, I'm curious. We can explore it together, can't we? At some point? Otherwise there's not much good in staying." Ryan's contempt—he'd curled his lip at Little Peter when the submissive had curtsied himself out of their room, and she hoped the slender man hadn't seen it—made her uncomfortable. Their hosts seemed nice enough so far, despite their unusual proclivities.

Ryan looked at her, his gaze traveling over her nude body. Tenderness crept into his expression as he sat on the bed next to her. "Maybe we should go." He tucked a strand of her hair behind her ear. "We could look at houses again, more seriously this time. And you could watch me practice at Raceway."

Did he think she failed to appreciate his surprise vacation? "Nah, you went to all this trouble setting it up, and we're here already. It could be fun. Besides," she joked, "if I do take that vice president position this might be my last vacation ever."

She felt his hand freeze, then lift.

"What is it?"

"Nothing. Hand cramp." He swatted her gently on the rump. "You should hop in the shower. Get ready for dinner."

"You sayin' I stink?" she protested, mock-fierce, but only got a wan smile in response. She could tell something bothered him, and she suspected it was her promotion. It wasn't worth the fight to bring *that* up again.

She tiptoed to the bathroom, a huge, tiled affair with a bidet, double sink, and enormous glassed-in corner shower with six different showerheads and attachments. Even if she wasn't all sweaty, she'd have made an excuse to try out such a shower as soon as possible.

She turned one faucet after another: a waterfall cascade from directly above, forceful needles from the right, pulsating jets from the left (at thigh, belly, and chest height), and a segmented flexible steel protrusion that danced on her fingers when she fondled it, pouring a steady stream of warm water wherever she aimed it.

She lathered up, shampooed, loofahed, then rinsed by turning in a circle with her arms wide open.

Sylvester's large, graceful body, as he unfolded from the front steps, appeared behind her closed eyelids. He wasn't even that attractive. . . . Kind of ugly, she told herself emphatically, even as the driving spray and rivulets of water relaxed her muscles and washed her clean.

His face was too serious, his nose too big and slightly crooked, his hair and brows unkempt. He had large hands. Probably was clumsy with them. Though maybe he wasn't. . . .

He'd scowled at her more than once. Didn't he like her? Maybe he was playing some role, the stern-faced Master of the Mansion perhaps. That was it: he was pretentious, she thought with relief at having pinned a fatal flaw on the man. Now she could stop thinking about him.

Except she couldn't.

She opened her eyes. The windows were steaming up.

What if he appeared in the bathroom? First as a faint shadow beyond the steam, then more solid as he approached . . . then opened the glass doors to the shower?

She smiled at the thought of her own fear and startlement, and his bestial expression of lust. He'd enjoy her fear; it would stimulate him. He'd already be naked, his cock enormous, rigid, and intimidating as he stepped inside, knowing she had nowhere to run.

Water pounded her from all sides. Nearly all sides. Her eyes half closed, she reached for the flexible steel attachment, warmed now by the constant strong flow of water. She aimed the flow between her legs.

Gasping at the sudden sensation, she saw him in her mind's eye more sharply than before. She turned slightly, and when needlespray assaulted her erect nipples, she whimpered. In her fantasy, Sylvester smiled cruelly at the sound.

He moved more quickly than she'd have thought possible, pinning her against the warm, wet shower tiles. He held her arms above her head, sealing her mouth with his palm. She was terrified, but more terrified to try to escape, to scream and have him hurt her, even though she could feel the powerful brute pawing at her roughly, parting her legs. She could feel her body slide against the slick tiles at her back, the sharp stings of spray as she tried to evade his rough touch, struggling against the assault. She heard herself pleading for him to stop, to let her go, crying out as she felt the insistent probing between her legs when he thrust against her. She heard all his contemptuous, foul curses as he shoved his cock inside, hurting her and yet filling her exquisitely at the same time, and she came under his fierce, relentless plundering. . . .

. . . and staggered as her knees went weak in the shower, alone with the sensation that went on and on.

She replaced the steel hose on its holder and let the gentle waterfall cascade over her again, washing her wicked thoughts away.

Her heels clicked on the smooth wood floor of the hallway as they passed room after room. "This place is huge," she said again.

Ryan nodded but didn't respond. He looked resplendent in a blue button-up shirt and slacks that fit his physique to perfection. He'd shaved, too, and she could smell the familiar scent of product in his hair.

He'd looked at her with approval when she'd appeared in a low-cut raw silk evening gown and strappy high heels. She'd decided to wear her hair down, and she enjoyed the feel of it whispering against her back as they followed Little Peter's directions to the vaulted great room and its adjacent dining room. She wanted to pause and examine the ceramic and painted wood masks hanging on the hallway's walls, and the framed erotic photos too, but Ryan urged her forward with a warm hand on her elbow.

Good thing she wore heels so frequently at work, she thought with a twinge of annoyance as Ryan rushed her. Her feet would be aching otherwise. The Sultan Room evidently claimed one of the farthest spots from the center of the home.

When they arrived, she forgot all about her feet. She made a small sound of admiration at the double-sided fireplace in the center of the room, not to mention the grand piano perched on a carpet on one corner, the movie theater–sized television against the wall, or the exquisite yet entirely comfortable seating groups scattered everywhere. One group of three people conversed over by the piano, much too far away to hear.

Who were they, and could any of them boast an intimate relationship with Sylvester? Not that it mattered. She was an engaged woman, she reminded herself.

The scent of good food and freshly baked bread wafted to her.

She spotted a pool table, and two game tables. There were even chaise lounges just begging for people to stretch out with a good book, positioned under lamps with Tiffany glass and Craftsman details. Soaring ceilings bisected by enormous beams from which descended half a dozen lazily rotating ceiling fans. Colors were neutral, with jewel-tone accents. A chef's kitchen that looked torn from the pages of a home-improvement magazine was clearly visible at the far end.

"Wow," she breathed, taken a little aback. For a lair of sexual deviants, the place struck her as amazingly tasteful. And comfortable. Weren't there supposed to be manacles attached to rock walls, people running around in leather masks, things like that?

As if in answer to her unspoken questions, an authoritative thud of boot heel drummed against the floors, and a woman strolled up to them. Nora couldn't help staring. If Ryan sneered at this woman, Nora would kick him. If the woman didn't first.

A red rubber mask covered her hair and the top of her face, leaving exposed her wide, red-lipsticked smile. A long, dark braid of hair lay against her bare back. Her clothes were outrageous, from the leather cutout bra notable for the rouged nipples emerging like offered candy, to the cream-colored rope dress that began at her muscular ebony neck and ended just above her tall, metal-studded boots.

Ryan, for once, seemed completely silenced.

"I'm White." The woman offered a long-taloned hand to Nora.

Nora shook it, unable to control her glance at the woman's deep brown skin.

"My name," the woman laughed. "White. Purity of heart. Absence of darkness. Black is over there." She indicated a pale woman leaning over the breakfast bar and into the open kitchen. A narrow blond braid trailed from under her white hood and half mask. Her backside, high and firm like a boy's, was packed neatly into a shiny black latex skirt. Black's choice of boot mirrored White's, tall and metal studded. Delicate silver chains encircled her back, leaving the front to Nora's imagination. "Wickedness of heart. Glory in darkness. And you?"

"Gray, I suppose." Nora remembered her recent fantasy, felt a flush of shame. "Dark gray, maybe."

"Your name, silly. What's your name?"

"Her name is Nora. I'm Ryan. Pleased to meet you." Ryan shook her hand briskly, eyeing her gumdrop-red nipples.

"Hungry?" White's eyes twinkled.

"Uh . . ."

"Dinner's about to be served. If you'll follow me." Without waiting for a reply, she preceded them into the dining room.

With its vaulted ceiling, potted plants, and two gilt-framed leaded windows with a view of lush ferns and maple trees, the elegant dining room was fit for royalty. An intriguing piece of art hung from a beam near one end of the table: what looked like a curled-up human form encased in a stretchy translucent pink material.

All of it was merely a backdrop to the people already seated at the table.

Her gaze darted to Sylvester, then away.

"Sit where you wish," said White. She circled the table to place herself on one side of a man who smiled a welcome to them both. Black had already claimed the seat on his opposite side.

He patted both Black and White on their masked heads.

Nora felt Sylvester's presence so strongly, it was as if the very air vibrated around him. She knew where he sat—at the head of the table, of course—knew he watched her, but couldn't yet bring herself to look at him.

She sat at the middle of the rectangular table, and was glad for Ryan's presence when he sat next to her. Now, if Ryan could be trusted not to be rude to these people, and if these people could be trusted not to act like freaks and weirdos, she might be able to relax. Maybe even enjoy dinner. She appreciated the good food smells wafting from dishes being served by Little Peter and a female service submissive, who glanced at Nora with a shy smile when setting a silver-encircled china plate on the lace placemat before her.

"That's Kitten and Little Peter," the man across from her said. "You've met my Black and White, I gather?"

Before she could answer, a lovely woman appeared in the doorway and simply stood there for a long moment. Her long, sleeveless black velvet evening gown clung to her curvy body in just the right places, and her upswept auburn hair and luminous pale skin seemed just another work of art lit by the window's green twilight and the room's soft lighting. Until she snapped her fingers, and both Kitten and Little Peter abandoned serving duty to prostrate themselves before her.

"Mistress Kiana," the man across from Nora protested. "Really. They were serving dinner."

For her part, Mistress Kiana looked at the service subs at her feet. "Rise. Speak."

Immediately Kitten said, "I'm sorry for not immediately attending to you, Mistress Kiana." Little Peter belatedly added, "I'm sorry, too."

"Tsk, tsk. Kitten, fetch a rubber gag. The one shaped like a penis," she called after the scurrying sub.

Only then did she address the man across from Nora. "Master Andre, you're aware this one"—she gave a hand gesture to Little Peter, who knelt—"is still in training. After I spent so many hours cooking this meal with only minimal assistance from Kitten, I don't intend to suffer the slightest disrespect from either of them. This correction will only take a moment."

Kitten reappeared holding a length of leather, with a fat, stubby rubber likeness of a penis jutting from the middle.

"Insert it into Little Peter's mouth," Mistress Kiana commanded. "Buckle it closed."

Kitten did.

"Very good. Little Peter, as a service submissive, your only goal in life is to give good service. That includes being aware at all times where your owner is, and addressing her properly. Do you understand how you failed me?"

Little Peter nodded, hunched his shoulders pathetically.

"Good. Now, get on with serving; you've wasted enough of everyone's time."

Nora watched as everyone was served, chatting amiably as if nothing had happened and there wasn't a full-grown man with a penis gag in his mouth placing food before them.

She swallowed, hoping she didn't offend someone and get a gag stuffed into her mouth too. Her appetite fled.

Sylvester spoke softly with Mistress Kiana for a short time, making Nora wonder if they were a pair. She felt an odd sense of loss at the thought. In fact, she felt odd in general. Shy. She managed to speak briefly about her job. People seemed interested enough when she discussed the ups and downs of travel marketing. Slowly, when nothing else bad happened, the excellent food seduced her appetite into returning.

The courses pleased her enormously. Mistress Kiana was an accomplished cook. The woman barely glanced at the man she'd gagged.

Nora wasn't at all certain about the protocol of things, here. When not serving, the service submissives knelt in opposite corners, attentive, occasionally rising to fill water glasses or remove plates.

Ryan radiated tension, she suddenly noticed. Clearly he was even more uncomfortable than she was.

It was too quiet. But if she spoke up too often, or complimented the intimidating chef, might she get a gag put in her mouth?

Nora snorted, tired of feeling afraid. She decided to chance it: "Mistress Kiana, may I compliment you on an exceptional meal?"

"Certainly." The woman smiled at her, and it transformed her face into something much more accessible. "Thank you. Cooking is my second-favorite hobby."

"Her first favorite is 'beating the bottom.' Little Peter is in for it later." Master Andre grinned. "Maybe Kitten, too, if Mage is still being antisocial."

Sylvester spoke to Nora directly, explaining. "Mage lives here part of the year. He often has Kitten bring him a late dinner up in his Painloft."

"Antisocial." Master Andre repeated. He offered Nora a small smile. "More fun for us having Kitten all to ourselves. Perhaps as a toy for Black and White. What do you say, Kitten?"

Kitten started to nod eagerly, then checked herself and looked to Mistress Kiana. "If it pleases you, Mistress Kiana?"

"I'll be busy attending to Little Peter's punishment," the dominatrix agreed. "A caning, I think. Leave him something lasting to remind him of his disobedience." She frowned slightly, rubbed her temples. "And then perhaps a long, soothing massage."

Ryan put down his wineglass and spoke too loudly. "Isn't that a bit excessive for the crime? The poor guy's already wearing a dick in his mouth."

Everyone turned to stare at Ryan.

"We haven't gotten to know our newest guests yet." Sylvester's voice rolled across the room, compelling. "I've explained my role as dungeon monitor and general consultant, in the welcome brochure. Perhaps you have questions."

Nora frowned. "I didn't see any—"

"Yes, you explained everything," Ryan interrupted. "When does the role playing start?"

Sylvester stared at Ryan. "I'm not sure you do understand. And why such a hurry? The activities on your play checklist don't even involve role play. Unlike Nora's."

She could suddenly smell the nervous sweat coming off Ryan. Why was he afraid? And what was this checklist they were talking about? "Ryan, what's going on? Why didn't you tell me about . . . hey!" she slapped his hand away as he pawed at her face.

He tried again to stuff his wadded-up linen napkin in her mouth. "You've been bad, very bad. Your goal was to give good service, and, uh, you didn't. You've failed me." Though his mimicking words were ludicrous, the look in his eyes as he tried again to force her mouth full of napkin reflected some strong emotion. She smelled the alcohol on his breath. "You've failed me," he moaned.

She didn't understand his pain, but she did understand he was trying to gag her. "Ryan, stop it!"

"Stop."

Ryan did, panting. He glanced at Sylvester, who'd risen.

Sylvester enunciated clearly. His eyes shot sparks. "In BDSM fetish circles—Bondage, Domination, Sadism, Masochism—we have a creed we follow. Everything we do must be safe, sane, and consensual. *Consensual.* That did not look consensual."

"No, it didn't." Master Andre stared coldly at Ryan.

"No," Mistress Kiana agreed. She looked at Ryan as if he were a bug.

"We should leave." Ryan stood.

"Wait." Nora remained seated. "Why did you just do that? What is the checklist you were talking about?"

"I don't have to explain anything to you." Ryan began to stalk away.

"Black, White? Fetch." Master Andre smiled as his companions moved swiftly after Ryan. Nora watched, too surprised to move, as White headed Ryan off, then tripped him, even as Black pinned his arms behind his back as he stumbled and sank to his knees. They dragged him back, struggling and cursing, but when Black sat on him with his arms held firmly he subsided. He couldn't see White behind him shaking her head, a slow gesture of amazement. The woman left the room, then returned with steel manacles, which she quickly snapped onto his wrists.

"Un-freakin'-believable," said Little Peter, before he remembered himself. "Sorry, Mistress Kiana."

"Understandable," she murmured.

Nora sat rooted in her seat, staring at her fiancé. His arms were twisted back behind him, the wrists overlapping each other and fastened securely with handcuffs that didn't have any give at all. He struggled to his feet . . . then sat down heavily in the nearest chair. "That didn't work out quite the way I'd planned."

"What the hell is going on!" Now that everyone else sat motionless and silent, Nora felt her own fury build. "Explain what this is about!"

The crinkle of paper sounded loud in the silence. Sylvester unfolded it, brought it to her. "This isn't yours, I take it."

She scanned the stapled pages, then slowed and actually read some of it. "This has my old knee injury on it? How did you get my medical records? A BDSM Play Partner Checklist? Anal plugs? Golden showers? Electric torture?" She saw something that made her go faint with shock. "Chase and Capture rape fantasy?"

3

She stared at Ryan. "This was your idea. You made this list up
for me. After I told you about my fantasy."

"It was supposed to be a surprise."

"A dozen red roses is a surprise. A long, romantic weekend
at a bed-and-breakfast is a surprise. Rape isn't a goddamn surprise. It's assault. Were you going to do the honors yourself?"

"You think I don't know you're a million miles away when
we do it, in your spare scraps of time?" Ryan screamed at her.
"Off in fantasyland. Who can compete with that?"

"Whoa." Her world felt as if it were tilting sideways. "It was
never supposed to be a competition. Hey . . . Please excuse me,
I need some air," she told everyone as she stood and walked unsteadily from the room. She walked blindly, only by luck ending up by the back upper deck. Sliding the glass door to the
right, she stepped through onto the wooden planks and let the
cool twilight air caress her.

Her heart hurt. Another part of her felt vindicated by the
justification of certain suspicions. Ryan's competitiveness, Ryan's

secretiveness, Ryan's easily bruised ego . . . He hated her long hours, and her success. The problem was obvious, in retrospect.

She heard the door slide open behind her. Ryan stepped through. She saw the others slowly gather just inside the doorway, silent. Curious. She could hardly blame them.

Ryan tried to shrug, but his pinned wrists made the gesture awkward. "I'm sorry. If it's any consolation, I probably wouldn't have gone through with it."

"Probably. Great."

"It's just that, you know, you're this ice queen."

She started. Ice queen? Her?

"You have this fabulous vacation-marketing job where you get to fantasy-travel to all corners of the world. You have this bold attitude, living life on your own terms instead of settling down and raising two kids in a suburb like all your friends. You want adventures, new experiences, despite your crazy hours at work. And now, you're going to be vice president of the company and make shitloads of money . . . *and I never see you anymore.* What am I, next to all that? An aging has-been of a race-car driver who can't even make you come."

She made a small sound of demurral, but he was continuing. "So I just figured if you got taken down a notch or two, you might realize I'm better than fantasyland. You might actually, you know. Appreciate me. Love me."

"I said yes to you, didn't I?" She held up her left hand, ring on display.

"I should take it back. I don't deserve you."

She yanked it off, in full agreement. What he'd said had turned her stomach. "No. You don't." And yet, her heart ached seeing the lost, agonized look when she handed him back the ring.

"Ryan, you signed me up for rape," she said matter-of-factly.

"Yes. I'm sorry for that now."

This conversation was insane. "Sorry for it? Enough to maybe take one for the team yourself? Huh?"

He looked at her steadily. "If that's what it takes."

She threw up her hands. "Oh my god, we're both crazy. You know what? It wouldn't be enough now."

"Anything you ask. Anything on that sheet. I'm so fucking sorry, I'll do anything. Put me under a golden shower. Lock me in a cell. Whip me till I'm bloody."

"Asphyxiation!" called out Black.

"Pony play!" called out White.

"Anal fisting!" called out Kitten.

Everyone looked at Kitten. "What? It's on the list."

"Do you wish to make amends to Nora?" Sylvester stepped forward, alongside Black and White. The others fell silent. "Do you wish to put yourself, as the lowest of slaves, into the hands of these two switches? Assuming Master Andre has no objection," he added.

Master Andre shook his head. "They've been bottoming too much lately anyway, wearing me out. Let them top for a change." He grinned at Ryan. "Oh, they have plenty of nasty tricks. I should know; they learned them from me."

"Ryan, it must be consensual. You have to negotiate your limits with those whom you play, but considering what you did I'd seriously consider agreeing to remove any and all limits. However, a safe word is mandatory. Say it, and all play stops. Safe words are respected here. Choose one now, in my presence. Any word."

" 'Nora' is my safe word. And I agree, no limits."

Sylvester's lip quirked down on one side. The hint of contempt was the only emotion he'd shown. "Heard and witnessed. For the next three days and nights, Ryan is everyone's property and may be punished by anyone present, at any time, in any way they wish. Three days from now, Nora will decide if his penitence is sufficient reason to take him back." He nodded to Black and White.

The two women surged to Ryan, touching him, pinching. "Hey!" he slapped Black's hand away from his nipple. She immediately slapped his face. Then pinched his nipple, twisting cruelly.

"Whoa." Nora froze.

Then, as Black's handprint rose in a palm-shaped red mark on Ryan's cheek, he smiled at Nora. "For you."

"Oh, man. You don't have to do this." She looked at him pityingly.

"Yeah, I do. Oh. Um." He tried to turn the front of his body away from Nora as White tugged his pants down.

Not fast enough. Nora gasped. "You're hard! You *like* it!"

Ryan blushed.

As they collared and bound him, he began to look as if he had regrets, but Nora no longer worried too much about him.

As they tugged on his leash to lead him away, she even giggled.

"I'm glad to see this isn't traumatizing you." Sylvester watched her from the edge of the deck, smoothing his hand once over the railing as if calming it. She noticed the deeper silence and saw everyone else had vanished. He interpreted her gaze correctly. "Mistress Kiana is in the dungeon disciplining Little Peter. Black and White probably can't wait to get Ryan over to the flesh hook clearing, to terrify him. Kitten is cleaning up after dinner. Master Andre hopes to spend time with you later. And I . . . I want to have a little chat with you."

"Good idea."

"Would you like some water?"

"Got anything stronger?" She knew he did, the good red wine that had accompanied dinner. She licked her lips when he nodded. He preceded her inside. "Actually, you're wrong. I am a little bit traumatized. Ryan and I dated for two years. How could he do something like this?" When offered a choice of wines, she pointed to the bottle of Cabernet. "Thanks. He and I had our problems, sure. I guess we had more problems than I knew. He hides a lot," she said, the full impact hitting her of just how much he'd hidden from her.

She gulped her wine.

"Easy, there." He glanced up at sudden movement. Master Andre flipped channels from a couch in the middle of the open room. The TV was a strangely normal sound, but it made Sylvester frown. "Come with me."

She did, still sipping. A pleasant warmth filled her stomach. She felt the stirrings of excitement as she followed the man down another hallway and into a large room far enough from the TV to renew the silence. Which ended when he flipped on the lights. The soft wail and steady beat of Enigma accompanied the warm, recessed-lighting glow.

He immediately turned it down, but Nora smiled. "I've heard Enigma is like the national anthem for BDSM."

He made a noncommittal sound. Then, "I don't invite people into my suite, as a rule."

"I like Enigma." She liked him, too, but she didn't tell him that. His reticence was kind of cute, especially paired with the commanding way he'd taken control of the situation earlier.

He wasn't ugly after all, she realized, trying to look at him surreptitiously. It was difficult with those eyes of his trained on her. Not ugly at all, just unusual. His dark brows made him look intense. The shaggy hair made him seem a bit wild. Masculine. Tempting, in a dangerous way.

"So . . . you own this place?" She moved farther from him, sat down on a silk print–covered chair. Only after placing her drink on the low table did she realize she had a clear view of the adjacent bedroom.

A large, four-poster bed. Of course. She caught herself squinting at the sturdy-looking posts to see if they had eyebolts on them.

"Yes."

She started. "Yes? Oh." He was responding to her question: he owned the place.

He walked toward her. Sat in the companion chair. She felt her body tighten in reaction to his proximity. She nudged her wine away.

"You don't like it?"

"I like it fine. Just need to clear my head." He wasn't going to carry her off to his lair, she wasn't going to do anything stupid, and why couldn't she look away from his bedroom? She glanced around. Bookshelves. She was up and at them in a heartbeat. She recognized many of the books, too. Favorites of hers. Disconcerting, this particular man owning so many of the same titles. Exciting how she may have found a kindred spirit. Literarily speaking.

"How are you feeling?"

She considered. "Healthy. Recovering. Slightly buzzed. You're very polite."

"Politeness is desirable." Sylvester sounded amused. It pulled her away from her head-tilted review of his book spines. "Common courtesy goes a long way toward avoiding misunderstandings and preserving people's feelings. Would you like to talk?"

"Yes, please." She strode back to her chair and folded herself into it with a sigh at how comfortable it was. She smiled at him, more relaxed than she should probably feel. Just being in his presence was at once stimulating and soothing. At the moment she didn't care to examine the pleasant new feeling too closely, but after all she'd been through in the past hour she appreciated it greatly.

He looked at her without expression. "Just because sexual conventions are freer here doesn't mean social conventions aren't used." He placed his own glass of wine gracefully opposite hers. "Your Ryan's actions appalled me."

"Me, too. That checklist. He made me sound like a perverted slut."

"That's not what I found appalling." Sylvester smiled at her for the first time. "I don't judge people's kinks. Even when I strongly don't share them. . . ."

"Such as golden showers?"

"A fine example." He sobered, stared at her seriously. "What do you want from the next three days? You expected something quite different, I realize that. It's my hope you don't wish to leave."

She felt her heart leap, a little. He didn't want her to leave. "Well, that's good. Because I don't want to leave." She thought about it. "I honestly don't. I find this environment very interesting. Foreign in the extreme, but interesting. The slaves bowing to Mistress Kiana, for example. And those two women—Black and White. Ryan's in for a wild ride, isn't he?"

She searched herself for jealousy but didn't find it. She wondered what that meant. Maybe she was still in shock.

"You're not involved in the local BDSM community." It wasn't a question. "But you're curious. Okay. Let's find out what sorts of things interest you."

"What are you, some kind of . . ." Pimp, she was going to say, but that didn't sound right. Or polite. "Facilitator?" she finished.

His raised eyebrow let her know he'd tracked her thought. "I bring together like-minded people, and make sure no one gets hurt. I host the party. I had this property built on twenty-one secluded acres to create a big retreat center that's sex positive but not sleazy. Guests are usually friends of friends in the local leather and fetish community, real free spirits—I don't have the inclination to host an overnight just for some businessman who wants to check in for a spanking. I enjoy watching. I like the diversity. But now it's your turn to talk. What are your fantasies, Nora?"

"Well, you get right to the point, don't you?" And yet she felt the warm glow in her belly expand to heat her nether regions as well. The way he looked at her, as if he knew her dirtiest secret, made her hot as hell.

But she wasn't going to repeat the mistake of telling someone her biggest fantasy.

"I'm curious about bondage." There, that wasn't so hard. But she felt her face heat with embarrassment for admitting it out loud like that.

"Giving or receiving?"

"Receiving . . . Maybe a little giving, too." It could be interesting to have someone all tied up and at her mercy. Maybe someone like Sylvester. She gave him a flirtatious smile.

His expression didn't change. "What else?"

"Um. I heard flogging could be sort of fun. And being blindfolded. And, uh, nipple clamps."

"What else?"

She blinked. "I'm not sure there is anything." Except the Chase and Capture rape fantasy specter she couldn't evict from her mind. The very idea of something so violent was abhorrent, and yet, just knowing it existed as one of the possible fantasies made her wet.

"This is fun," she told him, admitting that much at least.

"Negotiating is supposed to be."

"We're negotiating?" Her breath came faster.

"That's what it's called in the scene when you discuss play limits."

"Oh."

He stared hard at her. "Let's go down a checklist of things, the way you normally would have before you arrived. You can tell me a number between one and five to indicate how you feel about that activity: one means no way, five means it's a wild turn-on for you. Are you ready?"

"Who would I be . . . playing . . . with?"

"That depends on your answers. And their wishes, too."

His calm, aloof demeanor both set her at ease and excited her. She thought of the other men at the dinner table, evaluating them. Master Andre seemed cute. Little Peter seemed harmless. Sylvester attracted her the most. "I guess I'm ready." She returned his stare, feeling bold.

"Spanking."

"Okay."

He waited.

"Oh. Four?"

"Tickling."

"Three."

"Branding."

She cringed. "One!"

"Electrical torture."

"Isn't that the same as branding?"

Sylvester shook his head. "Not at all. For example, Mage has an elaborate muscle stimulation kit, with attachments I'd never seen before. And he has an astonishing number of other electrical toys. It can be quite sensual."

"Do you know this from personal experience?"

"We're not discussing me right now. A number, please?"

Her curiosity spiked again. Damn but this conversation was making her want to try everything . . . with him. "Four."

"Threesome."

She considered. "One. Well . . . it depends. Two guys, maybe a three."

"Feathers, fur, food."

"Four."

"Hair pulling."

"That doesn't sound fun. Two."

"You'd be surprised. Role playing."

"It depends." In her fantasy, the man stalked her, then had his way with her. Should she tell him that? She felt tempted, then pushed the fantasy back underground where it belonged. "Could you give me an example?"

"Doctor/nurse. Teacher/student. Boss/secretary. Torturer/ prisoner." He looked at her. "Predator/prey."

"Could you . . . explain that last one?"

He was quiet for so long she wasn't sure he heard her. Then, "One of the most common role-playing fantasies for women is to be taken against their will."

The air in the room seemed to turn electric, plucking at her nipples, teasing her intimately until she felt short of breath. She tried to hide her reaction. "Yes, I've heard that's a common one."

"Give it a number."

"I . . . can't."

His stare burned her. "You can't? I think you can." He gave her a fierce smile, showing teeth. "Is it being kidnapped and used as a sex toy? Or chased and brought down and brutally fucked? Maybe a date rape, or a home break-in, or a cruel ravishing while tied to a pirate ship's mast."

Her mouth went dry. She wanted to dash from the room, and yet she sat rooted, unable to even look away. She felt her eyes widen and her nipples stand erect, no doubt clearly outlined under the tissue-thin material of her dress. She tried to remember how to be the coolheaded, knowledgeable person she was at work. People consulted her, looked up to her for her experience, her capable management, her enthusiasm for researching anything she didn't know. But nothing she'd encountered in the workplace or elsewhere prepared her for this sensation of willing helplessness under his gaze. He was talking her language. If he wasn't careful, she'd . . . she'd what? Beg him to rape her?

To calm herself, she reached for her glass of wine. "I'm not sure that's . . ." To her horror, her hand was shaking. She set the wine down abruptly.

"Some men have the same violent desires. To take, to dominate a struggling victim. *As a fantasy only.* Nora? Nothing here happens that isn't consensual. You're safe, I promise."

He looked off into the distance. Then, "Some men mistakenly believe a woman doesn't care who stars in her fantasy. Of course she does."

He referred to Ryan. He believed she was still affected by Ryan's foul trick on her, she realized with relief. He had no idea what dirty thoughts played in her mind.

Or did he?

She went on the offensive. "Do you have those fantasies, Sylvester?"

"We aren't talking about me."

"We're talking about fantasies. You're explaining them so well. Do you dream of torturing your helpless victim, then spreading her legs and plowing her as she struggles underneath you? Do you fantasize about stalking a woman, capturing her, and forcing her to perform degrading acts on your filthy body? Does it do it for you, having a woman naked and whimpering while you press her up against the slick walls of her shower, begging you to stop and crying when you push your big cock up between her legs?" Oh god, talking about it was getting her way too hot. She decided to throw caution to the winds. "Do you want to force me, Sylvester?"

Sylvester found himself on his feet, looming over Nora. The woman clutched the edges of her chair as if afraid, but her fast breathing made her obviously hard nipples thrust up at him like pointy little invitations. Which they weren't. They *weren't*.

She didn't know what she was asking for.

He should know better than to be taunted into a lather by a

hot-talking woman. Know better than to believe such words at face value. He had, once upon a time. It had ruined his life.

He looked down at her. No denying she wanted something. Possibly him. Probably an effect of her rebounding emotionally from her boyfriend's betrayal. This had to be put into perspective.

Throttling back his own lust along with the agonizing memories she'd inadvertently evoked, he shook his head. "What I want isn't relevant at this time."

Knowing his erection tented his pants, and that there was nothing to be done about it, he slowly returned to his seat. "This isn't about me and my list of fantasies. It's about yours. What you want." He saw her heat undiminished, and marveled at her. Tempting. Refreshing, brave, desirable. In other words, extremely bad news for his hard-won equilibrium.

"It's just a fantasy, right Sylvester?"

"For some, yes."

"For you."

"Irrelevant. Taking me out of the picture, what does Nora Sabine want?"

"I want the world," she declared. She seemed surprised by her own answer.

Truth rang in her words. Struck by her hunger for life, even after the trick that was played on her, made him admire her more than a little bit. Then again, she might just be tipsy from the wine. "You'll have to narrow it down. 'The world' might be a tall order, even here."

"Do you generally participate in the playing?" She pulled off her high heels, wiggled her toes. Then stood. He knew there was no misinterpreting the challenging look on her face.

"As the resident dungeon monitor, I try to keep an eye on things. I need to be ready to help out when and where needed." Her scent, an alluring floral scent of light musk and the soap he'd chosen for all the showers, reached him. It made him blink

slowly, savoring. He stared at her. "If the help is welcome."
Now why did he say that? She looked at him, clearly wondering whether to "welcome" him further. He nipped it in the bud.
"Ethics forbid involvement."

"Ethics? Or fear?"

He felt stung. Was she suggesting cowardice? She had no idea who she was talking to. "Let's talk about you," he repeated. "You're curious. You want to play. You seem to have an interest in playing with me, but that's not something I wish to discuss tonight. You've met the other guests. Who's choice number two? How about Master Andre?"

After a moment in which he was certain she'd storm out, she merely shook her head. "Arrogant, much?" Her lips twitched with suppressed laughter. "What can he do to me that you can't?"

Nothing, he wanted to tell her. Instead he said: "Master Andre's an accomplished dominant. He has a solid reputation, and is well known for his Florentine flogging style."

"Dominants like submissives. I'm not a submissive person."

He looked at her, evaluating. Maybe she wasn't. But she wanted to be conquered, was begging for it.

The way she held herself, like a prize bitch daring him to take her down, kept him hard. She really had a sexy body, her curves and muscles in all the right places, her movements graceful as she moved about his room, stretching out. Making herself comfortable. Burning off excess energy? He'd like to help her with that. She would be more than a firecracker, she'd be an explosion of sensuality. The pinnacles to which he could take her. The delights they could share. His mouth filled with saliva at the idea of her welcoming his rougher attentions.

But she wasn't for him. That fantasy was too dangerous. He stood, prelude to escorting her to Master Andre.

As if reading his mind, she pivoted and stepped against him.

He didn't even have a chance to protest. He couldn't move for a moment. The shock of her warm body so unexpectedly fitted to his sent sensual forks of lightning all through him. "I want you," she said in a demanding growl that he felt as well as heard. She grasped his hard cock through his pants. It would have taken a stronger, kinder man to resist the temptation to pull her closer, take what she offered . . . and he was neither.

He grabbed the cheeks of her ass and hauled her onto his hardness. "You want this? No?" he asked as she recoiled from his size. "Too late," he said as she suddenly struggled against his obscene thrusting against her. He could rip off her ridiculously thin dress so easily. He could almost hear the tear of fabric, and see her cowering to hide her nakedness, ashamed, but not really . . .

He felt his eyes narrow in pleasure as she pressed her palms against his chest, pushing, and her small body made a convulsive, and wholly unconvincing, motion of resistance. He pinned her wrists above her head with one hand, and delved down the front of her dress with the other. "No bra. What a little slut you are." She tried to twist away, but he tweaked one nipple, pinching it cruelly just to hear her gasp. He cupped one breast. "Nice. Not too big, not too small." He weighed it like so much meat.

Then he pinched her other nipple. Hard. Harder. He needed to make her cry out, needed her fear, her pain and pleading and tears like other men needed moans of pleasure.

"Nooo," she finally begged, squirming against his cock, and it was as if she'd taken him into her mouth. Hissing, he pushed against the juncture of her thighs and let his hand leave her tits to cup her ass, to drag her hard against him. As his fingers sank with difficulty into the fear-sealed crack of her ass he felt himself teeter on the edge of losing control completely.

Again.

He couldn't let it happen again.

He backed away from her, shaking.

She swayed in place, lips parted, eyes glazed. "Don't stop."

God, she was tempting. He made himself take another step back. "I'm sorry. That was inappropriate." He watched her recover herself. Smooth her dress. When she again focused on him he saw anger in her eyes, and was glad for it. "You're in a vulnerable place right now. I want to help you, *but not that way*."

She looked at him, at the telltale bulge in his pants. She tossed her hair. "Bit of a drama queen, aren't you. It's just sex. You. Me. Bouncy bouncy."

"Thank you, but I'd prefer not to."

"But I could *feel—*"

"We didn't negotiate that. You don't have a safe word established. There are too many reasons to list why that was wrong and why it's not going to happen again."

"No means no."

He nodded. "Unless negotiated otherwise."

"I thought you and I were negotiating?" She looked at him hungrily.

It made him nervous. Her sexuality baked off her like a heat aimed right at him. How long had she buried it, denied it, dated people like Ryan who didn't have a chance at truly satisfying her? He reminded himself she had no idea how much danger she was in.

She was forcing him to rudeness. So be it. "This conversation is over, for the moment. Go. Play with Master Andre, or whomever else you wish."

Target hit.

She drew back as if he'd transformed into Frankenstein before her eyes. "Right. Got it." She turned her back, slipped on her shoes, walked away.

Too much? "Don't forget to discuss your list with him, and choose a safe word. I'll see you at breakfast," he called after her. "It's going to be—"

The door opened, slammed shut.

"—Belgian waffles," he finished in an empty room. "And berries." He let himself fall back into his chair, heavy and as helplessly riveted by his lust as if he were trussed to immobilization by Mage's most elaborate knotwork.

4

When her eyes focused again, she'd crossed the hallway connecting Sylvester's suite to the great room. A sense of being watched prickled her skin.

Master Andre stood in the middle of the room. The TV was off; his gaze was steady on her. He waved.

The simple, normal gesture made her smile. She waved back, veered toward him.

"Hello. How are you doing?" he asked when she closed the distance. "Considering everything," he added. His voice was softer than it had been at the dinner table. In deference to her supposed fragility?

Her body still tingled from Sylvester's rough touch. And still ached with need for more of his bruising, forceful assault.

So much for fragile.

"Pretty good. Considering everything." She looked around, appreciating anew the tasteful luxury of the large room, then at Master Andre. In her limited experience, mostly from the media, the S and M–type "masters" all wore sweaty leather vests and leered a lot, as if they'd just cleaned up from a porn shoot.

Master Andre wore a tasteful flannel shirt over black jeans. Standing, he was taller than she'd thought, and though he wasn't smiling, his lips naturally curved up at the ends. His thin brown hair wanted to recede, would doubtless begin to in a few years, but he had the shapely skull and elegantly casual bearing to get away with it. He reminded her of Bruce Willis. The only hint of leather was a pair of beefy Doc Martens, but she had a pair of those, too, and it didn't make her into anything but appreciative of good boots.

Master Andre didn't leer at all. He just stood there, indulgent, permitting her scrutiny. She remembered his proprietary way with Black and White. "They won't really hurt Ryan, will they?"

He didn't pretend not to know what she meant. "No." He considered. "If by that you mean any permanent physical damage. That's just not what it's all about."

"What is it all about?"

He grinned, an easy, cheerful smile that would've looked foreign on Sylvester. "You put your right foot in, you put your right foot out . . ."

"Sylvester explained a few things, but he didn't cover the Hokey Pokey." She cocked her head at him. "Master Andre."

Something flickered in his dark eyes. "That does sound nice coming from you."

"Does it?" He wasn't Sylvester, but if she wasn't mistaken, this very attractive, dominant man wanted to "play." Whatever that meant. She found herself excited at the thought of finding out.

"What exactly did our gracious host explain, Nora? I'll be happy to answer any questions you still have." He looked at her inquiringly. Politely.

"I'm curious . . ."

"Yes?" His voice was kind.

". . . about bondage. And S and M. And everything."

He raised his eyebrows. "Everything?"

"Not everything," she hastened to say. "But . . . well, there's a list." She felt strangely flustered again. He had charisma and self-assurance to spare. She wondered at all the things he knew. Hadn't Sylvester said Master Andre was an accomplished dominant? And what on earth was "Florentine"-style flogging? And where could they go to have him show her?

Suddenly he laughed. "You're all but in subspace just standing there, aren't you? I'd better get you down to the dungeon where I can deal with you properly. If you'd like me to?" Polite again.

Her curiosity about the dungeon, about the nasty, clever wiles he'd taught Black and White, about what Master Andre could do to her, emboldened her, yet at the same time she felt oddly abashed. She wasn't sure of the protocol.

"I'd like you to."

"Come with me," he said, taking her arm and placing it firmly in his as he directed their stroll to a wide staircase leading down. "Now, tell me the things on your list. But first and foremost, for a safe word, I'd like to use the default one, the traffic light system. Have you heard of it? Red, yellow, green? Probably self-explanatory, but red means complete stop. Yellow means pause. Green means . . ."

"Go."

"Very good. Now tell me all about your list."

By the time she finished, carefully omitting all mention of Chase and Capture rape fantasies, they'd entered the candlelit domain of the dungeon. She felt wonderfully sensitive, alive to the slightest shift in the air from talking about her fantasies again.

She stared around the room, marveling. The sun had sunk,

so the only lights came not from the glass on the two different French doors leading outside, but from the fireplace, the low-watt bulbs placed above the erotic pictures and freestanding art, and the countless pillar candles placed in corners and on shelves.

The art complemented a torture-chamber decor. She peered more closely at one particularly well-lit display of weapons. Steel helmets, short swords, a well-honed trident, and a weighted net pegged to the wall. She fingered it, curious.

"A retiarius net, used by gladiators to snare their adversaries." He waited for her, indulgent.

Did he think she was stalling? She swallowed, moved away from the weapons. Maybe she was.

A rug over a carpet gave part of the room a lush, opulent feel. Farther away, under low-hanging beams from which chains dangled free, the floor showed only bare concrete. In one corner, dangling from a large exposed beam, was a twin piece of art to the pink-encased man upstairs. It looked just as odd down in this den of exotic sensuality as the other one did upstairs in the elegant dining room.

Unfamiliar music throbbed, a sensual bass beat. She wet her lips, gazing at the bondage furniture. The beds and benches and other larger pieces could be nothing else; the straps and chains and eyebolts made them single-purpose devices. She recognized a converted sawhorse, and an enormous X-shaped cross of wood, and a tall human cage with a tall human male confined inside. . . . "Ryan!"

"Nora?" He wore a blindfold.

"Don't talk to the doggie." Black strolled by her, wrapped herself around the narrow cage. She cooed, "Bad doggie. I told you not to speak. And you're not erect. You know what I have to do to you now? I have a cattle prod in my hand." She displayed a long, red wand to Master Andre and Nora. Inserting it through the bars, she murmured, "I could zap you over and over until you screamed. I'd like that."

"She would," White told Nora, who jumped. She hadn't heard the woman approach. "But I'd be very sad. Maybe we could just zap him once, so he knows better for next time."

"You're too nice," Black complained, tracing Ryan's naked ribs with the probe. Down to his belly. She poked his penis, which stirred.

"Please, Mistress Black."

Zap! Ryan screeched and Nora jumped at the popping sound of the electrical burst. She covered her mouth.

"Just above his pubic bone," White whispered. "It sounds worse than it feels." She considered. "Though it doesn't feel good."

Black continued. "I didn't give the doggie a command to speak. Care to say anything else? No? Then I just need to decide where to zap you one more time.... The arm? The nipple? Oh, he doesn't like that, look at him tremble! The belly?" Before she finished the word, White triggered the prod. Ryan screamed and the smell of ozone joined the good wood scent from the fireplace.

Nora stared.

"He's okay," White assured her, still in a whisper. "Look," she said, and Nora did. Ryan's erection jutted up and out, straining through an opening between two metal bars. Black strode up to him, and without warning grasped his cock and balls, fondling them briefly yet expertly. "Good dog."

Ryan moaned, shamed but clearly in a state of bliss.

A strange surge of feeling rushed through her as she watched Ryan's arousal. His face was red, he seemed on the verge of dying of mortification, yet his penis leapt and danced the way it never had with her. A willing torture victim.

"How are you feeling?" Master Andre asked, watching her closely.

"I'm feeling . . . kind of good."

"Would you like to feel more of that? I'd be honored to guide you in your first submissive experience."

She wasn't feeling particularly submissive, but she liked the way Master Andre's eyes seemed to promise a world of dark delights. "Lead on! Um, the cattle prod thing? Probably only a 'two.' And regular sex is right out; I hardly know you."

He smiled, indulgent. "Not a problem." The mischievous glitter in his eyes made her wonder what sorts of irregular sex he was thinking about.

He guided her. "This environment is particularly intimate and welcoming. The far doors over there lead to a small balcony for smoking. Do you indulge? No? A pity; quality pipe tobacco is a soothing thing after a session. I go out there all the time."

He continued to walk her about the place. "Over here is a small, cozy area near the fire. Hardly anyone can see us, but we can see them, can't we? Black and White are making that poor boy squirm. Mistress Kiana seems fatigued; she's letting Little Peter give her a foot rub rather than inflicting her usual diabolical punishments. Sylvester's off doing Sylvestery things, and Mage is forever sequestered in his garret. Other than that it's just us . . . and this rack of toys. You haven't seen these before, have you? Sylvester's collection, and more. His guests buy toys from shops and vendors' fairs and Home Depot. They often leave them here. Lucky us."

He touched one after the other. "Spanking gloves, paddles, shackles, ropes, clothespins, single tails, floggers, canes . . . Any preference? No? That padded table"—he indicated a wooden table between him and the fireplace, covered only by a fitted gray pad—"will do for you."

She gazed at it. A bare expanse. Was she supposed to lie down on it?

He gave her a wolfish grin. "First: strip, Nora."

She swallowed. Just like that?

"Do you need help?" he asked, solicitous.

"No . . ." Her cheeks burned. Could she do this? She knew she could trust him, could trust everyone she'd met—if she said "red" her adventure with Master Andre would end—but could she take off her clothes in public before a man she hardly knew? She glanced at the others, busy with their own adventures.

If she didn't, wouldn't she always regret it? Here was her chance to claim some of the "world" she'd so vehemently told Sylvester she wanted. What was he doing right now, she wondered. Was he having as much trouble as she was, trying not to think about their intense connection? If only Sylvester would give her what they both needed.

But Sylvester had pushed her toward Master Andre.

Who was watching her, a polite question in his dark eyes as she simply stood. She wanted Master Andre, too, wanted his expertise on her body. Wanted his bondage, his flogging, his mysteries. She stepped out of her shoes, kicked them away. Slowly, she pulled up her dress. Folded it, placed it to the side. Feeling his eyes on her body, she bent to remove her black lace panties. Placed them on top of her folded dress.

Should she sit on the table? It felt odd to simply stand, nude. She kept her legs closed, then crossed them. She folded her arms across her chest, then clasped her hands, unable to find a comfortable position for her arms and legs. Master Andre watched, seeming to enjoy her ordeal.

Then he approached. She shook, a little, but not from cold. "Relax, please," he told her. "You're going to have a wonderful experience." He circled her as if she were only a piece of art to admire, as if it were unthinkable to touch her. "You're very beautiful. I very much like the taper of your waist, and your breasts. Your ass is firm and round. I hate a flat ass; they have no mystery. Your legs have good muscle tone. Do you run?"

"I . . . yes."

"I'm not the least bit surprised. You have a lovely body, and a lovely face. I'm going to put your hair up for you, to get it out of the way."

When she moved to help, he gently placed her hands at her sides. "Not necessary." With the finesse of an artist, his warm fingers gathered up her hair, twisted it around at the crown of her skull. He tied it off with a knot.

He let his fingers trail sensuously down her neck, tracing patterns on first her right shoulder, then her upper back. His voice in her ear was as soft as thought. "If I do anything that distresses you, or you wish me to stop, say 'red.' If you'd like me to pause, to ask me a question or for any other reason, say 'yellow.'" He drew a snaking pattern on her left shoulder. Then the nape of her neck. "Do you understand?"

Nora nodded. His touch made it difficult to focus on anything else. The light skimming of his fingertips felt gentle, not at all like Sylvester's punishing touch. She couldn't completely relax, knowing Master Andre planned his own kind of punishment using the toys he'd called to her attention earlier. But the slow movements of his fully clothed body and his delicate touch didn't seem sadistic, or cruel, or threatening at all.

Her instinctive grasp of Master Andre's rhythms guided her. He wouldn't mar the soft, erotic rhythm of such a masterful touch with something so crass as a sudden beating. His hands continued to stroke and explore her curves and planes and angles, probing here, tickling there, brushing against her nipples so lightly it might have been accidental. She felt her nerve endings come alive at his touch, a hot tide following in the path of his trailing fingers. She leaned into it.

"Nora. I want you to climb up onto this table. Please get on your hands and knees. Yes, parallel to the fireplace, facing this candle pillar."

She did as he instructed, wondering where her will had gone. It seemed perfectly natural to do as he said.

"Good. Spread your legs for me, Nora."

She complied, feeling a delicious vulnerability.

"Close your eyes."

She did, and the faint flicker from the fireplace at the edge of her closed right eyelid became the only movement in her world. As if an expression of that flame, Master Andre's hand grazed her back, then the cheeks of her ass, then her sides and her flanks, warming her far more than the fire. She trembled.

"Hold very still. Don't make any sound."

She held her breath. She tried not to move at all, waiting for who knew what else would occur, but nothing did.

Only the rhythmic beat of the music kept her company while she waited. The tension built in her.

Light as a butterfly's wing, his touch finally trailed from the top of her neat triangle of hair, down into the crevice, around her lips and back up to circle her clit. Not touching it, just circling. Teasing.

She twitched, exhaling harshly with the effort to remain still. Down, down went the fingers into her folds, even as he continued to flick at the skin just above her clit in time to the music. She could feel her mouth open in a wordless moan, yet she tried to stay motionless and silent.

Until his fingertips stopped teasing. He tapped her clit directly, in the same steady beat.

It yanked a gasp from her and despite herself her hips moved toward the source of pleasure.

Master Andre slapped her on the ass.

The crack of sound startled her almost as much as the sting. It didn't exactly hurt, but it surprised her. A second later, a strangely compelling, almost itching heat covered her ass where he'd slapped her. It radiated out, bringing a tingling to her every extremity. He spanked her again, then five more times.

His fingers working between her legs never missed a beat.

Where the two sensations met—the feeling of his devilish

tapping and the radiating heat of the spanking—rose a feverish wanting for more.

On the same wave rode an odd dismay at disappointing Master Andre so much that he had to spank her.

She was panting, ashamed of her desires but unable to keep herself from making the galvanized little leaps in response to his fingers.

"You keep moving. I'll to have to restrain you, Nora."

5

Nora nodded, fierce joy blooming in her at the thought of this man binding her. This S and M thing was starting to make a whole lot of sense to her. It wasn't Chase and Capture, and Master Andre wasn't Sylvester, but she couldn't remember the last time she'd felt so excited with someone else in charge of things.

Gently, Master Andre buckled a snug, soft contraption around one of her ankles. Fleece-lined restraints? Tight, but comfortable. Then he moved her other ankle farther out, and buckled another restraint closed. What was this? A cool breeze against her moist sex. She tried, but couldn't close her legs.

"It's a spreader bar. What a gorgeous ass you have, what an amazing body." He fondled her, and she felt diminished, embarrassed, just a sex object on display . . . yet achingly alive to his touch. She shivered and moved against him as best she could. He immediately spanked her again. Ten this time. "You need more binding." She could only gasp, awash in sensation.

He pushed her head to the table, guiding her gently down

with his palm on her forehead to cushion the impact. He pinned her arms behind her exactly as Ryan's had been earlier, only Master Andre used the same snug restraints he'd used on her ankles. She tried to wriggle out, to no avail.

"Yes." She heard her own voice, low and satisfied, and marveled at it.

"Am I going to have to gag you, too?" Amusement tinged his voice. "I'm beginning to believe you want me to punish you severely."

There wasn't much she could do to stop him, she thought. Her helplessness combined with the obscene position he had her in made her feel flustered, yet intensely aroused. She wriggled with delight as he ran his fingertips once more between her legs, down into her slit and up, his deliberate provocation impossible to resist.

Suddenly a line of fire bloomed on her ass cheeks. A moment later, the sting sank deep, and she gasped for the first time in true pain. "A rattan cane," Master Andre informed her, "offers a unique twofold sensation: the first strike offers a simple sting, and then the exquisite and deeper unfolding of a pain that fades almost immediately to an addictive, piquant buzz of warmth. You're feeling it now, aren't you?"

She nodded, marveling at the metamorphosis of pain into the sensation he described. Fearsome, yet delicious. She whimpered when he brought his hands into play again, plucking at her sensitive nipples, sliding clever fingers between her legs. Again, she couldn't stop her hips from moving.

This time, he slapped her with something wider, something that made a startlingly loud clapping sound. It didn't hurt, at first, not like the cane. But he continued, hitting her on the same fleshy spot of her ass until she heard herself making a small sound of distress. He stopped immediately. She heard his sharply indrawn breath when she twitched her ass at him, longing for more touches, more slaps, more of anything he cared to give her. God, she was feeling like an animal, pinned down and ready to mount, bound and helpless. Shudders of delight wracked her. If he were Sylvester, just the thought of his rough penetration and hard use would be enough to send her flying right over the edge.

But he was Master Andre, expert at bondage and torture and dominance, and sex was not on the agenda. Sex was an ending, in her experience, and she didn't want this to end. Curiosity consumed her. She wanted him to take her farther, show her more, diminish her completely. If he could.

"More," she whispered.

"Oh, you are precious." He ran the toy over her ass, letting her feel its thick, uneven rubber surface, its rough edges. "This is a tire tread slapper. Made from recycled tire rubber. I can tell you want to obey me, and yet you also seem to enjoy testing me." He whapped her with the slapper again, this time between her legs. Gently, repeating the blows in rhythms of one-two-three, he reached under her to tweak first one nipple, then the other, until she cried out.

"Such a very bad girl." With a cool, delicate touch, he quickly removed her wrist restraints. "You're enjoying this too much. Up, to your hands and knees."

She was quick to obey him. Of course she enjoyed it; even now his clever fingers slid over her skin as if unable to resist touching her in this new position. "So beautiful, so hot and wet and perfect." He traced a tiny figure-eight on her clit until she vibrated with urgency. "So responsive." He slipped a blindfold over her head, adjusted it over her eyes. The world went dark, and then his touch began again. The enforced blackness ratcheted up the intensity.

"How are you doing?"

"I'm . . . fine."

"What is your safe word?"

With her nerve endings singing to his touch, she had to make a huge effort just to remember the simple word. Her slow voice sounded thick and unfamiliar. "Red."

"Very good." A heavy cascade of leather strands fell on her back, slipped down her side to the table. Then again, slipping down over her ass to the table. "This is a flogger. If at any time the sensation becomes too much, I want you to remember your safe word."

"Okay." She shifted, bereft without his magical fingertips. "Flogging," she murmured. "You're known for your Florentine style."

"That's right. And you're going to be sorry if you continue to disobey me. I'd seal that mouth with a penis gag, but I have a better idea of what to put inside you. No, not that, you dirty-minded brat." He slapped her ass with his hand, reproving. "Though I said no sex, I did not say no penetration. Want to say your safe word yet?"

The smile in his voice both excited and worried her.

She remained silent.

He began the flogging.

It started slowly. The merest kiss of leather against her backside, gentle strokes in time to the music. One on her right cheek. One on her left cheek. Occasionally she'd feel just the leather tips skim her skin, and it stung. Then the heavier fall of leather began to sting, too. Master Andre let just enough time go by between strokes for the sensation to fade . . . and then his rhythm doubled in speed.

"This is the Florentine style. It allows for a faster speed and a graceful strike. It takes coordination and strength to do properly. Your ass should be heating up quite nicely."

It was. Without the recovery time in between, the heat seemed to build and build. She made a sound of distress, but this time Master Andre ignored it.

She twitched her hips, trying to relieve the fire, but he went on, remorseless. Her panting was audible to her own ears; couldn't he hear it? Her ass must be blistered and lacerated from the feel of it. And yet, the stinging fire seemed to refer to her nipples, to her clit, and she rejoiced when the sensation built upon itself, fire upon fire, steady and unstoppable.

At least until he stopped. "Would you like to say your safe word?"

"No! Keep going."

He didn't immediately. "Teaching brats respect is another of my specialties. A labor of love, even." She heard steel chains clanking, and metal against plastic from the direction of the toys. "Ah, yes. Nipple clamps." He made the clamps snap next to her ear. "These have nasty little claws, and should help keep your mind on matters other than defying me." He reached under, massaged her nipples. "Still rock hard. That does make it extra easy for me to do this."

The sweet, biting pain of the clamp pinching her nipple made her gasp, half in shock, half in wonder. Master Andre was right. They demanded her attention, insisted on it. The pain almost exceeded her threshold, worrying her—would she lose circulation? Would her nipple be severed?—but the pleasure spiking out quickly overcame the pain, though it still pinched cruelly.

Then the second one closed on her, and she couldn't restrain a whimper.

"Don't worry," he said, as if reading her mind. "They're adjusted to nearly the loosest setting, believe it or not. I can tell from the compression of your nipple the clamps grip you firmly, but not excessively. Even so, if you feel too much discomfort, you must say your safe word."

But she'd already gotten used to the steady pressure. The fierce pleasure of it seemed linked in some erogenous referral to her belly, her lungs, her crotch, and nerve endings she didn't know she had. She also felt a sinking pleasure at being naked and pinned and clamped, on display, a shameful and exhilarating sensation that excited her further.

He tugged the chains attached to the clamps. It won a cry from her, of pain and pleasure.

Master Andre patted her ass, approving. "That's right. Hmm." He fingered between her crack from behind. "One more thing."

She heard the impact of metal on padding and felt the weight on her nipples increase, a piercing sweetness. He'd let go of the chain. She heard him move to the toy rack. Then she heard a zipper, and a thump of plastic and rubber. Straining to determine what diabolical new instrument of torture he'd grabbed, she almost didn't register the vibrating noise.

Vibrating noise?

She didn't realize she was trying to close her legs until the inflexible bar between her ankles resisted her efforts.

Master Andrew returned, gave a single sharp tug on her chain. "Now, that's no way to obey."

A thrill of fear and excitement flooded her. What would he do this time? Would he really use a vibrator? She could feel the wetness between her legs at the thought. He had to do something extreme, something to satisfy the cravings he'd woken. Why wasn't he getting on with it? She frowned, listening. Silence.

Then she felt a warm, heavy length of something hard against her thigh. She jumped. Ready, Master Andre jerked on her chain. "Naughty. This isn't what you think. Feel it."

As if she could do anything else while bound and blindfolded, she thought. But she obeyed, and in the next moment her nerve endings informed her the hardness was rubber rather than man. A dildo. And yet, its dimensions were wrong. Maybe it was some sort of lumpy cane.

She wanted his clever fingers back on her. Even a dildo, if it pleased him. His sliding, thrusting motions with it made her want it embedded in her, whatever it was. Who knew giving up control could feel so rapturous, she thought. She moved sensuously against the length of rubber.

"It's an anal plug."

Another yank of the chain when she tried to close her legs.

"It's a small one, as they go. Only an inch in diameter. Lubed and ready. Would you like to say your safe word?" He caressed her with it, a deliberate touch that aroused.

Anal plug. She'd never experienced any kind of anal activity. Not for her partner's lack of trying. Whenever Ryan had attempted it, she'd shifted away and given him a quelling look.

But now, despite her reflexive fear, she found herself curious. More than curious.

She shook her head: there would be no safe word just yet.

A small, nearly subaudible moan reached her ears. She wondered at it. Was she affecting him so much as all that, just by enduring his erotic tortures? She felt Master Andre's body heat as he leaned in close. "You are superb," he whispered, and she marveled at the emotion in his voice, even as his talented hands brought her once more to the brink, rub-tapping her clit with the plug, tugging at her in the same rhythm with the chain attached to the nipple claws.

Then the lubed, hard rubber pressed between her ass checks. "Relax," he instructed, pushing it harder. The hard tip wouldn't be denied, though she tried to resist it for a moment, imagining it was Sylvester forcing himself on her.

She shouldn't have imagined that.

Her body trembled violently. Nora moaned, whimpered, and panted, the sensation and the fantasy together taking her higher and higher.

"Are you okay?" Master Andre's solicitous query interrupted her, and she nearly snarled at him until she remembered she wasn't supposed to speak.

She nodded instead, her hips moving of their own accord, following the delicious sensations. She pressed back.

Master Andre pushed the plug into her ass.

Her eyes opened wide behind the blindfold.

The rigid length of it invaded her, stretching her to the point of pain, but the pressure also shocked her nerve endings awake. It felt foreign, and very hard. Invasive. When she clenched, she could feel just how tightly it was lodged. When he wiggled it, it made all the fine hairs on her body stand at attention.

It was in her ass, for anyone to see. She suddenly felt grateful for the blindfold. She was impaled on a butt plug. Shame made her face heat, at this further reduction of her to sex object. She surely couldn't bear to meet anyone's eyes.

A flap of heavy leather landed on the middle of her back, and she wondered for a moment if it was a saddle as Master Andre looped it down around her waist, cinching it tight. A belt?

Suddenly the tugging on her nipples increased to a steadily biting sweetness, as Master Andre looped the chain down through her legs, up over the base of the butt plug, and up farther to fasten it to a point in the middle of the belt. His fingers, tugging always at either the chain or her clit or both, as he worked at the attachment, caused a white fire to rise in her mind.

He finally spoke with satisfaction. "There! Now you're ready."

She felt ready. Ready for anything.

"Beautifully done. She hardly seems like the same person."

Her breath stopped in her chest. That wasn't Master Andre.

"Sylvester! So good of you to join in our reindeer games." He sounded sincere. "What brings you out of the shadows? Usually you lurk worse than Mage does."

"He's here, too. Are you surprised?"

A grunt was Master Andre's reply.

"My compliments on your technique."

She fought down her panic and the galvanized response to try to close her legs; she'd learned how ineffective that was. Sylvester watched. Close enough to touch, by his voice. He was watching, damn him. Her shame swelled a thousandfold. How embarrassing, to have him see her like this. And yet, stimulating beyond anything else. Would he touch her?

Her body tingled at the idea.

The thought must've occurred to Master Andre as well. "You seem intrigued. Would you be interested in helping with this next bit? Nora has been exceptionally disobedient, a brat actually. I propose to show her what happens to naughty little brats. Though she'll probably enjoy it, slut that she is. Or . . . not."

"You realize she's never played before?"

Sylvester sounded concerned, caring. Unexpected, under the circumstances. Maybe that's why her heart throbbed with gratitude at his thoughtfulness. Was an emotional hair trigger a side effect of being tortured?

Master Andre flicked at the chain snaking up her ass crack, making her gasp at the twin tugs on her nipples. "I find it difficult to believe. Such responsiveness and lack of inhibition isn't common for beginners."

"Yet it's true. But, please continue." Sylvester sounded amused. Had she imagined the caring in his voice? "I'll be delighted to help in any way I can."

"In that case, I propose to give Nora a proper initiation ritual. I'm sure she won't mind if I paddle her ass until it's a nice bright red. Then pass the paddle around to whoever wants to take a whack. Will you, Nora?"

She felt her head sink down as if weighted by shame. Could she go through with such a humiliating initiation? They talked about her as if she were just some object. And what about the plug? What would happen to the—

Whack!

She cried out. The paddle landed squarely on the fleshy part of her butt, hitting both base of the plug and the fastened chain. Her nerve endings shrieked the message: sharp fire as the chain tugged her nipples, stinging skin where the paddle impacted, and a startling thrust inside her bowels.

Master Andre paused to fondle her. "Are you doing okay?"

She could only nod her head and whimper. And, as his fingers converted the residual pains into a rainbow of pleasure, she moved her hips.

"I think you need more. Much more."

"She seems to agree." Sylvester's voice, closer. Nora burned for his touch, needed some violent culmination of the teasing seesaw of pleasure and pain of Master Andre's. She craved Sylvester. Wanted him to carry her off, then throw her down, pin her with his body and split her open with his cock.

Instead, she got another whack.

Her nipples ignited, her ass felt like fire, her bowels contracted in a delightful spasm around unyielding rubber.

And another, harder.

And another.

Master Andre settled into a new rhythm, spanking her ass and her thighs. He used sharp blows interspersed with more teasing fingering, caressing her slit with fluttering taps or slow, deep, circular strokes, until the combined assault had her nearly out of her mind. The barrage of sensation seemed to split her off from herself, even as all her feelings fused to a single awareness of Sylvester watching this happening to her.

The thought of him as witness diminished her more than her spread nakedness, more than the butt plug, more than the shameful obviousness of her arousal. And she found, in the diminishment, further glory.

When the paddle impacted, she imagined Sylvester mounting her like an animal, shoving deep. When the nipple chain tugged, her mind transformed it into his cruel fingers pinching and twisting.

"She's not going to last much longer. Sylvester?"

"I'll go last."

"All right. Who'd like to participate in this little hazing ceremony, have a go at this beautiful reddened rump? Ah, Mage . . . an honor."

Silence.

Cool air chilled her bare skin, despite the nearby fireplace.

WHACK!

She yelped at the brutal hit, the pain overwhelming pleasure for a long moment. "Ouch . . ." She panted, riding out the yanked nipples, seared rear, and suddenly deep thrust of the plug. Mage had a heavy arm.

"She is noisy. I will give her a reason for such a production. Tomorrow. Yes, little one? You will present yourself to me." His voice chilled her further, making her skin pebble as if the low, gravelly voice stroked her obscenely. It sounded vaguely foreign. New. Exciting. She recalled Sylvester saying Mage played with electricity. She nodded, frightened yet feeling wealthy with the opulence of offered new experiences. Shivering with anticipation, she jumped when he touched her: just a simple stroke of her hair. "Tomorrow."

Everyone she'd met proceeded to take one turn with Master Andre's paddle. She surprised herself by being able to distinguish between each, even on such short acquaintance: Black's evil laugh and sadistic aim, which landed half on her pussy lips and half on her thigh. White's sympathetic cooing and gentle tap on a less-abused part of her left cheek. Kitten's butterfly-soft touch, barely felt at all. Mistress Kiana's brisk blow aimed precisely in the middle. Little Peter's awkward landing on her right cheek, more paddle's edge than flat surface.

Then Master Andre, who paddled her briskly until her ass heated to ignition once more, and fondled her until she gasped.

Then it was Sylvester's turn. He grabbed her hair, yanked her head back to speak in her ear. "You feel welcome now, don't you? A little ceremony to initiate you into the mystery of BDSM. It's quite the turn-on to watch how you respond to it. You're just a little pain slut, aren't you. Do you like it so much? Or were you lying about being new to this? I'm going to find out."

His words, spoken directly into her ear, slid right into her brain. She was afraid, but still so intensely aroused that it wouldn't take much to push her over the edge. He still held her by the knot of hair. His large hands grasped it by the base. It didn't hurt, much; it was just another sensation added to the melody.

He laughed then, and shook her head slowly by her own hair. Then he released the knot, letting her hair fall down to shroud her face in a sensual, silken slide.

"With your permission?" he asked Master Andre.

"By all means. I've always wanted to see how you do it. I've heard rumors—"

"Hmm," Sylvester made a noncommittal noise. "Please stand back."

Nora tensed, but nothing immediately happened. The silence engulfed them. She could hear White whispering something to Black, somewhere in the distance. The sound of Ryan rustling in his cage, and the crackling fire, and Master Andre clearing his throat . . .

Whack!

Only he didn't remove the paddle from her ass cheeks, but left it there. The authority of it pressing against her, trapping its stinging heat under its flat surface, was bad enough.

Worse awaited. As she reeled from the blow—ass, nipples,

plug—he brought his left hand into play, fingers adjusting the plug, thumb roughly massaging her clit. A final scratch with his thumb elicited her first scream, even as he drew his right arm back and paddled her again.

This time he left his left hand on her. He rubbed the paddle back and forth, making the plug press against first one of her inner walls, then the other.

He massaged.

And paddled, assaulting her senses inside and out.

It hurt, more than before, but the pleasure he gave was greater still. The brutal paddling picked up tempo, but so did his fingers, and his prodding of the plug.

Suddenly she was hurtling up, on the verge of orgasm, and as if he knew, he spanked violently, but there was no pain. Only a heavenly heat uncoiling in her belly and taking over her body.

And it was Sylvester again, in her mind, riding her harshly, without mercy, making her welcome his brutality, making her enjoy the perversity of his actions. The forbidden heat incinerated her as it always did: a gasping pleasure that drove her mind from her body, both up high into the farthest stars and down below to grub with the depraved, among whose numbers she surely belonged for enjoying such a thing.

She became aware that she'd screamed, hearing the memory-echo of it as she returned to herself.

Master Andre had removed the plug, clamps, belt, and unbuckled her leg restraints without her realizing it. And it was Master Andre who slid off her blindfold, covered her with a blanket, and gathered her into a gentle embrace, holding her and whispering soothingly. She surprised herself by clinging to him. It was a point of pride with her that she never clung, never truly needed anyone, yet she snuggled into Master Andre's chest. Her emotions surprised her: emotional vulnerability, cat-stretching physical contentment, confidence in her own desirability, affection for everyone present including Master Andre.

She listened more to his calming tone of voice than to his compliments and reassurances. She soaked it up as a much-needed balm.

But her gaze kept returning to Sylvester from the moment her blindfold was removed.

He looked back, expressionless. Completely unmoved.

6

"You were magnificent, superb, responsive. Your presence here is a gift. Welcome, my dear."

Master Andre's words penetrated the pleasant fog of her mind, and she tore her gaze from Sylvester.

"Thank you. You were amazing, too." Didn't hurt to return the compliment, and he certainly deserved it. He didn't need to know her nerve endings convulsed most strongly when she thought of Sylvester. Master Andre's skill was beyond reproach. "Remarkable. Unique. There isn't a word."

"Magic." Master Andre smiled. "But it's nothing compared to the ultimate submission of slave to master. To trust body and soul to his keeping, to wear his collar, to let him guide you to the stars and beyond." She could feel the heat baking off him, now that her own fire had been quenched. Through the folds of blanket and the material of his pants, his erection felt huge, overeager.

Still basking in the warm glow of comfort, she didn't mind it. His words intrigued her. But at the moment she only wanted to be held. "I'll take your word for it."

"No need."

She shifted to a more comfortable spot. The blanket began to feel claustrophobic. Master Andre's arms felt good, though, so rather than moving from his embrace, she looked around with her head still resting against his chest.

Her experience gave her vision a new lens. Instead of a strange, intimidating space of unknown people and dangerous-looking furniture and toys, she saw a welcoming dungeon, a place of fantasy. And the people were friends. Strange friends, she admitted, watching White adjust a full leather hood on Ryan's head. The woman positioned the sole opening, a tiny rectangular slit, over his mouth. It was his only article of clothing. When White refastened Ryan's cage and stood back to admire the effect, his nakedness made him look small and vulnerable.

Elsewhere in the dungeon, play appeared to be winding down. Mistress Kiana spoke softly with Little Peter. Mage had disappeared. Kitten wasn't anywhere to be seen either. Someone had turned the music down. And Sylvester . . .

She let herself look at him.

He was gone.

She felt a twinge of disappointment.

She'd wanted to view him with her new vision, as well. How might he look? She certainly felt different. More experienced. More desirable. She didn't understand it, but she felt it. Stretching, she basked in the newness.

Master Andre tightened his grip. "How do you feel?" The knowing, almost smug tone in his voice made her smile. She supposed he'd earned the right to a little smugness.

She laughed. "I feel drained. In a great way, but . . ."

"Mmm?" He bounced her on his lap as if she were a child. Once. Twice. "I imagine you're feeling sated and sore. The welts from the cane might last a day or two, but the redness and the prickly sensation on your skin's surface should mostly be gone by tomorrow."

"Good to know." He smelled nice. Of leather and clean sweat and fresh warm breath. She liked him quite a bit, she realized.

"Nora, I'd like to collar you and keep you. In my home. Naked, of course."

"Of course. Business casual is so dull."

He gave her a steady look. "Think about it. I pushed you pretty hard tonight, but it's nothing compared to what I can do. At my home, I have resources. And less distraction. Sylvester, for example. I don't know what possessed him to finish you off that way." He said it lightly, but Nora heard the irritation underneath. "You should know something. I do very well for myself, and enjoy travel. I keep a private plane, fueled and ready to go, for whenever I get the urge to visit Paris, or Amsterdam, or Australia. At dinner, you'd talked about your travel-marketing job, and mentioned your interest in seeing the world. Wear my collar, and you won't have to just look at pictures. I'll give the world to you." The words were offered up in all seriousness.

To travel. To travel the world, to see the source of all the pictures she viewed every day. To engage senses she'd only just learned she had. It tempted her.

"Think about it," he repeated. He patted her thigh. "You are a rare woman, and it would be an honor to collar you. Now!" He stood, letting her slide from his lap. She gathered up folds of blanket to hide her nudity, then felt foolish for it. He'd seen it all. "Drink plenty of water, and rest up for two more days of playing." He bent to kiss her, a chaste peck on the cheek. "Hopefully with me. See you later."

"See you later," she promised.

The chill on her bare shoulders reminded her the fire burned low.

She dressed quickly. Moved by an impulse to confide in Ryan, she approached his cage. Nodding to Mistress Kiana, who sat with her submissive, and waving a little self-consciously at Black and

White—White grinned at her, Black only stared—Nora observed her ex-fiancé. The cage backed to a generous corner space, strewn with more pillar candles, carved masks decorating the walls, and statues and artwork that drew the eye.

Ryan seemed almost a piece of art himself, lit from above by track lights throwing his well-defined muscles, his flat stomach, the gentle waves of his short blond hair, and even his flaccid penis into sharp relief. She saw the way his hands clutched the bars when he heard her approach. Was he frightened? She felt a need to reconnect with him, talk with him about how much she'd liked her experience. About how much he'd enjoyed his, too.

She touched his cage. "Hey, you. It's only me."

His blinded, mask-covered face turned toward her. "Nora." His mouth formed a thin line. "I saw you, earlier. I saw what they did to you."

She couldn't help her blush, her reflexive shame . . . until she remembered his erection from earlier. "I guess we're both learning a few things about ourselves, huh, Ryan?"

He replied with simple dignity. "I screwed up, and I regret it. I'm doing this for us." He aimed his leather-covered face at her. "What's your excuse?"

Great, now she felt ashamed *and* guilty. "What did you think, I'd just watch TV for three days?" She bit her lip in dismay. The lovely peace and sense of accomplishment she'd felt were slipping away.

"I thought you'd keep your clothes on, at least."

"Says the man who'd planned on getting me raped."

"It was your fantasy!"

"No it wasn't! Not like that. You don't understand anything about it." Her resentment flared. She could've been seriously hurt. She could've been psychologically scarred for life.

Sudden silence told her the music had been shut off, and the others all ceased their own conversations to listen to theirs.

Nora turned toward them, intending to apologize for raising her voice, when she heard breathing nearby. Not Ryan's.

Already disconcerted, she pivoted toward the heavy breather. She saw only the hanging artwork, the pink bag containing the fetal-curled statue of a man.

The statue moved.

Nora screamed.

"What? What is it?" Ryan tried to tear off his mask, but it was locked at the neck. "What the fuck is it?"

Nora stared. It was a man, a real man inside. The stretchy, pink-colored material smoothed his skin tone to look like marble, the pink wrapping minimizing human flaws and hair, and nearly disguising the catheter she could now see attached to his penis. His eyes had opened to mere slits.

"His name is Osmond." White had crept up beside them, speaking in a low tone. "The shouting woke him."

"I'm sorry, I didn't realize . . ."

"It's okay." She frowned at Ryan, who was still shouting. Black glided toward him like a malevolent spirit, a gag in her hand.

White urged Nora away. "Come with me upstairs."

"Nora! Don't go! What was it? I can hear someone nearby. Who's there?" He whipped his head back and forth, trying in vain to see. "Nora?"

"Good night, Ryan."

"Nora! God damn it, Nora, you bitch! Don't you . . . mmmpph."

White smiled. "Gag placed. Shall we?"

"We shall." Nora glanced back. Ryan looked cowed, with Black stroking his head in a gesture that might have been motherly if it weren't for her sadistic expression. Nora wondered how many hours Ryan would spend in the cage, listening to the breathing in the air near him, trying to guess who Osmond was.

And what it was that had made Nora scream. He'd conjure up the worst possible boogeyman, she knew.

Nora laughed, still looking back.

Black met her gaze. She finally smiled at Nora, as she wrapped a fist in Ryan's short hair and pulled his head back with a jerk. Ryan's erection stirred.

"Intense," Nora murmured. Her reality whirled as her own nerve endings responded to the scene.

"Hmmm. Interesting."

Nora looked at White, saw the evaluation in her gaze. "What's interesting?"

"You, honey. Seems you might like dishing it out, as well as taking it? A switch," she explained at Nora's look of confusion. "Someone who enjoys either side of S and M play. Top or bottom. Dom or sub. Like me. Maybe." She stared at Nora, then grinned, shaking her head. "There's something about you. Hard to pigeonhole. C'mon, let's get something to drink."

"Is being hard to pigeonhole a bad thing?" Nora smiled back. White's straightforward manner charmed her. But as they made their way upstairs, then to the now-deserted kitchen, Nora felt a return of her guilt. "Ryan . . . he'll be okay down there, won't he? In that little cage? And why is Osmond hanging in that bag?"

"Your guy will be fine," White assured her. "More than fine. You could see that."

"Um."

"Don't worry." White filled two tall glasses with tap water. "Good mountain water. Drink up; you'll have lost plenty in that scene. Okay, so about Osmond. Long story short, he's doing it for kinky and nonkinky reasons. He wants a rebirth. So he's being encased and cared for as a fetus right now—breathing through a snorkel, fed through it, too, wearing diapers. He's only taken out a few times per day during this "pregnancy." Soon he'll have the experience of being born anew. I just hope Kiana's up to the task of the birth. She's agreed to midwife, but she seems tired."

Nora shifted on her chair. Winced.

White noticed. "Master Andre's divine, isn't he? And Sylvester, too! Lucky you."

Nora kept her voice neutral with an effort. "I understand Sylvester doesn't usually participate."

"Never, to my knowledge. And I'm here once a month, at least."

"Why doesn't he? Participate, I mean." Nora drained her glass, then yawned, covering her mouth. White charmed her, the conversation fascinated, but her body and mind felt sluggish, as if being dragged down into sleep. "Excuse me."

"Post-scene plunge. Perfectly normal. You'll sleep like the dead, too." White tapped her long, lacquered nails on her glass. She looked at Nora sideways, and her demeanor became suddenly more guarded. "Sylvester is very gracious, to allow us to play in his home this way. If he doesn't participate, I'm sure he has good reasons."

"He said he likes to keep an eye on things. To be a . . . what did he call it? . . . a dungeon monitor."

White nodded her head. "And he's a damn fine one." She smiled politely, drank more water.

Even tired as she was, Nora could tell White held something back. Sylvester had loyal friends, and he had secrets. Good to know. Nora changed the subject. "You come here pretty often. Do you travel much, other than here?"

"Oh, no. I'd love to. I'd go to Italy. Eat Italian food until I'm round. But I have a little girl at home, and a full-time job. Police dispatcher," she said, with evident pride. "But, travel? No way, no how. They don't exactly give dispatchers a month off for their European vacations, if you know what I mean."

Nora did.

"Coming to Twisted Wood is my vacation, when the ex has his custody weekend. But enough about me." She put her empty in the sink, held her hand out for Nora's glass. "One of the service subs will take care of these. Isn't it great? So. Do you have a job that lets you travel a lot?"

"I've seen the world in photographs. But I've never been out of the country." Nora thought of her job. Her job dangled tempting fruit before her, she realized. Not just the generous salary. She tracked down the most alluring photos of ancient architecture, read tempting descriptions of white sand beaches in tropical paradises, edited reports about luxury cruises to exotic destinations. She wished she could be one of those tanned, happy-faced tourists in the pictures. But the fast-paced company said it couldn't get by without her for more than a week. They'd bitterly complained about just four days.

Nora frowned. If she accepted the position of vice president, she'd quickly accumulate enough money to go anywhere she wanted . . . but have zero time to do it.

Her conundrum of a career bound her up and teased her, in its own way, more thoroughly than Master Andre ever could.

As she heard herself explaining it to White, she felt a measure of self-directed contempt. What a complainer she was. No doubt she made more money than the friendly black woman, and her job had to be less stressful than a police dispatcher's. She made herself shut up.

But White surprised her. "Well, of course you need time off; being a workaholic's no fun. Got to go places and have fun, or maybe just sit home staring at a TV or reading a book. They're called mental-health breaks." She laughed. "As you can see, I don't get nearly enough of 'em."

Nora smiled, genuinely liking the other woman, but her words inflicted doubt: did Ryan have a point? Was she a workaholic, her priorities in need of a shake-up? She'd condemned him for what he'd done, and he'd accepted his penance. Even in the face of her letting Master Andre strip and penetrate her with a butt plug, he was still subjecting himself to discomfort and imprisonment. For her.

She didn't exactly have the moral high ground.

Guilt resurfaced, flooding her tired body with just enough energy for her to straighten, determined. She'd set Ryan free from his imprisonment. They would discuss things. That was how normal people in relationships handled conflict.

A small headache started. "I should probably say good night."

"Get lots of rest," White approved. "We sleep in, here. There's a late breakfast, informal buffet style, in case Sylvester didn't tell you. You should really ask him for a tour of the place; tonight you got kind of waylaid, didn't you?" Her eyes twinkled. "If I'm not mistaken, tomorrow looks like more of the same. You're like a new toy, you know. They're just getting started."

" 'They'?" Nora felt a smile play at the corners of her mouth. She was a toy, was she?

"Master Andre for sure. Mage, from the looks of it. Mistress Kiana, if she's feeling better. And maybe even Sylvester." White frowned, played with an edge of pale rope at the neck of her dress. "You should be careful with him. He's a heavy top."

"Heavy top?" Nora stepped sideways, preparing to head downstairs. She had to let Ryan out of his cage and have a discussion, though she'd rather do nearly anything else.

White noticed her movement. "Yeah, get some sleep. Oh, don't worry, really. I forget you're a newbie: 'heavy top' means a rough dominant, even a little brutal. But maybe you're up for that. Just . . . be aware of it, so you're not surprised, is all."

Nora felt warmed by the woman's concern. "Thank you."

White had begun to walk away, but paused when she heard Nora's tone. "Hey, no problem, sweetie." In a graceful and perfectly natural movement she enveloped Nora in a hug. "I'm glad you're here. We all are! Good night, luv." With a soft, grazing kiss on the cheek that traveled to the edge of Nora's lips and lingered a few seconds too long to be purely platonic, White laughed again, leaving Nora with a bemused smile.

Alone in the enormous kitchen and living room area, Nora found the total silence unnerving. She made her way back to the stairs and down to the dungeon. She'd sort things out with Ryan. It was the right thing to do, she told herself.

But when she entered the room, still low lit from guttering candles and the dying fire, she found it silent as well.

The cage was empty. Ryan was gone.

7

When she again entered the kitchen, bright late-morning sun-shine filtered through the tall forest of trees and dappled the clean slate-tile floor, granite counters, and carved wood cabi-nets.

Seeing Sylvester talking with Kitten as he assisted with dish-washing, Nora was glad she'd decided to shower and dress in clean jeans and a pretty top, rather than wear her comfortable flannel pajamas to breakfast. The owner of Twisted Wood and the service submissive both dressed casually, but had no hint of sloppiness about them: Sylvester with his all-black clothes that seemed so right on him, and Kitten with a short pink skirt and baby tee with rhinestones spelling, "Happiness in Slavery."

Nora's gaze kept returning to Sylvester. Even with his cour-teous domestic activity, he exuded a graceful masculinity that reminded her he was the man who'd captivated her from the day before. Her fantasy. The one who'd kissed her, and later, paddled and fondled her to orgasm.

It made it damn hard to know how to act around him.

"Nora." His eyes seemed to pin her. "Good morning."

She forced herself to approach, to be casual. "Hey, there. Hi, Kitten."

"Good morning, Nora. I have waffles and berries and toast— with or without butter or jam—as well as an omelet. Oh, would you like some coffee?" The service submissive didn't wait for her answer, but pulled a mug from the cabinet. She looked at Nora, appraising. "And a big glass of juice." She retrieved a glass as well.

Nora nodded. She had to smile. "Do I look desiccated?"

"Like a thousand-year-old mummy," Sylvester assured her with a wicked smile.

Nora tried to ignore the heat suffusing her face. She murmured, "Then I'd better take two." She pulled up a stool and sat at the breakfast bar with a grimace at the quick, bright pain it caused her ass cheeks. She'd chosen the same stool she'd sat in the night before with White.

Which reminded her. "Where is White? And everyone else," she added belatedly, blushing again. She should've probably asked after Ryan first. Or Master Andre. No doubt she'd bungled some sort of protocol again.

But Sylvester only poured batter into a waffle iron. Kitten handed her a steaming mug of coffee, and a moment later placed a tall glass of orange juice before her as well. "You anticipated Nora's needs. Good job," Sylvester told the service submissive in an approving tone. "Now get the bowl of fruit for me, the one I put in the fridge an hour ago with the strawberries."

"I'm sorry if I'm late," Nora began.

"You're not." His words allowed no doubt. "Black and White are still sleeping, Master Andre had his usual early morning bagel after watching the news, Little Peter is . . ." He looked at Kitten, inquiring.

"He's taking care of Osmond and washing the toys." Kitten danced from one foot to the other. "May I be excused? Mage said to attend him this morning."

"You should have informed me of this initially, before committing to helping with breakfast. You can't provide service in two places at once." Sylvester's reproof was mild, but Kitten wilted. "You've done well, other than that," he added. "You are dismissed."

Kitten ran.

"You're just a big softie, aren't you." Nora grinned when he gave her an aloof glance. She'd seen the way the corners of his lips turned up for a split second.

"Here's your waffle." He dumped it on the plate Kitten had placed. "And berries. Drink your juice."

"If I say 'no,' will you take a spatula to me?"

"Would you like me to, brat?" Now he did smile. Just a tiny one, and only momentarily, but she saw it. "You know what they say about brats—that's a bottom who enjoys struggling against control, someone who's always a challenging pain in the ass?"

"Um, no?" Nora forked waffle into her mouth. It was divine. More than made up for his calling her a brat.

"Some brats are only testing their dominant. Other brats have a desire to be conquered. Tamed."

She swallowed despite a sudden bright flare of lust. Conquered and tamed. Suddenly she wanted nothing more than Sylvester conquering her. He played on her erotic sensibilities in a way she'd never known before. She closed her eyes for a moment in a long, savoring blink. Then asked him, "Are you my dominant, then?"

Sylvester didn't answer her question. He disassembled the waffle-iron plates and placed them in the sink. Then, "I've never seen a vanilla take to BDSM as quickly as you did. Master Andre took you so far and so fast, you should still be sleeping it off."

She replied, noncommittal, "He seemed to know what he was doing."

"He does. You've infatuated him. I can see why, of course, but you should know he'll want to collar you."

"Yes, I know."

"Don't get full of yourself. It's the novice aspect of you he wants. The breaking of you."

She pushed her empty plate away. Sylvester scooped it up and placed it in the sink.

"Breaking me. I'm not sure I like the sound of that." At least with Master Andre.

Sylvester gazed at her as if he could read every thought in her mind. "I'd never place you, or anyone else, in a permanent collar."

"Really?" She fingered the fading dents in her wrists where the restraints of the night before had dug into her flesh. Her butt cheeks still felt sore, but not in a bad way. "Why not?" Satisfied with good food and coffee, her belly felt content . . . but now the rest of her body had woken up. She wanted Sylvester. She wanted his body on hers, his touch, his rough handling. Badly. "Isn't it strange for the dominant owner of a place like this to say he doesn't want to collar anyone?" A horrible thought occurred to her. "You don't want to be collared yourself?"

"Oh, no."

She relaxed again, or as much as she could in his presence. The idea of such dominance and expertise, such controlled poise as Sylvester's being brought low would have been appalling. She didn't try to hide her relief. "Good."

He looked at her with a knowing smile. His eyes were half lidded and dark. "To answer your question: the reason why I wouldn't collar a slave for myself is I prefer a woman's rebellion to cowed, obedient submission. I enjoy spirit."

"So you can conquer and tame it?" She held her breath. Her body felt tingling and alive, her nipples hard as rocks. She wanted him to conquer her right now. She could use a little of his kind of taming. Or a lot.

Again, he sidestepped her question. "The dom/sub lifestyle isn't for me." He intercepted her look. "Lifestylers don't just role-play, they adopt the master and slave dynamic in every part of their lives. Being a master becomes integral to their personalities rather than just a game. Collared means twenty-four/seven. Some lifestylers don't even use safe words." He frowned, then shrugged. "It works for some people, and that's great. I have . . . different interests."

"Such as?"

"We can discuss that another time."

Exasperating man. Her blood sang in her veins, mingled irritation and lust. Sylvester only tossed back his juice and strode to the sink once more. He moved like a panther. His body, in those black jeans and frame-hugging shirt, redefined masculinity for her then and there. His deliberate movement of simply washing out a glass riveted her. Paired with a body that looked strong and capable enough to engage with any challenger and come out on top, he made a mesmerizing package. Plus his voice. And his ideas. And his intensity. Everything about him drew her with one hand while warning her off with the other.

Irresistible.

She wanted him. No, that was too mild of a word. She craved him, his punishing kiss, his particular brand of handling.

Unless she was mistaken, Sylvester craved her, too.

She was about to suggest the conquer-and-tame idea to him in no uncertain terms, but just then there was a terrified scream.

"That was outside," Sylvester said, already running to the deck.

Nora followed. "It sounded like . . ."

Sylvester slid the glass door open with enough force to make it bounce partway back, then cursed when he reached the railing and looked down.

Nora had guessed the screamer's identity, but when she saw what was in the clearing at the front of the house, she gasped.

A large bear batted a doghouse back and forth with its clawed paws. Within, Ryan screamed again.

"Stay here," Sylvester snapped, running back indoors.

Nora covered her mouth with her hands. The bear snuffled at the arched opening of the small doghouse. Growled.

What was Ryan doing in there? Black must've put him inside it. Nora never should have left him alone in that cage, alone with Black. She should never have agreed to this whole plan in the first place.

Dismay and guilt propelled her down the stairs. She'd drive off the bear herself. She'd distract it so Ryan could get indoors. With her marathon training, she could outrun it. Probably.

"Hey! Bear!" She waved her arms. Only when she felt the low heels of her slip-on ankle boots crunch the small rocks edging a walkway did she realize she wasn't dressed for a marathon. She kicked them off, never taking her eyes from the beast. A minor hysteria gripped her. "Beary beary bear! Over here! Ryan, when we get out of here, I'm going to kick your ass good!"

Ryan remained silent. Prudent, she thought, taking a step closer.

The bear looked from the doghouse to Nora, then back to the doghouse. Undecided.

With the loudness of a rifle shot, a whipcrack sounded. Watching the bear, Nora saw it flinch at the noise. Cautious, it sniffed the air.

Another whipcrack. With impressive calmness, Sylvester passed her, approached the bear. "Go on," he told it, then underscored his request with another snap of the bullwhip.

It worked. The bear backed off. With one last longing glance at the doghouse, it ambled to the edge of the forest, then disappeared into it.

"Are you okay?"

She tore her gaze from the spot where the forest had swallowed the bear. Sylvester bent to retrieve her boots with his free hand. He offered them to her.

She swiped them from his grip. "Peachy. Thank you." She trembled suddenly, feeling the way she did after an extra-stressful day at work. Now she'd have to collect Ryan and go home. No more BDSM fun. No more Sylvester. Time to be a grown-up.

Sylvester looked at her. The look in his eyes reminded her of the bear's.

Ryan screamed again, now profanity-laden abuse. "Was that supposed to be part of it? Huh? I don't fucking *think* so!"

Nora stared at him. Ryan peeked out of the doghouse, a turtle emerging from its shell. She saw his bare shoulders and realized he was naked.

"He must be freezing," she said, uncertain.

"Inside there's an arctic-rated sleeping bag. He wouldn't freeze," Sylvester assured her.

As if to demonstrate, Ryan pulled it out with him, wrapping himself in it as he continued to curse. His face was red with rage or embarrassment, or both, as he shouted at them.

Nora took a step back, confused. Why was he yelling at her? She didn't want or need it, not after she'd tried to help, not at the tail end of her truncated vacation. Not right when she was deciding to be responsible, take the stressful vice president position, embrace a normal life.

She no longer felt her original impulse to rescue Ryan. In fact, anger flared in her. Big anger.

"Shut up! You ungrateful . . . *dog*."

Ryan stopped as if she'd slapped him.

"Good job," Black told her. The pale woman had slunk up

unnoticed beside her. "You can't let them disrespect you. Disrespect is a difficult habit to break, once they have it." She drifted toward Ryan, smiling. "Right, dog?" Nora noticed her elegant cream-colored skirt and blouse, her delicate small-heeled pumps. She might have been one of the VIP clients who occasionally visited GoGlobe.

Nora felt her tension subside. Nothing made sense anymore, but Black's actions seemed exactly right.

Ryan sputtered. "I . . . you . . ."

Black stopped. "Would you like to say your safe word and end all play? And all chance of Nora's forgiveness?" She drummed her short, sharp nails against her skirt.

Ryan stared at the woman as if hypnotized. "No, Mistress."

"Very good. You stayed in the doghouse all night. You must need to relieve yourself. Is that right?"

"Yes, Mistress."

"Then do so. Crawl to that bush and lift a leg like the dog you are."

"What? No!"

"What did you tell me?" Her low, dangerous voice had Ryan swallowing visibly. "You will be punished for your disobedience and appalling lack of manners. But first things first."

"Hardcore," Nora murmured. She heard a noise like muffled laughter, but when she looked, Sylvester's face was impassive.

On the verge of reassuring Ryan he didn't have to do *that* for her sake, Nora glanced down his body. She swallowed her words.

Ryan's penis jutted up, as hard and ready as she'd ever seen it.

"I need to stop worrying about him," she said to herself, even as she felt an answering heat in herself—not for Ryan's erection, but for his reveling in the humiliation. It made her remember her own desperate need the night before, naked and shamed and toyed with . . . and aroused. She saw Sylvester nod out of the corner of her eye. In the meantime, Black had collared Ryan, and was retrieving the six-foot leather leash coiled on its hook on one wall of the doghouse. She attached it to his collar. "Heel," she commanded, and without waiting, tugged Ryan toward the bush. Ryan crawled awkwardly, his erection bobbing.

Nora leaned on Sylvester, weak with lust. The contact of his body, not embracing her but not moving away either, aroused her further. He knew she wanted him. She remembered very clearly how much he wanted her, too. His discipline over his own reaction aroused her further.

His body didn't move at all, not even to avoid her. A statue. She frowned. Had she misjudged? Had his interest in her faded?

Turning her back on Ryan's leg-lifting attempts, she stared her challenge directly into Sylvester's eyes.

A small shudder ran through him. It vanished the very next second. But she smiled. Not impervious! She curved her body farther into his, feeling his hardness.

"I think it's time you visited Mage," he finally said, backing away. "He's up to the taming of you, if I don't miss my guess. He won't be distracted by possessive, softer feelings. Unlike . . ."

Her breath stopped in her throat as she waited for him to finish his sentence. He had to say, "me." Had to admit he had feelings for her. She craved it suddenly even more than his hard, driving use.

". . . unlike Master Andre." It was his turn to smile, derisive.

She gritted her teeth. "Mage sounds fascinating."

"Oh, he is. He came down from the Painloft and watched us at dinner for a while, did you notice? Easy to miss him, with that quiet stealth of his. You'd think he's shy, the way he avoids crowds, but it's not that, exactly. He's intense, and self-aware enough to realize his level of intensity wouldn't necessarily be welcome at the dinner table."

"Is he foreign? His accent last night . . ."

Sylvester began walking toward the house. "I think it's Eastern European. I haven't inquired."

She didn't need to ask why not. She'd already gained more than a little appreciation of Sylvester's respect for his guest's privacy. "Doesn't he stay here full-time?"

"He travels. But yes, I believe this is his primary mailing address."

"He must have a lot of money."

Sylvester grinned, wolfish. "Of course."

"Last night, he said I should visit him today. Or tonight? I wonder which he meant," she mused, watching Sylvester.

The smile vanished, leaving an impassive expression in its place. Then, "Mage prefers to take his time. The elaborate rope patterns alone can take hours. Electrical play also is well suited to his patient temperament." He didn't look at her. "And that's simply foreplay." He reached the lower door to the house. Stopped. Faced her.

Desire unfurled inside her. Only it wasn't Mage, the owner of the exotic accent, whom she envisioned touching her patiently with hours of electrifying foreplay.

How convenient, she thought wryly, that she'd made her chosen fantasy man so versatile.

Then she just enjoyed the fantasy: Sylvester torturing her sensuously, denying her release. What might ropes and electrical play be like?

That was when she realized she was in trouble. Sylvester wasn't just her latest and greatest forced-sex fantasy. He'd vaulted to the top of her lust-o'-meter, as the all-round perfect sex partner. Plus, she liked and admired him. A lot.

It shook her.

She'd known him less than twenty-four hours. She hadn't even seen him naked.

"Why are you looking at me like that?" His voice sounded low, intimate. It stoked the growing fire in her.

"You know why." Her voice trembled. Just an emotional reaction to the bear attack, she told herself.

He gazed down at her. Not admitting or denying anything.

She sighed. He'd said he was off limits. Clearly he meant it. "Okay. I'm going to take a quick shower and change into something more playful. Then you can take me to Mage." Last chance, she thought, praying Sylvester would change his mind even though Mage did intrigue her. Surely Sylvester wouldn't deliver her to Mage if he had any personal interest in her.

Sylvester nodded a few more times than strictly necessary, as if acknowledging her thoughts. Or his own. "I'll come for you in an hour. That'll give him time to prepare for you, as well."

She made herself tilt her chin up, smile. "I'll be ready."

But despite her disappointment with Sylvester, anticipation trilled her nerves pleasantly. As the danger grew greater, the disconnect from her normal life grew wider. First there'd been the bondage in the dungeon. Now ropes and electrical play. These were things to make her vacation—probably her last for years to come—a truly memorable one, a vacation to savor.

So long as the danger didn't get out of hand.

8

"What's eating you?"

Sylvester's wandering mind returned to the present, and to the sliding glass door before him. He liked to watch the stars come out as twilight faded to clean, cool mountain nighttime. Cool but not cold; his breath didn't mist the glass the way it did in winter.

He must've been standing there for a bit longer than usual. His stiffened muscles protested as he walked back to the corner of the living room where Kiana lounged on a sofa. "Just thinking," he finally remembered to answer.

"You're a million miles away."

He smiled. Kiana's gleaming auburn hair draped his largest, jewel-toned upholstered couch. Both were a treat for the eyes. Kiana's face, however, looked pale and drawn. Earlier, typically, she'd waved off his concern. He seated himself in his favorite spot, a roomy leather recliner before the fire. He responded without thinking. "More like eight hundred miles away."

He checked his watch. Five hours, now. He'd reminded Nora to use a safe word when he'd brought her to Mage's door.

When she'd only looked at him mockingly, he adjured her in his firmest tone to use it if she felt uncomfortable, or frightened, or just wanted the play to stop for a while. Mage would respect it, of course. If she used it.

He hoped she used it.

He shouldn't be so bothered by the image of Mage teasing her to an explosive edge, taking his torturous time the way he did, then mounting her if she pleased him.

He knew she'd please Mage.

And he really wasn't enjoying all the images of Mage fucking her. She could have been his instead. She should have been. She'd offered Sylvester his fondest fantasy with an eagerness that reached into his nervous system and squeezed.

His reaction to it scared the hell out of him. He couldn't succumb to the temptation. He couldn't go through that hell again.

"Do you miss Los Angeles?"

He went still. "I don't recall telling you where I'm from."

Kiana smiled. Even with the wan complexion and tired eyes, her catlike expression seemed to toy with him. Her words, however, had the effect of a bucket of ice water. "You don't think I'd ask about you before playing here? Letting Little Peter run around naughty and naked? I've heard some interesting things about you."

He held her gaze and kept his face carefully expressionless. She knew. Was this an effort to blackmail him? What exactly did she know, or think she knew? "If you have something to say, say it."

Her expression softened at his tone. "Oh, surely you don't think I'd believe those rumors? I would never dream of staying here if I did. Or recommend Twisted Wood to so many people. You've built quite the unique bondage and breakfast. It's larger, better equipped, more luxurious than any I've been to. More expensive, too. Worth it for quality, though, of course. I've found there's often a correlation between expense and quality in life. . . ."

He allowed her to change the subject. Kiana believed what had happened was just a malicious rumor.

It wasn't, of course.

But with the threat of exposure past, his thoughts slid back to Nora. Was she okay? Would she discover Mage was even more to her taste than Master Andre? Perhaps she'd decide to join Kitten as one of Mage's slaves. Perhaps Sylvester had lost his last chance with her.

He stood with a curse, startling Kiana.

"What is it?"

"Nothing."

"I recognize a non-nothing when I see it." But she said it with a tolerant, even tired, smile.

He looked more closely at Kiana. "You should take it easy, rest a bit. Have Little Peter give you a massage."

"I did. It didn't help." She slumped into the couch cushions. "Training him is such a chore, but he's so fragile, so completely unsuited to handling the vanilla world. I have got to get him up to speed on being a good domestic slave so I can place him with a caring dom. Someone with more energy than me."

Now Sylvester was worried. Mistress Kiana had trained and placed subs before, but she'd never admitted weakness.

But she sighed. "I sent him home so I can take a break. This place rejuvenates me even when I'm not playing. The rural quiet, the wonderful surroundings of your lovely house and friends . . . it's so very soothing. Nowhere I'd rather be than right here, relaxing at Twisted Wood. The Portland leather community had nothing like this, until you left smoggy Los Angeles and opened this delightful B and B."

"You're too kind."

"Just honest." Kiana closed her eyes. "We really are grateful to you, you know. I truly am." She yawned, covered her mouth.

Her gratitude touched him. Almost as much as telling him she didn't believe the rumors about him in Los Angeles. As he left the living room, he took the long way by her sofa. He paused, scooped one of her hands up from its resting place on her thigh, and kissed her elegant fingers. "Thank you."

Her eyes slit open. She smiled and nodded, regal as a queen.

Sylvester passed the bagged Osmond—now hanging near-but-not-too-near the living room fireplace—and made his way down the stairs to the dungeon to check on his other guests. Mistress Kiana owned the gift of diplomacy and a light hand when needed. He appreciated her friendship and support more than ever. He smiled to himself until he remembered Nora.

As much as he wanted to rush up to Mage's sanctuary and snatch Nora away from him, he simply couldn't. Mage's Painloft was off limits.

So was Nora, for that matter.

There couldn't be any more play, and certainly no intimacy, with Nora. He couldn't risk having his reputation ruined again, his friendships destroyed again, his joy in his local kink scene snatched away again.

It'd be best for both of them if Mage magicked her into his service, the way he so often did with the more attractive women visiting Twisted Wood.

Sylvester looked at his watch again, shook his head. Mage probably had Nora begging for more by now.

Nora wriggled against her bonds. Enveloped by a crisscross pattern of ropes, she felt the whole shift slightly. Pleasantly.

The elaborate rope sheath separated and raised her exposed breasts, encased her torso and legs in dozens of small diamond shapes, and pressed just beneath her pubic bone in a teasing knot that jiggled with Mage's movements.

This time, he'd placed her standing face-out on an X-shaped cross, her rope-looped wrists and ankles fastened to tie points in the wood. He still threaded and tightened the rope, always adjusting.

His Painloft had much of the same equipment as Sylvester's dungeon, and even more that was unfamiliar. Mage had placed her on, and sometimes bent her over, nearly every vinyl-padded surface in the room. He'd bound her in positions both demure and blatantly erotic, and he'd tortured her. He'd used a bug zapper to spank her, he'd bound her long hair into a fancy rope restraint and attached it to a sawhorse to force her to kneel, and he'd used various sharp instruments to dent and poke her flesh. He'd been gentler than she'd expected. Sylvester had led her to expect a fanatic, a deviant of the first order. But Mage was . . . very reasonable.

She felt a sneaking sense of disappointment.

The ropes whispered over her body, the twisted ridges of the cotton vibrating the spider web of the whole as it crossed over, then under. Mage certainly took his time. With his deliberate, slow touch and the frequent breaks in between each bound position to keep her muscles from cramping or overstretching, it felt more like a trip to a masseuse than a bondage scene.

Not that she was an expert, of course. Nora tried to stretch, but felt the rope's restraint. And the corresponding shifting and tightening of the rope sheath. Liking the resistence, she tried to stretch again.

Always solicitous, Mage asked her, "Are you uncomfortable? Would you like to try another position?"

She was comfortable. If she was any more comfortable, she'd fall asleep. A tiny rivulet of sweat tickled as it ran down her back. Mage kept his Painloft warmer than the dungeon, even without a fireplace.

She noticed Mage didn't seem to sweat at all.

Carefully keeping the impatience with his slowness out of

her voice, she replied, "I'm good. Thanks." Wouldn't do to be rude.

Why had she been so frightened of Mage at first? His appearance? He had an inoffensive face. Short, tamed dark hair. A longish nose. Even, white teeth. The curvy lips of someone with a foreign background. His body was harder to determine—he wore a long shirt the color of a bruise, and black pants tucked into matte black leather boots. On anyone else it'd look pretentious, she mused. But Mage pulled it off. In fact, he'd look right at home wearing a vampire cape.

Must be his accent, she figured. It whispered of cruelty, of dirty deeds witnessed, of atrocities performed without emotion. When she'd heard his voice while blindfolded down in the dungeon, she'd felt a shiver run down her spine.

Strange how the different dominants compared. Master Andre seemed the most approachable, the most normal of them with his imperfect hairline and his ready grin. Mage was the most exotic. Quiet and deliberate. Sort of relaxing, despite his creepy voice initially, and surprisingly tame: was that bug zapper paddle the extent of his electrical toys?

Then there was Sylvester. The "heavy top." The one who made her loins clench just remembering the way he'd spoken to her in his room, the way he'd made her so wet talking about their shared fantasy before grabbing her and starting to make that fantasy come true. . . .

Nora moaned at the thought.

"Are you well? Is anything too tight?"

"Everything's fine. Thanks."

Sylvester had seemed resolved and distant when he'd brought Nora up to Mage. *Seemed* resolved. She knew his body burned for hers. He wanted the same violent coupling she did. He wanted to make her whimper. She knew it. He knew she knew it. But he didn't do a damn thing about it except deliver her to yet another man.

He'd all but thrust her at Mage, after assuring her the man could be trusted. He'd also reminded her to use her safe word if she felt the slightest discomfort.

Nora smiled to herself. Of course she felt discomfort. That was kind of the point, to have little discomforts and some larger ones, physical and mental, then having them soothed away. Poof, catharsis. All of it simply a sensual sort of play, with its ritualized giving and taking of power.

She remembered Master Andre's enjoyment of having power over her. He'd basically asked her to live with him and be his pampered sex slave as he traveled the world. She'd liked Master Andre. She'd enjoyed playing with him. She hadn't felt afraid even once, in his power. His proposed traveling setup had undeniable benefits and might actually merit some consideration.

Was Mage enjoying having her in his power, too? Trussing her up and down, spread-eagled and hog-tied and over a padded sawhorse . . . She stifled a yawn.

Disappointment scratched at her. Nora suddenly felt jaded. Was this all there was to it?

"There." Soft warm breath tickled her neck, where Mage fiddled with some final knotwork. Now he'd torture her gently for a while, untie her slowly, then do it all again. Nora briefly considered saying "red" just to end the scene faster. And, to be honest, so she could go in search of Sylvester.

Mage tugged on a back section of rope.

Hard.

The knot just above her clit dug in, twisting.

She felt the heat of his tongue as he licked her from shoulder to earlobe. "Salty. Wet. I think we are finally ready to begin."

"Begin?"

"Do you remember your safe word? Red for stop, yellow for pause . . . and let us make your right fist knocking five times against the wood, here, a signal for 'stop' as well, yes? For when you are speechless." Mage laughed, and Nora recalled why she'd found him frightening.

He brought before her a small black rectangular box, about half the size of a guitar case. He set it reverently on a low table in her sightline. With a glance to make sure she watched, he flipped the metal catches and opened it.

Her disquiet deepened when she saw colored wires, curved tightly in concentric circles. So this was the real electrical device. The black box—a battery?—had the center spot in the case, nestled in the dark gray foam. Radiating out from it, each in its own discrete depression, were clamps, two tubes of conductive gel, round adhesive pads, and a number of probe-shaped devices that seemed a little on the small side, if they were what she thought they were.

"I am very interested in electro torture."

Her gaze reluctantly left the objects on display. Mage was watching her. A new light in his eyes, and the sadistic curve to his lips, made a brief shiver ripple through her.

"Cattle prods. Stun guns and batons. You do not want to know the damage these things do to a human body. They make a person very . . . cooperative, shall we say? My toys are gentler." Mage considered. "They will still make you scream."

Nora swallowed. When Mage stepped closer, she involuntarily flinched, her head hitting the pad he'd placed behind it. It made him smile. "Electricity is edge play. The biggest danger is its potential to interfere with the normal electrical impulses that make your heart beat. But playing with electricity, like hang gliding or mountain climbing or scuba diving, is not inherently dangerous. It is merely unforgiving of mistakes. Lucky for you, I do not make mistakes."

Arrogant much? she wanted to say. The comment seemed inadvisable at the moment. She tested her bonds surreptitiously. Still secure.

"In a hurry to leave? I am only beginning." That smile again, as he lifted the wires and electrodes, snapping their ends to the pads and coating them with gel. He attached more wires to the clamps. When he flipped on the black box she could hear its low hum. "The juice." He said it with relish.

Despite the danger, she felt curiosity rise in her.

He reassured her further, even as he attached the electrodes to her butt cheeks, thighs, belly. "This toy, the Eclectrik EL-321, is like a TENS unit–TENS stands for transcutaneous electrical nerve stimulation. Doctors use it in medicine to treat muscle pain, as the electricity interacts directly with the muscle's nerve endings. It is said to relieve pain. That is amusing, yes? Feel its bite."

With his words, he pushed a button.

"Oh." The areas beneath the electrodes suddenly felt very odd. Alive, crawling, tingling. She looked down, and the one on her belly was making it twitch involuntarily.

"This is the low setting. Here is the next higher one."

She jumped as the juice hit her. There was the "bite" he'd mentioned. The ropes dug into her body as she twitched. She felt the muscles beneath the electrodes spasm. The knot above her clit twisted, adding its own type of bite. She gasped. It all happened so quickly, her body moving outside of her control. But before the pain grew unendurable, Mage tapped the button again.

For the first time, he touched her with affection. He stroked her hair, then let his hand glide down her neck and chest to her left nipple. He pinched, then rolled it between two fingers. "Your body is firm, young, healthy. You are warmed up, so an involuntary muscle spasm is less likely to cramp. And, of course, you are restrained for my pleasure and your safety. I think you can take a lot more."

She tried to concentrate around the riveting pleasure of his touch. "You like seeing women in pain," she said, only just realizing it. "You actually enjoy it."

"Screams, tears, they are the sweetest nectar to me," he agreed. "Though moans of pleasure are also delightful. And now I will have to ask you to shut up. Unless it is screams and moans. Or your safe word, of course. Oh, and do not move unless I instruct you."

"For safety?"

Instead of answering, he shook his head mockingly: Naughty Nora. He let her watch him turn up the setting. And push the button.

She gasped as the electrodes surged the juice into her muscles. Ass, belly, and worst of all into her thighs . . . the pain! She whimpered, trying not to move despite her muscles shrieking for her to do so, anything to relieve the lightning-stab of electricity pummeling her deeply wherever the electrodes touched.

She panted, sweat running freely. She looked at him pleadingly.

He pushed the button, and the pain was gone as if it hadn't existed. "You see?" He yanked off one electrode. "Not a single mark. Amazing, is it not?" He gazed at her expectantly as she fought for composure. She glanced at his finger on the button, and remained silent.

Mage grinned, the first real pleasure he'd shown. "Very good! I am going to have a lovely time breaking you."

"Break—?" Too late, she cut herself off.

Another mocking shake of the head. But this time, he took the nipple he'd fingered and applied a wire-attached clamp to it. He snapped another clamp closed on a generous pinch of pussy lip.

Apprehension surged and grew in her. This wasn't going to feel like Master Andre's nipple clamps. Not at all.

But her curiosity rose, gamely, to the occasion. What would it feel like on something as sensitive as a nipple? She craned her neck to watch him adjust the lower clamp. Less than an inch from the teasing rope knot.

Again, he let her watch him adjust the level—downward, this time, she was relieved to note.

But only until he pressed the button. The current penetrated her nipple, a delicious bite. It sank its electric fingers deep into her, a pleasure that magnified the sensation of mere touch by a thousandfold. It flirted at the very edge of pain. Mage knew his stuff, she thought, amazed.

Butterflies in her stomach seemed to rise to her throat, even as the sweet pain assaulting her nipple sent a corresponding message to her pussy. Her whole body trembled in Mage's complex rope net, and feeling the resulting pleasure from trembling against the knot, trembled some more.

It seemed impossible she should be close to orgasm just from a little electrical stimulation. She let out a little moan of pleasure. The current stopped immediately.

"But you seem pleased with your chastisement. That will never do." Mage's silky, insinuating voice seemed to penetrate her mind as the current had her body. He brought out a small, wavy metal cylinder, coated it with lube. He meant to insert it? Wires connected it to the small black control box, she saw with a return of dread.

He wouldn't. Would he?

Mage paused, the thing glistening in his hand. "Would you like to beg me not to do this to you?" he inquired with insane courtesy.

"May I speak?"

"Only if it's to say your safe word." He waited, a knowing smile playing at the corners of his mouth, while her fear battled curiosity.

When she didn't speak, his smile disappeared, replaced by a stern compassion. Her poise seemed to bother him. "You do not take it seriously. You will, though." Dewdrops of perspiration made his skin begin to glitter. She didn't need to hear his savoring deep breaths as he adjusted the wire attachments to know his anticipation rivaled hers.

She shouldn't let him do this, she knew. Foolish, irresponsible in the extreme, dangerous . . . Her intellect listed all the reasons she should scream out her safe word and escape not only Mage but Twisted Wood entirely. And yet . . . Sylvester trusted him.

Nora shifted, breathing faster. The real reason she would let Mage toy with her body—Mage, a man she suspected of involvement in central European violence!—was that she craved this so-called edge play. After the duty-bound predictability of her existence, the part of her coming to life in the aftermath of Ryan's revelation wanted the greatest possible vacation from it.

She clamped her lips shut on anything that might resemble the word "red."

Mage was on her so quickly she didn't have time to flinch. His large, clothed body pressed against hers dug the ropes into her flesh deeply enough to make her grimace. The rough-hewn wood of the X-shaped cross pricked her shoulders and arms. With one hand he grasped her jaw, forcing her face up. With the other he gathered up strings of rope, as if pulling in a fish in a net, and shook her. Only she had nowhere to go. The ropes tugged at her flesh, vibrating the knot obscenely even as small splinters pierced her and she was given what felt like an all-over Indian burn.

Adrenaline poured into her body, and she trembled with fear at last.

The word felt shaken out of her: "Please."

"Nice." He shook her again. "Beg me some more. You like it rough. Loosened up, now, yes? You can take these little pains. And some not-so-little pains. I must play, too, you see."

Nora looked into his eyes and realized what Mage meant by "play."

But even as her mouth started to shape her safe word, his

hand slid down between her legs. He crooked his index finger in a come-here gesture, stroking her slit.

The sensation felt nearly as electric as the electrodes and clamps he activated a moment later.

He touched her clit as her nipple leapt and trembled in response to the voltage, and her flesh under the electrodes crawled. "Too much," she gasped.

Then gasped again when he pinched her clit tightly. "That? You think that is too much? It is not enough," he declared, a look of disapproval on his face. "You open your mouth only to complain about nothing. You learn too slowly." He cruelly twisted her clit. The pleasure spiked, on waves of electricity.

Then he released her. He cut the power with the button on the black box, ripped her electrodes off . . . then grinned as he let her see him grasp the wire to the clamp on her nipple. "Ready? Brace yourself." She clenched every muscle in her body, but it didn't help her against the sudden searing pain of Mage yanking the clamp off her nipple. She shouted. It hurt.

Craning her neck, she looked down to make sure her nipple hadn't been ripped off, too.

Then looked up into Mage's bright eyes. The man was obviously in his element as he closed in on her once more. She cringed, but he only massaged the hurt out of her nipple.

Then he nodded, his hand sliding up to encircle her throat. He blinked, long and savoring, as his fingers sunk into her flesh. With his other hand, he adjusted a bit of his rope, meticulous. Repairing a diamond shape to make his design more attractive, she knew, and shivered with a fear heavily flavored with lust and adrenaline. What would he do next?

She didn't have long to wait.

"Guess where this is going?" Mage held the jelly-covered steel dildo before her. Her eyes widened, and he smiled at her reaction. His hand moved from adjusting the rope, to sliding down her body. He tapped the indentation where her labia met inner thigh. "Not here." He slid his hand, smooth, relentless, up and over to her other inner thigh. Tapped. "Not here, either." He stared into her eyes, clearly savoring her fear.

She shook her head. Her emotions surged—the fear he enjoyed, but also lust, helplessness, other emotions she couldn't name—and to her amazement, she felt tears filling her eyes. She wriggled against her bonds. She tried desperately to close her legs. If the electricity did that to her nipple, what would an electrified probe inside her feel like?

A wild desire to find out warred with her sensible plan to stop Mage. Now. All she had to do was speak up.

"Don't. Please." She begged him, knowing her words were sincere even as she knew they only egged him on. He wanted to hear her begging. He liked it. Her tears visibly got him off. So why did her voice tremble, and her body shake with fear, when all she had to do was say "red" and everything would stop? There was something wrong with her, she thought, even as the tears spilled over to trickle down her cheeks. Something had to be wrong with a person who could revel in such treatment.

"Are you ready? Here it comes." Mage moved the probe between her legs. She lunged away, shaking her head in an ecstasy of terror, frustration at her captivity, and a delicious sinking sensation of pleasure. There was no escape. "No!" She wriggled frantically, but only succeeded in making the ropes pinch her.

Ignoring her struggles, Mage started to push the wet probe into her. After a moment he exhaled with frustration. "Be still." Then, "All this flinging about. I will make it that much harder on you." With a cruel grip, he pinioned one of her legs, then shoved the probe hard up between them. She let out a cry of defeat as she felt the coldness of metal lodged firmly inside.

He was still moving something between her legs. More rope? She was already tied so elaborately she could barely move, her arms and legs too open for comfort.

When he cinched the knot, she felt the rope tighten and ride up into her slit to nudge the bottom of the probe. She understood, then. He merely secured his toy inside her. Possibly against more expected "flinging about."

The coldness inside seemed to radiate threat. She tried to dislodge it, but failed entirely.

In shocking contrast to the cold intrusion, Mage stroked her nipples with warm, clever fingers. In helpless response, she clenched around the cold probe.

Then he held up the small box with the dials and the button that wasn't too much smaller than her nipple. With a sadistic grin, he pressed it.

9

The electrical pulse that surged into her pussy made her cry out with surprise. The force clenched her muscles for her, as if she were having an orgasm. Which, perversely, brought her that much closer to the edge. It didn't feel like torture, unless delicious sensations were supposed to be torturous. She panted, looking at him with confusion and growing pleasure.

"Low power. Not intense. Boring for me." He flicked it off. He made her watch while he slowly turned the dial up.

And pressed the button.

Every muscle in her body seemed to convulse, jerking against her ropes. She yelped, feeling as if the spasms between her legs would tear her apart. The bite of the probe was like lightning, and like an enormous cock violating her repeatedly. It was intense, and it hurt, and it frightened her . . . and she felt fascination even in the midst of it, at such a new sensation. Her body contracted involuntarily, her breath stolen as each new pulse hit. Her skin, slicked by sweat, danced against the ropes. She whimpered, the pain growing too much to bear.

As if reading her mind, Mage touched the button.

The stillness of her body felt like heaven. Sweat ran freely from her.

"Medium power. More intense. But it can go higher. Would you like me to turn it higher?"

She shook her head so hard the perspiration flew from her.

"But I want to. Just once." He slowly turned the dial higher. Instead of pressing the button right away, though, he reached between her legs, fingered her clit instead. "You are doing wonderfully, and bearing it well. You are very brave. It hurts, doesn't it? It is supposed to. But there can be pleasure in pain. I am going to hurt you even more now," he said even as he stroked her until the pleasure was pure and explosive. "You will feel agony." His eyes were luminous with lust, his lips parted.

"Please don't," she begged. "Please . . ."

With his touch, and her emotions on a hair trigger, her tears flowed freely as her sweat. She moaned, pressing herself against his finger. He met her urgency with a rougher touch that brought Sylvester's visage immediately to her mind. "Yes," she gasped, a heartbeat away from coming.

She closed her eyes.

Her world exploded.

The jolt that hit her made her shriek, her eyes flying open in shock and disbelief. The pain of her muscles contracting made her cry out in fear, and the tiny probe felt the size of a fist, the size of the biggest dildo she'd ever seen, far too big. It thrust and burrowed and tormented. The spasms stole her ability to think, even as the forced penetration assaulting her flung her dancing body against the slick knot at her clit and transformed the pain into something else, a force that would shatter her if it continued. Oddly, that make her think of Sylvester, too.

The pulsing contractions deepened, lengthened, and heightened rapidly to the agony Mage had promised.

His voice was an intrusive growl in her ear. "Say your safe word, if you want me to stop. Say it."

"Stop! Stop!" She rode the pain, pummeled and penetrated, crying for mercy she knew he wouldn't deliver. She couldn't find pleasure as she knew it with this device set on maximum, could she? She couldn't help but respond to its raw power, to explore it. It delivered pain for Mage's pleasure, surely she couldn't enjoy it, it hurt too much! Yet she refused to say the word "red." Not just yet. Her entire body contracted, agonized, as her pleas grew hoarse. She stopped begging, knowing it was useless. She submitted to it, and an awful pleasure began to rise as the world started to gray out.

It stopped.

She shifted in her bonds, bereft and relieved both. She hung limply, unable to even lift her head.

Mage's compassionate voice sounded as if it came from a great distance. "More might have damaged you." She heard the whisper of clothing. "We are finished with this toy." The ropes vibrated, and she felt air cool her crotch as he removed the probe. She began to breathe again, and marvel at how even the memory of pain seemed to vanish with the probe. And the memory of its pleasure. She bit back a whimper.

Mage put the probe, electrodes, and box aside. "I have one more toy for you tonight. A very special toy."

She slit her eyes open to gaze at him. She blinked.

Mage stood, naked. One hand rested on what appeared to be a large suitcase. "I travel to all places. Europe, Scandinavia, Russia, Thailand . . . so many places. Uncommon destinations, exotic ones. I have acquired many electrical toys. But this is my favorite."

She blinked at his hand patting the mysterious suitcase, then fixed her attention back on his body. Without clothes, he looked thinner, younger, with whipcord muscles under hairless skin. Here and there she could see old scars marring the skin: a raised ridge encircling a divot just below his shoulder, a long white stripe bisecting the taut skin over his stomach, a generous pattern of jagged splotches on his forearm. She tried not to look, but her eyes were drawn to his penis.

No scars, just a flawless erection that would make any man proud. It jutted straight out and slightly up, the bulbous head a good distance from its root. Mage was well endowed.

The smile on his face told her he knew it. "The scars," he said, unlocking the case, then facing her once more. "They are a roadmap of my pains. Not happy pains. A gunshot in Russia." He touched the round scar. "A knife attack in Pakistan." The long stripe over his belly. "A napalm explosion in Serbia." The splotches. "Dangerous places."

"Not a fan of Club Med, huh?"

Nora couldn't help flinching when this dangerous, scarred man who owned such painful toys suddenly walked toward her with a large hunting knife.

"No." He didn't smile. But his eyes twinkled as he brought the blade to within an inch of her face. "I am not."

Nora watched the knife. He didn't move or change expression, only stood there with the knife—to let her view its honed edge?—before walking around the cross to her back.

She swallowed, trying to forget he held that knife. When he spoke she latched onto the sound of his voice. "I am a—how do you say—a thrill seeker. Danger is my drug. And, of course, the delight of certain agonies." She felt the tip of the knife prick her in the middle of her back. Then the flesh of her shoulder. "You are too, Nora." It was the first time he'd said her name. It seemed intimate coming from a naked man with a knife to her back. "And I want to give you the thrill you seek."

The tormenting itch of Mage's poking knife prodding her over her shoulder blades, arms, and finally her vulnerable neck both focused her and made her want to purr. He didn't break her flesh. He wouldn't harm her. Hadn't he stopped the probe's assault when it grew dangerous?

Living on the edge had its appeal.

With a skilled flick of his wrist, her ropes loosened. He pulled them from her, and helped her from the cross to the large bed in the corner of the room. Her legs unsteady, she was grateful for his support.

He held her, guiding her down. "Yes. Sit. Just sit for now. Watch. I will give you a wondrous show with my violet wand."

He saw the look she couldn't control, and burst into laughter.

"No, my sweet one. Not this." He stroked himself once, bringing glistening pre-cum to the tip of his cock. "At least, not yet. It is true you have made it nearly the color of violet. The color of frustration." He looked down at her with tenderness. "I very much enjoy that. I enjoy you, Nora."

"You're not so bad yourself." She rolled her hips, feeling the gentle burn of her frustration saturate her, making her limbs heavy and her skin sensitive to every stray air current.

"Yes. I know." He grinned at her, and fetched more rope.

She watched him. He wasn't Sylvester, but a naked Mage was a thing of beauty. She just wished he'd finish her off, sexually. Her nipples ached. Her pussy hungered. She felt compressed, sensitized, and ready for an unimaginable explosion of pleasure.

"Lie on your side, facing me. Yes, good." She felt more of his now-familiar three-quarter-inch rope sliding over her skin. Decadent, arousing, relaxing . . . She let a pleased rumble vibrate her chest as Mage wrapped loops around her forearms, folding them in front of her. He crossed her ankles, and secured those, too. The crossed-ankle position left her thighs parted.

The bondage seemed skimpy compared to his earlier, more elaborate designs. She tried to free herself without success. In the ropes securing her forearms she detected a tiny amount of give, but her ankles were immobilized.

Skimpy restraints, but effective. She looked at him curiously.

"This is my violet wand." He held what looked like a glow globe attached to a handle. He nudged a floor pedal with his bare foot. She heard a low hum. The globe sparked to pinkish purple life.

She stared at it, mesmerized by the ever-moving forks of electricity. Mage cupped his hand, moved it around the globe without touching it. The lightning extended tentacles from the glass to Mage's palm with a snapping buzz, moving with him. The smell of ozone filled the air. His eyes glittered with reflected violet light.

In that moment he looked every inch a magician.

He nudged the foot switch, and the lightning danced more violently.

"Static electricity. When you grasp a doorknob, and get zapped? This toy offers a similar sensation, only it does not stop."

He suddenly moved it near her belly. The lightning seemed to latch onto her skin with a buzzing snap. She cried out as the electrical whip struck her, tried to wriggle away. His free hand restrained her. "Be still. Feel. It is not that hurtful now. Some people find it soothing." She stilled, and found he was right. It sounded worse than it was. Though she would hardly call it soothing.

"When skin touches the glass, there is no sensation." He touched the cool globe to her, and the angry buzz faded again to just a hum as the sensation stopped. "It is only in the gap"—he demonstrated, moving the globe slowly away from her again—"that the current finds you and punishes you. It must jump the gap. Farther away, it becomes more intense. . . ."

The angry buzz grew angrier as the lightning licked at her with its sharp heat. She hissed. The pinpricks of pain increased.

Mage continued. "A bit more painful, until finally, the distance is too great and the electricity cannot jump the gap." The buzz broke off when the globe gained enough inches of distance.

"Unlike the Eclectrik EL-321, my violet wand zaps just the surface of the skin rather than the muscle." He demonstrated, bringing the globe near her right nipple.

The moment the electricity surged across the gap and touched her, she jerked back at the sensation: stinging bees and scraping teeth and pulsating fire. It hurt, but the pinpricks of energy seemed to tease each individual nerve ending, blending pain and pleasure until she couldn't distinguish one from the other, and it all became pleasure. Delightful!

She almost didn't notice the angry buzzing, but the sight of the steady yellow current of lightning affixed to her nipple disconcerted her. "Will it burn?"

When he frowned at her, she remembered he didn't like her to speak while he tortured her. But he answered. "Not permanently. At worst, it can be similar to a sunburn."

He massaged first one nipple then the other with the lightning, around in circles, occasionally inflicting its bite directly on her tip. When the electricity struck the tips, the sharp shock of it made her suck in her breath. "That's intense."

He nudged off the current and announced, "I will gag you now. When you wish to communicate 'red,' open and close your fist five times."

As he inserted a small ball gag into her mouth and buckled its soft leather strap behind her head, she realized something. He'd said "when" not "if."

What did he have planned that made him so confident she'd utter her safe word?

She watched him replace the globe with a rake-shaped attachment instead. Its pronged edges drew her gaze.

Without any explanation, Mage nudged the floor pedal. As the machine buzzed to life, she noticed his erection hadn't faltered. Then he was holding the rake over her heart. He smiled without humor as he drew an X. Then he pulled the electricity sideways, over her shoulder, down one bound arm, onto her lower belly. The streams of electricity from the edges of the rake drew agonizing parallel lines. She made a muffled sound, trying first to shift her arm, then to suck in her belly to protect her skin from the casually inflicted pain.

Mage gazed at her, slit-eyed. "The skin is a sensitive organ." He grasped her bound forearms, turned her onto her other side with easy strength. A second later, she felt the rake on her lower back. She protested and wriggled from it.

He slapped her on her buttocks, the first time he'd struck her. "Be still."

She tried, as the static electricity fried the skin over her spine, her neck, her ass, but when he drew the rake over the side of her back, she convulsed—half tickled, half stung. He slapped her ass again, and trained the buzzing electricity on her nipples again.

His cock felt large, warm, and incredibly inviting against the crack of her ass, and she wriggled against it.

"Bitch!" He slapped her ass again, repeatedly, as he electrified her nipples. "One simple command. Be still. I tie you, pleasure you. I give you good pains, and still you do not obey. You will wish you had obeyed." His clever, intrusive fingers burrowed lower into the damp hair, delved into her slit to find and stroke her clit. Tickled it. She gasped at the sensation of his long fingers teasing her, the same fingers that had held a knife to her minutes ago. The electricity trained on her nipples buzzed and popped, sending delicious pinpricks of pain into her. His voice, honeyed with compassion, didn't fool her. She knew him now, knew a compassionate Mage was a dangerous thing. He was about to hurt her.

She still couldn't help trying to hump his fingers. After the hours of his rope bondage, the slow teasing and relaxing, binding and releasing, she was burning up.

Mage's fingers flicked, making her squirm and writhe. "You are very disobedient." His voice sounded oddly rough in her ear, low and rough, almost like Sylvester's. He flipped her onto her back, making her feel like so much meat, a package, nothing remotely resembling the travel-marketing executive she'd been upon arrival at Twisted Wood.

She shuddered with pleasure. Her attention was divided between his fingers and the sweet pain of electricity now travelling down the underside of her breasts, down over her belly button, down . . .

Her eyes flew wide open. She protested around her gag.

The rake sent its parallel electrified whipcracks into the smooth skin just above the soft triangle of her pubic hair, then into the delicate, sensitive flesh of her inner thighs.

He wouldn't.

She jackknifed, galvanized by fear, but Mage was ready for her and held her in place.

She yelled, but the gag strangled the sound.

He heard it, though. His body shifted slightly as he checked her hand for the stop signal. He chuckled at its stillness, lifted her by her hair, and spoke into her gagged face: "Scream all you want. Muffled screams get me hard. See?" Tears sprung into her eyes from his grip on her hair. Her gaze flicked down. Sure enough, he throbbed as if ready to explode.

As if eager to hear her scream as soon as possible, Mage gave the nub of her nipple one last cruel twist, then spread her labia wide, and raked her with the attachment, starting from her ass and pulling it up. The zaps assaulted her horribly, and as the device traveled it just got worse. At her anus it felt like a hundred stinging bees. At her pussy it felt like a welder's arc. And then . . .

She screamed.

Nothing could have prepared her for the blinding pain, the intensity like a sun exploding as the static electricity snapped her clit. It faded as the point of the rake temporarily left the sensitive nub of flesh, then returned as if the sound of muffled screams were truly music to Mage's ears. She obliged him, the sounds she made sounding desperate to her own ears. She threw her hips right and left trying to sever the relentless connection of energy connecting the rake to her skin, but Mage followed her movements, allowing her only the tiniest of reprieves.

She heard him laugh. For a moment, she hated him.

Then, the impossible happened. The on-again, off-again rhythm of electricity began to build into a perverse heat, not quite pain anymore. The whipsnap of buzzing current began to have a certain sweetness. And she began to anticipate each delicious raking torment of her clit by lifting her hips to better receive it.

"Yes. Now you see." He pedaled the energy off, and in the silence she heard her own muffled protest.

He laughed again. "Truly, you astonish me. You fight my tortures, you scream and plead so convincingly—I am convinced!—and then, you turn toward the pain. You transmute it. This"—he slicked one finger down between her legs, pushing it into her with only minimal difficulty—"is proof." He held his finger up, coated in her juice. He inhaled with relish.

She recognized truth in his words, not to mention on his hands.

Maybe it wasn't the whole truth. True, she enjoyed his tortures. But there was something she'd enjoy more, something Mage wasn't quite qualified to give her.

The ache of frustrated need made her moan through her gag. She let him see her gaze drop to his cock, then back to his face, pleading.

"Of course," he answered, smug. "But not just yet, my dear."

His smugness blunted her desire, but only enough to bring her senses back under her own control. She stilled her hips, becoming aware she was grinding against the bed. Her nipples felt tight and achy. Hell, her whole body burned, and she needed relief.

"Ungag me," she said, or tried to. The gag turned her words into meaningless grunts. The sight of his stiff cock bobbing as he moved from the suitcase with yet another tool tore from her another sound, a moan. Would he never tire of playing with her, and just ravish her the way she craved?

But even as she thought it, she knew he couldn't satisfy her that way, not like Sylvester could.

Still, she was willing to test the theory. As he approached, she shifted her ankles to let her knees fall farther open. He'd have to untie her ankles to do her properly, but at least now he could see what she offered.

Mage laughed. "Very nice. I will make you as slutty as Kitten, in time."

She blinked. Kitten. She'd forgotten about his service submissive. He wanted to add her to his collection of submissives? She wasn't submissive. She wasn't his. Her legs closed slightly.

One warm hand on her knee stopped her movement. "No."

His other held what looked like a metal spatula with a thick, flexible rubber-covered wire. He plugged the end of the wire into the violet wand's handle.

When he nudged the floor button, she heard the buzz, but nothing else happened. Mage smiled at her and waved his fingers—hocus-pocus—over the flat surface. Unlike with the rake and the globe, no yellow current leapt out to zap his flesh.

It was dead.

Then Mage let his hand slowly leave her knee. The fire leapt from his fingertips! With a familiar angry buzz, the current zapped her skin.

He saw her expression, and his eyes crinkled at the corners as he smiled. "Magical, yes?" He seared her all around her kneecap, tracing fire down to where ropes encircled her ankles, then up the other leg. She shuddered at the prickly, hurtful-but-not-really sensation as she marveled at the wizardly appearance of electricity shooting from his fingertips.

The current emerged from his palm as he tilted his hand. He caressed her thighs with current. So, it could come from anywhere on his body?

He'd placed her body halfway up the bed. When he knelt over her crossed ankles to kiss her thigh where his palm had just zapped, she expected a soothing relief. Instead, the current leapt from his lips to her flesh.

She yelped in surprise. His lips?

He kissed her higher on the thigh, then laved the seared flesh with his hot tongue . . . which then also zapped her when he moved back an inch. The spark jumped the gap, whipping the tender inner flesh of her thigh unmercifully. Mage had an electrified tongue.

The idea made her helplessly wet, even as she laughed in disbelief.

Mage murmured to her in between whip-kisses. "This body contact pad turns the entire body into an electrical conductor." He let it slip from his fingers to the bed, then placed his forearm onto it. He levered himself into position, his hot breath teasing her wetness. Apprehension, then sweet anticipation swirled in her head.

Her body suddenly ravenous, she made a small wanting noise around the gag.

And then he was there, his tongue in turn sliding over, and electrically zapping, the most sensitive spot on her body. Fully primed for it, the pain of the electricity now transmuted immediately to pleasure, a deep pleasure that took her into realms she'd never known before.

The sensation galvanized. Her hips bucked, her thighs trembled, and if she still had the use of her arms she'd be using them to keep his face planted right there for as long as it took.

Which wouldn't be long at all, she realized suddenly. The

long slow buildup of the past hours, the teasing and then stopping, the binding and the torture that didn't quite result in an explosive orgasm, gathered in her gut. The unbearable tension built, incredibly, still further as his lips and tongue and the buzzing electrical whips connecting him to her worked their diabolical magic.

She cried out around her gag, alarmed. She was going to fly to pieces. She might hurt him.

Then she laughed, a quick gasp as the tension spasmed throughout her body. Mage would like that.

She screamed around her gag as it hit. Mage lapped her up, electrifying her into unbearable bliss that went on and on.

The aftermath shudders continued long beyond what she expected, and she fell back, only then realizing her body had jackknifed. The steel plate now lay under her left hip.

Mage held her, gentle with her as her orgasm subsided. "I am going to fuck you," he said. His voice held lust long restrained. His cock nudged his own stomach as he shifted, bent to untie her ankles.

But after the hours and hours of buildup, the torture, and then the glorious release, all Nora wanted was to crawl away to her room and sleep for twelve hours. Couldn't he see she'd gone boneless? Limp as a noodle, grateful and happy. She wasn't his submissive, to be used if she didn't feel like it.

She moved slightly, made a distressed sound.

He gave her a smile of pleasure, unraveling the ropes with more urgency.

Exasperation gripped her. Would she have to use her safe word? She hated to do it. She didn't want to recognize any limits on her adventures, not yet. She felt using it declared herself fearful and predictable. Things she no longer wanted to be. Though she was still unclear on what other things would take their place.

And yet, Mage had been so attentive, she almost felt inclined to give him a mercy fuck. He'd given her amazing sensations, unlike Ryan.

Which reminded her of all the times she'd let Ryan use her, when all the mercy in the world wouldn't have made them right for each other.

It was a revelation. But the situation called for immediate response.

Her gag meant she had to give the hand signal instead. Her hands fisted, then she let her fingers curl away from her body as far as the forearm ropes allowed. A few inches of give. Enough to get his attention.

She felt the cool metal plate under her hip.

She thought. Then smiled.

His cock, as he drew the ankle ropes from her and tossed them to a far corner, was positioned perfectly.

She tilted her body toward him, grabbed with one hand and electrically stroked with the other.

Mage went very still.

So odd, to hear the buzzing and know her body conducted current into another person. She let her gaze flick up to him, checking his reaction. He looked stunned, but uncomplaining.

The velvet heft of his large cock seemed to delight in the combination of sensual hand job and electrical whipping. When she cupped around the thick helmet tip, not quite touching him, he flinched at the lightning's kiss. How well she remembered what that felt like. She tormented him a bit longer, then stroked him again, faster. Her awkward position made her movements inventive, experimental, rough . . . ah, success.

He throbbed in her hand. When he would have pulled away, she gripped him tighter, menacing his testicles with her cupped hand. Threatening. Cowed, Mage remained still, breathing hard and looking at her with an expression suggesting he'd never been more surprised.

It didn't take long.

Cursing in a language she didn't understand, he suddenly thrust hard against her gripping hand. With the slickness of his ejaculate, he moved fast enough to heat her palm with friction.

Nora laughed, a muffled snorting sound, when he collapsed next to her. The room smelled of sex and ozone.

She laughed again at his rueful glance down at his now-flaccid cock.

"This is funny to you?" He looked fierce for a moment, but couldn't sustain the expression. He grinned. "It is funny." He laughed, sitting up on one elbow long enough to unbuckle her gag, fling it away. He untied her forearms with quick, straightforward movements rather than the sensual tugs and sliding pulls he'd applied earlier. Her arms felt itchy from confinement, and strained from her recent awkward hand activity.

Mage cocked his head, listening. He sighed. He sat up, scooted to the edge of the bed.

Nudged the violet wand off. The buzzing ended. He remained at the edge of the bed. Glanced at her.

They regarded each other.

He shook his head, rueful. He no longer looked magical in the slightest as he eyed her crotch. "That was not the ending I intended. Would you be interested in playing again while you are here at Twisted Wood? We can finish properly. I promise you would be glad to have me fuck you."

She considered possible replies, rubbing her forearms against each other to soothe them. "Maybe later," she told him.

10

It was the third day, Nora thought. Her last day at Twisted Wood.

She walked alone down the center of the gravel road, enjoying the late-morning warmth and the press of nature on either side.

Tonight was the Chase and Capture fantasy rape event.

And tomorrow morning she'd drive back down this road with Ryan, leaving behind the erotic bed-and-breakfast. Maybe forever.

Her ass cheeks felt less sore today, at least. Her nipples, however, were distractingly raw and sensitive after the electrical play, even encased in a tight sports bra.

The confusing thoughts she'd awakened with rose up again, clamoring and insistent.

She broke into a jog, her running shoes making poor traction on gravel, then better traction on dirt as she turned off onto a narrow trail. Trusting her sense of direction to not get her lost, and her natural stamina and speed to outdistance any forest nasties, Nora ran, her ponytail slapping the bare skin of her back above and below the green bra top. She ran, trying not to think at all.

The path grew steep, curving first away, then gently back toward the main house. She breathed steadily, climbing, feeling a new chill on her skin as perspiration began to cool her. Ignoring other branchings from the path, Nora made for a clearing she could see through the woods.

By the time she burst into it, she felt the paradoxical energy and clarity running always gave to her. Bouncing on her heels, stretching, she let the peaceful beauty of her immediate environment wash over her like a balm.

Near the entry to the clearing, a beautiful huge Oregon maple erupted from the dark soil like a giant moss-encrusted hand. Ferns and blackberry bushes ringed it and continued all the way around the cleared patch of sun-dappled ground, which was covered only in sparse clover in a few spots. Vines wove through the ferns, climbed a grove of young cedar trees. The spot was as pristine and perfect as a framed painting, and smelled of packed dirt, oxygen-rich air, and mystery.

Nora just breathed deeply, appreciating it. How wonderful it must be to own twenty-one acres of such land, with a jewel like Twisted Wood at its center. Maybe if she worked enough years as vice president, she could eventually earn enough to buy something similar. Ten or fifteen years, tops. If the long hours without a life and little hope of vacation didn't kill her.

Her mood soured and she started stretching more vigorously. Time to run again.

She stopped. Frowned at something she could just see through the trees. A building? But Twisted Wood wasn't in that direction, she was sure of it.

Curious, she stood on a large root, trying to see better. A tiny house, maybe a shed? But it had a window, and a steeply pitched roof, and a small porch.

She squinted. Was that a bell hanging on a cupola?

What could it possibly be? A church?

Even as she pondered it, she was walking, making her own path past the maple and through the low ferns and grass. Vines clutched at her ankles, and once she was pretty sure she broke a spider web, but she only brushed at the web and walked more forcefully through the vines. It looked like a really old building.

As she approached it, she smiled. It wasn't a really old building. The single-room schoolhouse didn't have enough of a run-down appearance to quite pull it off: artfully peeling paint and roughened wood shingles didn't make up for the way the three front steps failed to sag with age, and the windows didn't have any cracks or pits.

If she was correct, Twisted Wood sat only half a mile downhill from this structure. Which meant Sylvester owned it.

Which meant it probably had some kinky purpose.

Compelled, she let her feet lead her up the stairs and to the front door, which opened easily.

Enough light filtered through the windows to allow her to see the teacher's desk front and center, behind which a large chalkboard dominated the single room. Filling the rest of the small room's space, short benches created neat rows and a stool was placed in one corner.

She walked over to the desk. On it sat a dictionary.

The loud clanging of the school bell made her jump. She whirled.

Sylvester stood in the doorway, backlit. She could see the shadow of his extended arm, and knew him instantly from outline alone. He'd dominated enough of her fantasies to recognize his silhouette.

He let his arm fall to his side. The bell stopped. "The only wiring in the place." He walked to the teacher's desk, reached under it, and pulled out one kerosene lantern, then a second. He quickly lit them. A warm yellow glow bathed both of them, banishing the room's remaining shadows.

He stood behind the desk. Spread his arms. "Welcome to Twisted Wood Academy." Lowered his arms. "Where naughty girls and boys learn interesting lessons."

She grinned, saw the answering small smile on his face. "You're the instructor, I presume?"

"Of course." He bent, brought out a long synthetic rod, and placed it next to the dictionary. "I'm quite the disciplinarian. Spare the rod, and all that."

She laughed. The sight of him standing there with his hand resting lightly on the rod sent an unexpected jolt of lust though her. They were in the middle of wilderness, nobody nearby to hear her scream. . . . He could do whatever he liked to her and there wasn't anything she'd be able to do about it.

He fondled the rod, looking at her appraisingly.

Her knees became weak.

"Would you like a lesson? Something simple. Complexity might discourage you."

She looked at him. Had he just insulted her?

"Something . . . elementary." He picked up the dictionary. "Sit, please." He didn't even look at her.

She thought about disobeying, just standing there with her arms folded. Or leaving. But what would be the fun in that? She sat. Then she folded her arms across her chest. Then unfolded them, feeling like an awkward grade-schooler.

She couldn't deny part of her thrilled to the game. Especially the part where they were totally alone, far from anyone who could come to her rescue if Sylvester chose to take advantage of her, if he decided to throw her down to the bare wood plank flooring and rip her clothes from her body. . . .

Nora made a small sound.

Sylvester marked his place in the dictionary with one finger. "Are you feeling well?"

"Yes."

"Yes, Professor Vincent," he corrected.

"Your last name is Vincent?"

He waited.

"Yes, Professor Vincent." She locked eyes with him, feeling her control over the situation slip away. She felt like a child before him. How did he shatter her poise so easily?

"Nora." He said her name, then waited.

When she didn't reply, he picked up the rod, strode to her. "Hold out your palms!"

She hesitated, then extended them.

"When a teacher calls your name, you stand. One stroke." The rod flashed down, raising a line of fire in the middle of her left palm. She cried out.

He didn't wait for her to compose herself. "There will be discipline in my schoolroom. Nora."

She stood quickly.

"Spell 'mischievous.' "

"Okay. M-i-s-c-h-i-v-i-e-o-u-s." She looked at him, half in hope, half in dread.

"Wrong. Hold out your hands."

"But—"

"Did you say something?"

She held out her hands. Received one whack. Then another. "For unruliness." Sylvester gazed at her. "Why are you still standing?"

She sat.

"Nora."

She sighed, then stood.

"Hold out your hands."

"What for?"

"For being a filthy-minded little slut."

Her body tensed. A bright flare of lust shook her, and she felt herself yielding to the searing desire he always inspired. She craved him. Craved more than his rough words and toys. She held out her hands slowly, defiant. He liked spirit, he'd said. "Do you feel manly, holding a long stick in your hand? Overcompensate much?"

Their eyes locked again.

"Hold out your hands."

"Here they are, big fella. Ouch!" She pulled her smarting hands back. Sat down.

"Nora."

"Go to hell."

She barely saw him move. One moment he stood before her, the next she dangled over his shoulder.

"Hey!" Fear made her tense up. Where was he taking her? What was he going to do?

He slid her off his shoulder, sat on the stool in the corner, and put her over his knee, facedown.

"Hey!" She struggled, but he just pushed her face back down until she enjoyed a scenic view of the wood planks and his black leather boot.

He yanked down her pants.

She struggled, enjoying the struggle even as her face suffused with mortification. Her body was all sweaty, dirty, and she wasn't wearing panties under the running pants. She squirmed, lunging away, but he simply pulled her back.

When he placed his large, warm hand on her bared ass, she stilled. "I'll have to pound the defiance out of you, won't I?" The velvet menace of his voice made her instantly wet.

Instinctively, she responded the way they both needed. "Don't hurt me."

She felt the tremor pass through his body. If anything his

voice grew even more chill, more cruel. "You deserve it. You've earned it. You need it." He punctuated each sentence with a hard spank. Each time, the force of it made her lunge forward under the stroke.

Then he picked up the cane. "For your appalling lack of decorum in not wearing panties." He striped her fanny three times with the cane, pausing torturously in between each strike. The compressing of the skin with his hits faded to deeper pain. Tears stood in her eyes by the time he pushed her off his lap.

"I'm sorry," she said.

He averted his gaze from her, as if she were not worthy even of his attention. "Place the hat on your head, and seat yourself. No!" he said when she went to pull up her pants. "Sit just as you are, to remind yourself just what a slutty little thing you really are."

Her hands trembled, putting on the tall, conical dunce cap. She collapsed more than sat on the stool, feeling the roughness of the wood against her assaulted bottom. She looked down. Her expensive running pants pooled around her ankles.

She wanted Sylvester driving inside her so badly she saw the thick stool limbs and her mind's eye imagined them penetrating her body. Didn't he know what he did to her? The dormant sexuality of her body had been awakened, here at Twisted Wood. Her fantasy no longer existed only in the privacy of her own mind. She ached for Sylvester's touch to make her fondest fantasy come true. She felt her mouth tremble, and knew she was on the verge of begging him. But that wouldn't work.

He didn't want her begging, unless it was for him to stop.

"Stay seated. You will give me correct answers to the following questions. If you hesitate—or worse, if you lie—you will be one sorry girl."

Her mind whirled. What would push him over the edge, make him seize her and force her? Should she defy him further?

Or continue to play the chastised dunce, the helpless victim? She'd grown a little tired of the spelling challenges and palm canings. Time to ratchet it up!

But as it turned out, his next words altered the game yet again. "Your checklist. I want to revisit it." Sylvester stood at the front corner of the broad teacher's desk, staring at her. "You gave a number of items a score of 'three' or higher. Spanking was a 'four.' Did you experience this activity? Yes or no."

"Yes." She wanted to remind him he'd been there, but seeing the look in his eyes she didn't quite dare.

"Would you want to repeat the experience?"

"Yes." Now would be fine. His large, warm hands on her ass, on her body, touching her expertly and tormenting her mercilessly . . . and then thrusting up between her legs with enough power to split her in half. That'd be okay.

His voice brought her back. "Tickling. A 'three,' I believe. Did you experience this activity?"

"Sort of."

Three strides and he was beside her, his hands wrapping in her hair, grasping a thick wad at the back of her head and pulling it to a craned-back position to meet his gaze. "*Yes or no.*"

Her eyes were pulled into slits. The pain in her scalp made her gasp. "Yes." Mage had half-mockingly tickled her under her arms after tying her. It hadn't done much for her. Unlike Sylvester's possession of her hair and scalp. Sylvester's grasp felt more like pressure than pain, now that she got used to it. A seizing of control that went to the heart of her psyche. She let her eyes broadcast her wants and desires to him.

He remained impassive. "Would you repeat the experience?"

"No."

He released the handful of her hair, but remained standing over her. "Electrical play."

"Yes."

"Would you want to repeat the experience?"

"Yes."

"Feathers, fur, food."

"No."

"You didn't experience those? Do you still want to?" His silken voice caressed her even as his hands touched her hair, stroking it until his fingers found her ear. He rubbed it between two fingers, making her want to purr.

Until he pinched the top of her ear once, just hard enough to remind her.

"Yes. Maybe a little."

Seemingly oblivious, he continued. "Role playing."

She caught her breath. Looked up at him. "No."

Surprise flickered in his eyes. "No? You haven't done that?" He raised one eyebrow and tapped his palm lightly with the cane.

"That's not the kind of role playing I want."

He stared down at her. The air between them grew electric.

His voice became soft, almost a whisper. "Don't you think you're in a dangerous position right now? A vulnerable one? Look at yourself."

She didn't have to. Flushed face, parted lips, traces of recent tears, bruised hands, sore ass-cheeks, pants around her ankles. She knew what she looked like.

She trembled with desire. She was aware the trembling looked like fear to Sylvester. She knew what the image of her like that did to him.

She brought her legs more tightly together. Made a small sound of anguish.

He dropped the cane.

Pulled her to her feet by her hair.

Sealed her lips to his, once, a bruising dry kiss. "Bitch," he said. "Get those pants off."

She pushed at him, started to pull her pants up. "Don't. Please. You can't do this."

He slapped her hand away. Yanked her pants back down.

She hit him, a weak punch that he probably didn't even feel. Stumbled away, pulling her pants up.

He caught her, collared her neck with his hand, walked her backward until she felt the cold edge of the teacher's desk. He whirled her around, bent her over it. "How about I fuck you this way. Like this." He ground his hardness against her crack.

"No!" She struggled, splinters stabbing her fingertips. The little pains were only hot goads to her, with Sylvester's enormous cock so near, almost there. He still wore his clothes. Damn it, why was he still dressed? She was about to come just from his pinning her. The thought of him penetrating her with his cock while scornful and violent made her pant with an animal lust she'd never felt before. "Let me go," she pleaded, making sure a thrust of her hips brushed against his rigidity. She didn't have to fake the desperate sound in her voice.

He cursed. The sound of his zipper was loud in the empty schoolroom. She closed her eyes in silent gratitude, until she remembered to whimper.

It acted on him like an aphrodisiac, and his castigation of her grew more vicious as he dry-humped her, a promise. "No," he snapped when she struggled too hard. He grabbed a handful of hair, yanked her head back, spoke in her ear. "You're not going anywhere until I'm done with you. And I'm going to fuck you so hard you won't be able to walk." When her head fell back, movement caught her attention. A shadow in the window. Someone watching?

Sylvester saw it, too. He froze.

A moment later, the wooden door flew open. A man entered, his apologies panted out. His frantic air made her not recognize him at first.

Tense, Sylvester pushed away from her with, "Time out."

All she could do for a long moment was gape at the intruder. "Mage!" A thin sheen of sweat gave his olive-toned skin a frenetic glow. His hair stood up in wet spikes. His clothes stuck to his body in places. He looked as if he'd run a four-minute mile.

He didn't seem to even see her.

Mage got his breath back. "Kiana, she has collapsed, she will not let anyone call an ambulance. She is asking for you."

Sylvester nodded. He walked as he buttoned. His brusque voice galvanized. "Nora. Get dressed. Mage? Wait for Nora." Sylvester disappeared through the still-open door.

Nora dressed, unselfconscious. "What happened?"

"Kiana. Stubborn, willful woman. I do not know what is wrong with her. No ambulance. She is foolish." His tone of frustration with a woman's stubbornness made laughter well up unexpectedly in Nora.

"We'd better go, then. Help protect her from herself."

Mage nodded, serious. "Yes."

She snorted but followed him, her mind at odds with her body. Her mind mulled over the latest development, filled with curiosity and concern about Kiana, along with a tiny jealous worry that Kiana inspired Sylvester to drop everything to rush to her assistance.

Her body still burned. Her skin prickled with the memory of Sylveter's harsh touch, and butterflies in her belly reminded her of him with every step. He'd raised her to a cataclysmic threshold of physical desire . . . and just left her there.

Mage moved with surprising grace and speed through the forest. He seemed able to avoid the vines catching at her ankles. He never stumbled, even when the moist ground broke and slid under his feet on the downslope.

Possibly his past military experience. He looked back every few minutes, checking on her.

He seemed pleased Nora kept up.

When they stepped from the forest onto the circular driveway, he offered her a bemused smile. "You seemed so small and weak last night. And also up there, with Sylvester. So powerless. But you have speed."

His praise warmed her. The sense of kinship evoked by his words took her by surprise. She had something in common with Mage, other than the kinky play? How strange to feel a bond with a special-ops torturer.

Then they were in the house, joining the circle of people surrounding Mistress Kiana.

11

Sylvester entered the living room to see White cradling Mistress Kiana. As he got closer he could see the black woman actually had her hands full trying to restrain the long-haired Mistress.

He took in everyone else at a glance: Master Andre paced behind the couch. Black and Kitten bracketed the arms of the couch, Kitten kneeling near its foot, Black in a studded white leather catsuit at its head. Ryan sat some distance away.

Even Osmond was there, his bag hanging from a beam near the fireplace.

"Some water might help," Black said when she spotted Sylvester. "And a thermometer." She hissed when one of Kiana's flailing fists connected with the side of her head. "And some damn restraints." She said that last with exasperation and a pointed look at Little Peter.

"No restraints for Mistress." Peter folded his arms.

Black frowned at him.

Sylvester dropped to his knees, took Kiana's hand. It felt

cold, clammy. Her face had a gray tinge that worried him. She turned her head from side to side, mumbling.

Sylvester addressed everyone. "What happened?"

Little Peter answered. Tears stood out in his eyes. "She just collapsed. Mistress was disciplining me. With a flogger. It's my fault."

"It's not your fault," Sylvester said automatically, trying to see Kiana's pupils. She moved around too much; he was afraid he'd poke her in the eyeball. He sighed. "We should call for an ambulance."

"No doctors. No hospital." Kiana glared at them all, trying to sit up. "Can't . . . think." She lapsed into an incomprehensible mumble.

Sylvester looked at Little Peter. "Get her water."

The submissive leapt up, ran to the kitchen.

Sylvester addressed White. "How long has she been like this?"

"Twenty minutes? Something like that." Her voice soothed, and she rocked Kiana like a small child and crooned to her. "You overexerted, didn't you, honey. I warned you, didn't I?" She looked at Sylvester. "Maybe I should drive her down there."

Kiana shook her head, possibly in disagreement.

"It's all my fault," Little Peter moaned. His hand shook as he handed the glass of water to Sylvester. Water sloshed over the edge. "I got turned around. I was scared. Mistress said if I got like that, I should pull over and call her, so I did and she talked to me, helped me find my way back here. I asked her to punish me. I begged her to." The service submissive hugged himself, trembled.

"It's not your fault," Sylvester repeated. He looked at Little Peter. The boy couldn't be any younger than twenty-two, maybe twenty-three, but he came across like a helpless child.

Sylvester lay a hand on him. He spoke as he would to a

frightened kid. "She'll be fine. I promise. Now, sit down and take it easy for now, okay? Help her by staying calm. Okay?"

Little Peter sniffled, then shrugged Sylvester's hand off angrily. "You don't know she'll be okay. You don't know everything."

Kiana tried to sit up. "Don't speak that way to Sylvester. He's not guilty. They found him not guilty."

A prickle of recognition crawled up Sylvester's spine. He thrust the glass of water at Kiana, who gazed at the air between him and Little Peter. Her glazed eyes didn't see either of them. They looked into the past.

"Drink. Help her drink," he told White. *Get something in her mouth to quiet her,* he prayed.

White looked at him oddly, but took the glass. "Hey, honey. Want some nice water?"

"Sylvester admitted raping her. They arrested him."

Sylvester needed Kiana to shut up. Fast. He considered gagging her.

As he ran a hand through his hair, he noticed two more join the gathering: Mage and Nora.

Kiana spoke as if to an unseen person standing next to Little Peter. "Yes, she was banged up pretty badly. I saw the same pictures. She told everyone Sylvester raped her, ruined her, wrecked her life. He never denied it."

Sylvester stood rooted. All the old guilt and rage and helplessness rose up, savaging him.

Silence.

White spoke, her voice carefully soft. "She's passed out again. I think we should call the doctor, find out what to do."

"Yes." Sylvester made himself walk toward the kitchen and the nook that held his landline phone. He forced his neck muscles to raise his head, turn it. He met Nora's gaze.

It was as bad as he'd feared. Her eyes were wide, horrified, for the long, painful moment she looked at him.

She averted her gaze.

As he pulled out the directory, looked up the number, and dialed, he swallowed hard with the effort to concentrate. His world was about to fall apart again, just as it had before. But first, he had to get Kiana the medical help she needed.

After she felt better and wasn't in any imminent danger, he'd consider strangling her.

Mage cleared his throat, drawing her attention.

Though he patted her arm, Nora felt him growing distant. His gaze jumped around the room, never resting for long on any one thing. "Crowds make me uncomfortable," he explained without looking at her. "But I would like to see you again. Tonight?"

Nora nodded, on automatic. Her thoughts were elsewhere. "Tonight is the Chase and Capture."

"Ah, yes." He stared at her. "You are participating?"

"I'd planned on it." Her voice sounded wooden, dead to her own ears. She wasn't planning on it anymore. The flare of heat; the pleasurable, guilty clench: it was all gone. At one time, Sylvester had starred in her fevered fantasies. But now Sylvester was a rapist, a real one.

It killed it for her.

She put her hand over her mouth, feeling loss like vomit rising in her.

Mage edged from her, obviously ill at ease in the crowded room. He looked back at Nora. "Are you not feeling well, either?"

"I'm fine. Thanks."

He was already leaving. She felt abandoned, though she hadn't craved Mage's company.

Maybe the connection she'd felt to these people was all in her mind.

Maybe it was a sign: her rape fantasy should stay locked in her head, where it couldn't make anyone judge her or hurt her.

She watched as Sylvester hung up, rushed to Kiana's side, and spoke urgently to her. Her response made him speak in clipped tones Nora could barely hear from her distant position near the sliding glass door.

Little Peter slapped his own head. The young man ran from the room. When he returned, he carried a syringe.

"She's diabetic."

Nora jumped. Ryan stood so near she could smell his familiar spicy deodorant. "Don't sneak up on me!"

He held his hands up, a warding-off gesture. "Sorry."

"No, I'm sorry." Nora reached out, touched his arm. "I'm a bit jumpy right now." Ryan's words sunk in. "Really? Kiana's diabetic. Huh. So her injection should set her right again. That's good."

"Are you okay?"

The warmth of his body and the caring in his tone weakened her. She swallowed with difficulty and found her voice. "I don't know."

"That must've been hard on you, finding out Sylvester's a real rapist. Or does that make you want him even more?"

Her nerves tensed. She closed her eyes. Opened them. "You don't understand. You never did."

"But I do." He spoke with a quiet, but desperate, firmness. "This was a wild vacation. For both of us. But it's time to leave fantasyland behind and go back to real life."

His repeating the thoughts she'd had in her head moments before shook her. She whispered, "Maybe you're right." She felt a strange numbed comfort at the idea. Go back to her predictable routine. Go back and accept the promotion that would give her such a large paycheck and long hours. Go back to Ryan.

Which reminded her. "My 'real life' comes with a job you don't like. My long hours." She felt tired just thinking about it.

"None of that matters now. Only that we're together, and away from this place."

She looked at him, surprised by his bitterness. "I thought you were kind of enjoying yourself."

"Enjoying being beat on, treated like a dog, locked in cages?" His face suffused with color.

Ah. He liked it but couldn't admit it. "There's nothing to be ashamed of."

"I said I didn't like it!"

White glided up to them both. "Is this creature annoying you?" She said it kindly, with a smile, but her slender black fingers snaked to Ryan's ear, twisted just enough to make him yelp. His eyes widened and his breath came faster. Ryan didn't move away or strike White's hands from him.

White looked at Nora. "You don't have to talk to him, if you don't want. He's technically still a slave for the rest of the day. In fact, you haven't really punished him yourself yet, have you?" White shook his head by his ear, making him grimace. "Would you like to?"

Ryan's face reflected distress deeper than physical discomfort. The flushed skin of his face dampened with new sweat. "Nora, don't."

Black joined White. "The doggie said don't." She reached for Ryan's other ear. She twisted harder than White had. "Bad doggie. Down."

Ryan sank to his knees, staring daggers at Black.

Nora knew she should look away, leave Ryan to the women's untender mercies. But as she looked at her former fiancé on his knees, she had a strange sense that she didn't know who he was. She could barely remember what it felt like to be in a relationship with him.

An erection tented his pants.

Ryan was past tense, she realized. At least for the possibility of marrying him. From his shamed, pleading gaze, she could tell he knew it, too. What did he want from her? Domination? Or for her to rescue him from his submission fetish?

She frowned. She didn't feel much like rescuing him, even if it was possible. They were here because of him, and she'd just suffered a horrible disappointment. Her fantasy, ruined. Her image of Sylvester, tarnished.

Sylvester, who hadn't denied raping a woman and ruining her life.

Nora narrowed her eyes at Ryan. She had a heartache now, damn it, and here was one of the men responsible for it.

The two women waited patiently.

Remembering how Sylvester had grasped a handful of her hair just above the nape of her neck, she reached out, let her fingers explore the familiar silky curls of Ryan's blond hair. It was long enough to grab a handful, she discovered with some satisfaction.

She pulled, and the women stepped back. Ryan was in her hands now. Literally.

She craned his neck back the way Sylvester had done to her. Ryan's expression went from shame to dreamy and pained, the same feelings she remembered having with Sylvester. So Ryan still wanted her, did he? Wanted this, at least. Not that she cared what he wanted, at the moment. "I haven't forgiven you yet, slave."

Ryan became a submissive right before her eyes. "Please, Mistress Nora. Tell me what to do." And yet, when his gaze met hers, she still saw anguish.

That made two of them. This dominating of him felt wrong, somehow. As if she were a child playing grown-up. She felt awkward. She felt deprived of her true desires. She felt *angry*.

Holding his hair, she shook his head. Seeing the glint of tears in his eyes made her want to let go, get away from him, from all of them.

Instead, she smiled a Sylvester smile of contempt and said, "Lick my shoes clean." She flung his head from her as if it were a soiled thing.

The speed with which he bent to the task made Black and White nod approvingly.

Nora could only look down at the top of Ryan's head as it bobbed over her shoes. He tongued clean her dirty, well-used running shoes. Ryan was her slave. She could flog him, dominate him, do anything she wanted to him. As a submissive, he'd do it; not just at Twisted Wood, but at home as well. It was in his nature to enjoy such treatment; his reaction made that clear.

Ryan gagged on the dirt, coughing. "I'm sorry, Mistress." He began licking again.

A muted thrill ran through her. The power intoxicated. But the feeling was overshadowed by a looming sadness. Their relationship was truly over.

More important, she realized she didn't crave a submissive partner.

She frowned. She didn't want a dominant partner either, not exactly. It wasn't that simple. While the floggings and paddlings, bondage and electrical play had given her pleasure, not to mention memories for a lifetime, they weren't her fantasy.

Reflexively, her gaze sought Sylvester.

He stood some distance from the couch, staring at her. Her breath caught at the raw attractiveness of him, and her heart flipped over in her chest even as the new knowledge twisted and turned inside her.

Nora yanked her gaze away, looked at the couch instead. Mistress Kiana sat up, tired but aware, attended by Little Peter. Master Andre sat next to the revived woman, holding her arm, his fingers positioned at her wrist to check her pulse.

Osmond hung in his bag, silent and paradoxical.

Futility crept over her. Her vacation was over.

"Stop," she told Ryan.

"Mistress?" He looked up, saliva making his chin shine. "Am I not doing a good enough job?" His eyes brightened. "Do you need to punish me?"

Nora couldn't suppress her shudder. "No, Ryan. Just get up. I'm done playing."

Ryan didn't move. Confusion crossed his face. "But . . . you're good at it. We can keep going . . . ?"

She couldn't miss the erection in his pants. He was really into it, she realized. But she shook her head. "Sorry, a slave isn't what I need." It was horrifying to her, suddenly, seeing him at her feet. "Please just get up."

The color drained from his face. Then flooded it again, a blush of embarrassment as he climbed awkwardly to his feet. He wiped at his chin so hard he left scratch marks. He stared daggers at her.

"What?" she asked him, mystified by his anger.

"Nothing."

White stepped forward, buckled a collar around Ryan's neck. "It's okay, honey, he's just disappointed." She attached a leash, tugged at it playfully. Ryan resisted, a look of such fury on his face that Nora flinched from him. "Oh, he's really craving punishment. I think we have time for some of that before tonight's big event, don't we, Black? The boy clearly deserves it."

"Make the doggie howl?" Black smiled sadistically. "Always fun."

"There won't be a Chase and Capture event tonight." Sylvester's resonant voice carried his words to the far corners of the large room.

"Says who?" White demanded.

"Says me." Sylvester's tone was final.

White handed Ryan's leash to Black, then stalked toward Sylvester. "You've been looking forward to this one all weekend. The weather is perfect, Kiana is feeling better . . . so that's no excuse. Kitten said even Mage would participate."

"I doubt that's the reason Mage wants to participate," Sylvester said with a wry glance at Nora, before looking away from her once more. "Not that it matters now."

"I was looking forward to it, too," Master Andre cut in unexpectedly as he walked toward them. "Doubtless for the same reason." He winked at Nora. "Why the sudden cancellation?"

White was shaking her head. As all of the people gathered around Sylvester, stern faced, he looked with surprise first at White, then everyone else creating the circle. One person made him frown. "Kiana, you should be lying down. Or at least sitting still."

"The shot fixed me up. Thank you." Her face remained pale, but now it had new strength and determination. "I think I may have said too much. About that rape accusation against you in Los Angeles. I apologize." She took a deep breath, brushed strands of her long hair from a face still damp with the perspiration of recent illness. "In case any of you didn't know, those charges were dropped. She lied," Kiana explained to the group.

"No. She didn't lie." Sylvester looked above her head. His voice sounded flat, emotionless. "I'm a guilty bastard, all right."

White made a rude sound. "Nobody believes that. We've seen how strict you are with checklists and safe words. How protective you are of everyone in your home."

Sylvester gave a slight shrug. "It doesn't matter."

White glared at him.

Nora saw the way Sylvester's lips thinned and tightened. Pained. This subject hurt him. Good, it should hurt him if he'd done such a horrible thing.

And yet . . .

She had to know the truth. She spoke up. "Sylvester, did you actually rape someone?"

He looked at her. "Yes. The blame rests with me, totally and completely. I couldn't regret it more . . . but yes, I did it."

White threw her arms up in a gesture of frustration. "Your guilty conscience strikes, and so you cancel the event you know you need, and that these guys have been talking about all weekend. Thanks a lot."

Sylvester snarled, "My house. My rules." His eyes blazed dark fire. He visibly gathered his self-control. In a tight voice, he explained, "I thought I was ready for it, but I'm not. Too bad."

"Too bad? No, Sylvester." White's voice rose in anger. "I knew all about your reputation. I heard about Sylvester, the sadistic lover, the heavy top, the accused rapist, way before I met you. And the silly twit who went into it with her eyes wide open, then cried 'rape'? Common knowledge. Everyone knows. You need to get over it. We all have."

"Not everyone knows."

Everyone looked at Nora.

12

She tilted her chin up, staring at Sylvester until a cool mask replaced his angry expression. Something about his control soothed her, gave her hope. Or maybe she just didn't want to believe the worst. Even now, he radiated a vitality that drew her like a magnet. She tried to fight her physical response to him, to concentrate. "I'm new to the kink scene. All I know about any of you is what you've shown me. And I've never seen a more welcoming, caring group of people," she said, looking at White, then Master Andre, then Little Peter, then Sylvester. "So, this rape accusation. Everyone seems to know all about it, except me."

Sylvester's nostrils flared for a moment. He said nothing.

White explained. "He didn't know we all knew. He's stunned." Her lips twitched, and she almost smiled. "That's his stunned look, don't you know. Our Sylvester, he projects. He's got emotional range like a Hollywood star."

Nora stepped closer to Sylvester. There had to be a plausible explanation. She chose her words carefully. "You seem to feel very guilty about what you did. I'd be grateful if you'd explain what happened."

He stared at her. Something was flickering far back in his eyes. He spoke, his voice neutral. "A scene went wrong. I misread it. I hurt her ... raped her. She was ... deeply affected by it. Damaged psychologically. I did it. I became a pariah in the kink scene there, and in my neighborhood, deservedly so. I ended up leaving, moving up here for a fresh start. Or so I thought." He shuddered as he drew in a sharp breath. "The Chase and Capture is a bad idea. I can't let something like that happen again. That's it."

"Bullshit!" White vibrated with ire. "If I'd known that's what you thought of it, I'd have slapped some sense into you a long time ago."

Sylvester turned a look on White that should have incinerated her where she stood, but even as he began to speak, Nora heard a loud thumping coming from the living room.

As a unit, the group turned toward the noise.

Osmond's bag swung and jerked, spasmodic. When it neared the light-olive matte-painted wall, the impact of a bare heel thudded again. And the smaller thumps of hands, elbows, knees.

"He's going to hurt himself," Kiana fretted.

"He's ready to come out. It's time," White said, anger fading from her face, replaced by eagerness.

"It's early," Black corrected. But the blond woman shrugged, her fingers playing with Ryan's leash. "Osmond will be a preemie, I guess."

Master Andre and Little Peter had already fetched the ladder kept near Osmond, climbed it. They brought his bag slowly down, absorbing the occasional kick coming from inside with stoic expressions.

Mistress Kiana dashed to the stereo, put on Native American

flute music. The heavy drumbeat and male chanting gave the proceedings a portentous feel. White dimmed the lights to a soft, comforting glow.

Nora looked around, but everyone had dispersed to perform a previously assigned task. Even Ryan, with a mutinous expression, brought in more firewood under Black's strict supervision to stoke the blaze in the living room's fireplace. It already felt too warm for comfort, Nora thought.

And she'd lost the chance to question Sylvester, to get to the bottom of the crime he'd committed. If it had been a crime. If it had been nonconsensual.

Nora felt cramped, cranky, and suddenly more tired than she should be in the middle of the afternoon. This was pointless. She didn't belong here. She looked for Sylvester. Found him stacking heating pads and spreading blankets not far from the fireplace. He wore the same pants he'd unzipped behind her at the schoolhouse.

When he crouched, then stood, his body moved with the same masculine grace she remembered. His rough-hewn face, arrogantly surveying his domain, was just as handsome to her.

Again she was assaulted by her sick yearning for him.

Kitten joined her, carrying a bottle of milk. She pressed it to her wrist. "Not too hot," she murmured, her eyes not leaving the activity.

"I should go," Nora murmured back, not wanting to disturb the birthing scene. "I don't belong here."

Kitten glanced at her in surprise. "Of course you do." As Nora stared down into the large, innocent-looking blue eyes of the younger woman, she realized anew how young Kitten had to be. Twenty-two, twenty-three tops. How odd that being a submissive to Mage, the scariest and most scarred person in Sylvester's house, hadn't tarnished her innocence.

Kitten continued in a more practical tone. "Anyway, it'll be good for Osmond to see an unfamiliar face or two here to welcome him. He really needs it, a fresh beginning where he can feel safe and loved, you know?" She tapped one pink painted nail on the hard plastic of the bottle, lowered her voice farther, until Nora had to strain to catch her words over the music. "His father killed himself when Osmond was fifteen. His mom had mental issues, and she abandoned Osmond later that same year. He grew up never feeling wanted, or anything better than unworthy and anxious and depressed. The only time he feels loved is when he wears diapers and people treat him like a baby." She shrugged. "So this is a way to give him a new birth to maybe wipe the slate clean, maybe give him a sense of acceptance that stays with Osmond longer than just when he's indulging his fetish. You know? It's Sylvester's idea." She looked at Nora sideways. "He's a good man."

"Osmond is?" Nora stared straight ahead, tender feelings threatening to overwhelm her.

"Sylvester." Kitten looked straight ahead, too. "It looks like Osmond's a breech baby."

Sure enough, a naked foot squeezed through the pink bag's opening to rest on the blankets Sylvester spread. Another foot kicked the opening wider, and two bare, glistening, hairy knees appeared. Sylvester grabbed them, not ungently. He pulled. Osmond slid out.

Immediately, Kitten jumped. "Oh, that was fast. Come on!" she said excitedly, pulling Nora forward.

Master Andre wrapped the man in blankets, and Mistress Kiana hugged them both as Sylvester tucked heating pads in all the gaps. Little Peter touched one of Osmond's feet and said, "Welcome. Happy birthday. You are loved," before making way for the next.

Kitten hurried forward. She touched him on the brow. "Welcome, Osmond. You're so loved." She worked the snorkel free from his mouth, replaced it with the nipple of the bottle. Osmond suckled on it, his eyes still closed. "Happy birthday, sweetie."

Kitten eyed her, looked pointedly at Osmond, then back to her.

Nora approached, reluctant. She felt awkward, at first. But with each step forward the ritual seemed to pull more strongly at her. She didn't even know him, yet he needed her, depended on her along with the rest of them. She couldn't let him down.

She looked at the naked man swathed in blankets. His moisture-darkened hair stuck to a face so thin its bone structure showed clearly. He had a cleft in his chin and tear streaks on his cheeks. She couldn't remember ever seeing a more vulnerable-looking adult.

Her hand reached out as if it was under someone else's control, touched the chin's cleft. "Welcome. Happy birthday." Osmond sighed, snuggled into his blankets. Her voice shook with emotion. "Welcome, Osmond. You are loved." Strangely, as she said the words, they became true. No matter what had happened to this man earlier in his life to deprive him of peace and acceptance, he was here now, surrounded by caring people, and she was able to love him.

She let others nudge her away from him, and heard familiar voices welcoming Osmond. Kitten laughed, once, a carefree, happy sound.

Nora remembered Kitten had said Sylvester was a good man.

Giving in to the urge to feast her eyes on Sylvester again, she finally looked for him, her heartbeat instantly increasing tempo in anticipation.

She saw him not far from the cluster of people, straightening after giving Little Peter soft instructions. The service sub scampered past her toward the kitchen, but she couldn't pry her gaze from Sylvester.

Sylvester looked at her as if trying to memorize every detail.

Her heart jolted in response, and her pulse began to pound. How could she still feel this way? How was it possible to want him so much after what he'd admitted? He was so disturbing to her in every way.

Little Peter placed a glass in her hand, and immediately filled it with Dom Pérignon. His impish smile was infectious. "To Osmond!"

"To Osmond." She sipped, then simply held the glass and looked at the birthday boy. Kiana wrestled with one of his legs, trying to thread a large diaper through his crotch. Laughter and the clink of glasses filled the air. Even the music had turned lighter, happier, the chanting giving way to a soaring, exultant choral. Black and White sandwiched Osmond, holding him and rocking him slowly back and forth.

It was a scene of such warmth and tenderness it made Nora blink back tears.

It was Sylvester's idea. The entire healing scene, Sylvester's doing.

She looked at Sylvester, and the heat of his gaze made her draw in a sharp breath. It seemed he hadn't stopped staring at her. His eyes met hers without flinching. The cord of tension stretched tight between them. A delicious shudder stirred her body. He was a good man, damn it. Why shouldn't she have him?

She sipped again, for fortification, then walked across the carpet runner to stand before Sylvester. She tilted her chin up and met his gaze squarely. "Maybe you shouldn't cancel the Chase and Capture just yet."

As she'd expected, he showed no reaction. But a small tic under his left eye jumped. Also, if she wasn't mistaken, he'd stopped breathing. "Sylvester, ever since you mentioned the event, I haven't been able to get it out of my mind." She laughed, a little nervously. "It's the only role-playing game I want. But it's not just a game. Not really." She looked deeply into his eyes, was satisfied with what she saw there. "You want the same thing."

She could sense him struggling against his own lust. He couldn't hide it from her. Her desire for him briefly made way for a passing admiration for his control. Then the lust rose up, swamped her once more, setting off tremors in her body.

"I won't damage anyone else due to my dangerous proclivities." His voice was soft, reasonable.

"Safe, sane, consensual. We've got all three." She shrugged and tossed her hair over one shoulder in a gesture of defiance. "Catch me if you can?"

The ghost of a smile played about his lips. His gaze speared her. "You are incorrigible. Brat."

"Punish me for it. If you can catch me. I gather the event's outside? Is it like a game of hide and seek? Or tag?" She touched his arm, playful. Its hard stillness gave her more shivers. "You never explained the rules," she said, and hoped he didn't notice the catch in her voice. His proximity kindled feelings of fire. She peeked up at him through her lashes.

"I haven't said we'll be playing." Male amusement, mixed with confusion. "I can't believe I'm even discussing it." He looked at her. "Why aren't you afraid of me? You know what I am."

Nora thought about it. She stared up at him. Try as she might, she couldn't see a criminal. He'd shown her too much thoughtfulness, too much caring for the feelings of his guests. Too much guilt. "She signed up for it, didn't she? On a checklist." She waited for his nod. "I'm guessing she didn't use her safe word either."

Sylvester shook his head. He looked uncomfortable, his lips tight with sudden tension. "No. But it doesn't matter." He drew one hand through his dark hair, making it even more unruly. "People made me into the devil. There was this one time, not long after the accusation went public. Afterward. In a parking lot, right? This woman. Sloppy housewife type, her lips loose and her hair this bleached-straw gray-blond. She tore the plastic lid off her fountain drink and came at me. She tossed the whole drink at my crotch and started screaming about marking me so women would know I'm a cum-stained rapist, a piece of shit, a kiddie raper—I don't know why she called me a kiddie raper, maybe so someone would hear it and beat the crap out of me?—and she didn't stop screaming the whole time I got in my truck and drove out of there." His dark eyes had become dark and unreadable as stone.

"And then the woman—your victim—dropped the charges."

"And then she dropped the charges."

She swallowed, holding raw emotion in check. How he must have suffered. And he was still chewing himself to bits with guilt. Nora leaned toward him, exhaling with agitation. "Sylvester. You said it yourself: it was a scene that went wrong. Horribly wrong. But it wasn't all your fault. It wasn't even mostly your fault. You've paid. Let it go."

"Don't tell me what to do, Nora." His voice was chill and exact.

It heartened her. Anything but the raw, desperate tone he'd had when he spoke of the housewife in the parking lot. "I'll do what I want. That includes you."

He blinked, then made a small sound that might have been a suppressed laugh. "Do you think so."

"Depends. Will you still have the Chase and Capture event?"

He stared at her for so long apprehension flicked through her. When he spoke his silky voice held a challenge. "You do realize I wouldn't be the only man chasing. Another might capture you."

Nora managed not to cheer. He was going to do it! "I'm a runner. I doubt anyone here can catch me." Her words were a deliberate goad. She smiled at him, feeling bright with confidence and eager as hell for him. "The real question is, would you know what to do with me if you did?"

His lips quirked briefly into a knowing smile, but his words were serious. "Be sure of this. I won't hold back, I won't be gentle. It will be real. Your safe word limit is sacred, but every bit of you outside that limit is fair game. I don't want to hurt you. But I might not be able to . . ." His resonant voice trailed off, as if the motivating power behind it waned, a brownout. He seemed overcome by just the thought.

Nora stared in fascination, but his face gave so little away. A moment later, he turned a stern, dispassionate gaze on her. "I might hurt you."

She spoke from instinct. "You need this, too. You need to accept your desires just as much as I do. It's consensual. It was then, and it is now. Sylvester, forgive yourself."

She could hear the shuddery intake of his breath. Then, he nodded once. Fire flashed into his eyes. And something more, but she couldn't believe the intensity of the emotion she'd glimpsed had much to do with her. It had everything to do with him. She could only smile back, throbbing with desire and weak with gratitude and awe, helpless before his power.

He nodded once more, then turned. "Everyone! May I have your attention. In honor of new beginnings, I'd like to announce the Chase and Capture event is back on for tonight!"

"No!" Ryan's angry voice bruised the happy atmosphere. The crash of his glass shattering on the wood floor hurt it further. "It's too much. I've suffered enough. Nora, get your things. We're leaving."

13

With his tense, petulant expression and his khakis-and-polo clothes, and the distance he kept from the others, Ryan looked like the only one in the large room who didn't belong. The collar around his neck seemed a jarring affectation.

Nora stared at the man she'd once agreed to marry and felt little for him. But she approached him. "Ryan. Please lower your voice."

"For these freaks? No!" He stared at her. "Don't tell me you're actually considering letting these guys chase and fuck you!"

Her whispered response was scathing. "It was your idea. Or don't you remember?"

"It was a mistake! I messed up, Nora, and I've been trying to make it right. For us." He glared at her. "Doesn't that mean anything to you?"

She sensed the disturbed serenity in the room, the heavy silence. Poor Osmond. Nora felt a surge of anger. "I'll think about it. For now, I need you to be quiet."

"And I need my fiancée to stop acting like a slut! What about what I need! What—mmnph." Black slid the gag into Ryan's mouth in one smooth motion. White jerked his leash warningly. Ryan got the message, lowered his eyes submissively.

Only Nora saw his look of muted rage.

She shuddered as she turned her back on him, feeling resignation and relief. She'd nearly spent the rest of her life married to him. They'd have been miserable together.

Five hours later, Sylvester presided over the group of event participants. There were the "predators" in the game—himself, Mage, and Master Andre—sitting on the longest couch some distance from the low-burning fire. The warm indoor air felt comforting, if a bit close. With Osmond napping in his nursery, and Mistress Kiana speaking in low, easy tones with Black over Ryan's prone form at their feet, the early-evening vibe should have felt relaxed, even lazy.

It didn't.

In honor of the event, Kitten reclined nearby in her flirty little miniskirt, which showed off firm legs and just a hint of ass. White perched on the edge of her upholstered chair, her long, strong body draped, for a change, in a simple summer dress. Her ebony skin gleamed almost as brightly as her eyes. She watched Sylvester and Nora, doing everything but eating popcorn.

Sylvester felt his gaze drawn irresistibly to the woman who'd agreed to play the part of "prey."

His victim of choice wasn't wearing something traditionally feminine and frilly. No dresses or skirts for her. Nora wore a track suit. And serious-looking running shoes. A small band pulled her glorious dark hair into a long ponytail. The bells bunched around the band.

She sat with unnatural stillness. He could see her chest rise and fall—her lovely breasts were compressed by a sports bra— as she inhaled and exhaled with deliberation. She would be difficult to catch, he knew. She seemed confident. Was she as calm as she looked?

Her gaze flickered briefly up to his. He felt his own breath catch, seeing the nervous excitement in her eyes.

She looked away. Just as well.

He cleared his throat.

"I've already explained the basics: prey wears bells, prey gets a ten-minute head start . . . If prey is captured, the noncapturing predators return to the house . . . no facial wounding or broken bones allowed." Sylvester glanced at his rivals. They looked nearly as hungry for Nora as he felt. "After one hour, Mistress Kiana will ring the brass bell to indicate the event is over." He looked back at Nora. "The safe word is 'red.' Aftercare is the predator's responsibility, and should be especially long and thoughtful. Any questions?"

Nora shook her head. Mage and Master Andre shook theirs, too.

"Then, Mistress Kiana will do the honors." He seated himself in a recliner, folding his hands in a pose of tranquility.

Mage would be the real competition. Master Andre's only regular workout was his whip wielding, but Mage kept himself fit. The man also probably knew a dozen ways to kill a rival, likely with inventive, unconventional methods.

It was worth the risk to capture Nora.

Mistress Kiana seemed fully recovered as she let her legs slide from the human footrest and straightened gracefully to her feet. Little Peter moved to help her, but she edged away, stepping carefully around Ryan.

Ryan, no longer gagged, now wore only a single brown sack-like garment Sylvester finally recognized as a hair shirt from the dungeon. It had been hard to spot due to the brown color blending with the floor Ryan knelt down on, arms straight, knees bent. A footrest.

Sylvester smiled, approving Mistress Kiana's taste.

"Ready. Set. Go!" She held up a large brass bell by the handle. The next moment, she brought it down, making it clang with a surprising loudness.

Instead of choosing the deck with its stairs, or the front door, Nora bolted in a different direction. Everyone listened to her bells jingle as she disappeared down the stairs to the dungeon.

"There are outer doors down there, too," Mage said, echoing Sylvester's thoughts. The man looked thoughtful, and not a little sadistic. Probably imagining all the things he'd do to Nora. Sylvester decided he'd never liked Mage much, and would probably evict him.

Master Andre shot a rueful smile at them both. "Hopefully she's decided to hide in one of the closets downstairs. Then maybe I'll have a fighting chance."

Sylvester stood, paced. Had it been ten minutes yet? He looked at Mistress Kiana, who eyed her watch. "Eight more minutes."

He lunged into a stretch, ignoring Kitten and White's snickers. He was going to be the one to capture Nora. The woman spoke to his soul, not only his fetish. She'd made him feel whole again. At peace with himself. For the first time in years, he felt no burdensome chains of guilt.

He was going to be the man to fulfill her deepest fantasy.

He looked his impatience at Mistress Kiana. She'd evidently dismissed her footstool, as Ryan was nowhere to be seen, but Little Peter flanked her with doglike devotion, clearly urging her to sit. She protested. "I've lounged all day, I need to stand! But"—she lifted one slender hand, caressed the service submissive's jaw—"you're doing a very good job. Your attentiveness is commendable." Little Peter glowed at the praise.

She looked at her watch. "Ready? And . . . go!"

Amid cheers and encouragement, the three men went.

14

Nora looked at the man who closed the sliding glass door behind himself with such gentleness. "Hello, Master Andre."

"Nora. I hoped I'd find you here." His smile broadened in approval. "I didn't bring my pipe tobacco. But, we have more interesting things to do this evening."

She spoke quickly, before he could get more of the wrong idea. "This isn't what you think. I just wanted to talk with you privately for a moment."

He looked at her, considering. "Talk." He stepped closer, inhaling deeply. "It's a lovely night, isn't it. The stars are out. And no one will be concerned when you scream."

He was speaking her language. Despite herself, she felt a twinge of desire. She shook her head with a regretful smile. Her bells tinkled with the movement. "I'd probably enjoy every minute of it. But I've been thinking a lot about your offer to wear your collar and travel the world. It was an incredibly generous offer. But I can't do it. Being a submissive, even a pampered, world-traveling submissive, isn't my kink. Having multiple partners isn't my kink. Those aren't the fantasies in my head. Well, the world traveling, maybe."

"Ah. I know where this is going." His mouth quirked into a small smile. "Sylvester."

A bright flare of desire shook her. She got off on just hearing his name. God, she had it bad. "I didn't know what I wanted until I tried things on for size, physically and mentally. And I keep coming back to the one thing."

"One thing Sylvester is admirably, naturally equipped to provide," Master Andre concluded. He grinned at her, and she was struck again by his impish good looks. "I'm glad," he confessed. "Sorry, but also glad. Sylvester has been needing someone exactly like you for way too long. Now, may I offer you some advice?"

"Um, okay." That had gone easier than she'd expected. Or was Master Andre about to tackle her? It would be a while before she felt completely at ease with the kinky rules of the road. "I'm all ears."

Master Andre's expression became serious. "Don't try this 'just talking' with Mage. You won't stop him with anything short of a safe word. And you might not have time to say it."

She smiled back, appreciating him. "You are amazing and kind and sexy, and if I wasn't crazy about Sylvester we'd be having some pretty serious sex right now." She patted a backpack sitting on the wooden seating bench encircling the private deck. "I have a plan."

"I hope you do." His expression went wry. "Now, get going, little temptress. Your man's out there."

Nora kissed him on the cheek, slipped on her backpack, and ran.

15

As she bolted out the door into the star-filled summer evening, she heard the shouts of those who'd spotted her from their balcony-edge viewpoints. She ran across the circular drive and down the gravel road, darkening twilight enfolding her.

Nora laughed. She felt an awakened sense of life, a rush of confidence and strength. The threat to her was real, in a way that alternately thrilled and frightened her. But compared to the pale hopes and muted monotony of her life before coming to Twisted Wood, it felt exhilarating.

Of the two remaining men, she thought Mage might be the fastest. She remembered the whipcord leanness of his body. And his scars, from his military background.

She suspected the man rarely failed to achieve his goals, and fucking her was one.

A rush of wind and shadowy movement at the corner of her eye was the only warning she had. Dodging before she even knew who she avoided, she felt the graze of fingertips against her hand as she fled. A curse in another language told her it was Mage.

She ran, her small bells jingling.

Nimble. Fast. Can't catch her, not until she wanted to be caught. Desire swirled inside her. It made her consider slowing a little, just enough to let Mage capture her, have her.

She laughed aloud again, pulling farther ahead with an effortless burst of speed. Behind her, she could hear feet slapping the gravel, then a quieter thud against the dirt on the path leading up toward the schoolhouse. Her calf muscles tightened, then began to loosen with a pleasant heat as the path grew steep. She concentrated on her rhythm and pacing so she didn't exhaust herself. It was no marathon, this distance to the meadow near the schoolhouse, but neither was it a sprint, and the uneven incline made for hard going.

After a few minutes, she chanced a glance over her shoulder. She'd pulled ahead by quite a bit. She picked up her pace. She needed even more of a lead for her plan to work.

Her backpack grew heavy, but she didn't consider ditching it.

Her breasts bounced slightly within the confining sports bra, her erect nipples rubbing against the material. Would her bra be ripped from her, or just pushed up? Would her rapist of choice pull her pants roughly down, or would he force her to undress for him? Would she be bound, or simply overpowered by brute strength?

She stumbled. Correcting for it, she regained her rhythm. *No more daydreaming*, she chastised herself. Soon enough, if all went as planned, she'd have the real thing.

The remembered clearing opened before her, its rich soil black under the pale light of the moon. Its surrounding ferns and blackberry bushes and cedar trunks were hard-edged against the deeper dark of the forest. A half-rotted fallen trunk bracketed the far end of the clearing.

When she saw the enormous hand-shaped maple, Nora smiled. And got to work.

Less than two minutes later, she crouched over the path on a fat, moss-covered branch of the maple tree. With one hand she gripped the weighted retiarius net she'd taken from the dungeon. With the other, she clung to the trunk, holding herself still.

Just in time: Mage pounded up the path. But just before the entrance to the clearing, he paused. Nora cursed his fine-tuned instincts.

Fortunately, before he thought to look up, she heard a faint vibration and the brief tinkling of bells some distance away.

Mage had heard it. She watched the cunning smile appear on his face. He moved again, with the silent stalk of a predator, toward the bells.

When he passed under her branch, she threw the net.

It worked better than she'd dared to hope. Taken totally by surprise, Mage flung his hands out, only entangling himself more. The weights swung the net around his legs, making him kick at in reflex, tangling his feet as well. He lunged sideways, falling hard and rolling until the blackberry bushes stopped him. His curses continued nonstop as he fought first to free himself from the bushes, then from the net that had snagged in the bushes.

Long before he succeeded, Nora had climbed back down and fetched the vibrator with her bells wrapped around its tip.

She checked on Mage. Nearly finished freeing himself, but breathing hard. She grinned as she wrapped the bells back in her hair. She felt well rested. Ready to run a marathon, if needed. Mage would never be able to catch her now. The vibrator buzzed in her hand. She tossed it to the ground next to Mage. He looked at it, panting. Then he chuckled.

"Bye, Mage!"

He didn't respond, but then, she hadn't expected him to.

She ran, then, toward the one place she hoped Sylvester would know to look for her: the schoolhouse.

16

He wasn't there.

Nora could tell from the moment she opened the door and nothing but the scent of dusty air rushed out that Sylvester hadn't been there.

She hesitated, torn between wanting to go inside and simply wait, and moving on before Mage freed himself and came after her. The unwelcoming dark interior decided for her. She closed the schoolhouse door, wondering what to do next.

Suddenly a hand covered her mouth. A low voice spoke into her ear. "Don't move. And don't scream."

Panic swept through her. Reflexively, she twisted and shoved, and then she was free, off and running again. This time there was no sensation of strength and confidence to buoy her. She ran spooked. What if that wasn't Sylvester or Mage? What if there was a real predator after her?

She ran blindly, not pacing herself at all, her instinct guiding her direction.

She realized she'd found another clearing only when the moonlight dazzled her with its comparative brightness. Sparse grass and clover covered an otherwise bare ground. She heard labored breathing, and realized with surprise it was herself. Her side ached, too, a stitch in it like she got when she pushed too hard and too fast. Which she supposed she had. How silly, to run like a B-movie heroine fleeing a monster.

It was only Sylvester.

A voice spoke from the shadows. "Hello, Nora."

She choked back a cry, fear rising again.

Sylvester stepped into the clearing.

Her nerves tensed immediately. He wore gray pants and a lighter shirt, but his eyes were dark as she'd ever seen them. His mouth curved in a cruel smile. A thrill of frightened anticipation touched her spine.

She backed away as he approached.

He shook his head. Spoke softly. "There's a fence behind you. The property line. Nowhere to run." He continued to approach, arms by his sides but his palms facing her as if ready to prevent her escape.

She tried it anyway, lunging to his right to slip into the forest, lose him in the dark.

She almost made it. Just as the moonlight was cut off by tree canopies, Sylvester grabbed her, held her arms above her head. He breathed heavily and so did she, as both anxiety and lust flared in her, turning everything complex. She wanted to cry, she wanted to plead for her freedom. She wanted to laugh her triumph, she wanted to wrap her legs around his hips.

She wriggled and fought to free herself from his grip. "Please! Stop!"

His grip tightened. He walked her back until she felt a tree's rough bark abrading her through her jogging shirt. He pressed against her firmly enough to feel every inch of his hard body.

One of her wrists twisted free of his grip. She pounded his chest, hard, before he recaptured it, brought it back up, where he enclosed both wrists in one cruel grip. His other hand roamed her body arrogantly, roughly. The tree bruised her and Sylvester did, too, but she couldn't move. It made her feel afraid. "Please . . . don't."

He yanked her shirt up. She whimpered as he brutally pinched a nipple, the fiery agony turning instantly to pleasure and taking the little pains of her bruises and abrasions with it. Her knees weakened with desire, and the old shame over how she could be brought to such a state with such treatment. She blinked away tears as he twisted the other nipple, and she couldn't be sure if they were tears of joy or pain.

Sylvester thrust himself against her, making animal noises of lust that reverberated through her body.

Then suddenly she heard a bass thump, and Sylvester crumpled to his knees.

Nora stared with horror at the man who threw a heavy serving bowl down, then grabbed her arm and pulled her toward him. "Ryan!"

"Yes. Remember me?" He slapped at her breasts. "Nice. Real nice. Couldn't wait to get yourself banged by him, could you? Well, guess what. I'm the only one who gets to fuck my fiancée."

"I'm not your fiancée anymore." She pulled her shirt down. Her hands were shaking.

"Yes, you are. I did everything they asked. And you know what? I'm no one's submissive, or doggie, or footstool! I'm your goddamned fiancé." He flung her down some distance from Sylvester, unzipped his pants.

"I don't want you. Red. I said red!" Ryan wasn't stopping. He was going to turn his inability to accept his submissive nature into something truly ugly unless she convinced him otherwise. She supposed she could fight or run as a last resort. And she didn't feel like running.

He sneered at her. "I can rape you as well as anyone else. And you'll get your fantasy fulfilled. Lucky you."

"Unlucky you." Sylvester's voice made them both start. Nora hissed with sympathetic pain as his fist met Ryan's face when the man turned to look.

Nora scrambled back from the fray, but it was over. Ryan lay moaning, clutching his jaw.

Another shadow detached itself from the forest, glided forward. "I will take care of this one." Mage pulled Ryan up by the hair, making him yelp. Mage grinned at Sylvester and Nora. "Enjoy. Good-bye."

Nora waved to him from where she sat on the ground.

Sylvester turned a still-fierce expression on her, but she met his gaze without flinching. He was okay. Not hurt. Relief and adrenaline warred in her. She looked at his thick hair and her fingers itched to play with it, and then to explore the rest of him.

She made her hands lay against the ground. Obedient hands. "How's your head?"

He stared at her. "I just punched your fiancé."

"Ex-fiancé." Her hands felt the grit of dirt and the silkiness of the clover. It was steadying, calming, to have the earth under her fingertips. Just not her first choice. "Thanks."

"*Why aren't you afraid of me?*" His voice was a harsh demand.

"I am." As she said it she realized it was true. Her insides still spiraled with the dangerous excitement of his proximity. He was a strong, potentially brutal man, with a body that punished and hands that did exactly what they pleased. "I just want you more than I'm afraid of you."

She saw him swallow. Then his face went expressionless as he nodded. "You don't know shit," he told her in a harsh, raw voice. "I'm going to do you a favor. I'm going to give you ten seconds to get the hell out of here. One."

A thrill of fear flashed through her body, followed by scorching heat. He wanted her to run.

"... five, six, seven ..."
She jumped unsteadily to her feet, stumbled away from him.
"Ten!"
She ran.
He tackled her, sending her sprawling. "Too late."

17

It felt terrifyingly real, not role play. Fear surged through her body. On her belly, she tried to crawl away from him, but he hauled her back by her ankle. "Uh-uh," he chastised, looping his hands around her stomach and pulling her tight against his erection. "Feel that? That's for you."

She felt it. It was impossible to miss. It felt as large and hard as a tree root.

"I'm going to pound it into you, slut." As he ground it against her, hurting her, tears blinded her eyes. Yet the degree to which she responded stunned her. She struggled, whimpering, as he yanked at the elastic edge of her pants, shoving them and her panties down around her knees.

Even as she tried to escape him, her body ached all over for his touch. The feeling was much more than sexual desire. It was a culmination of years of forbidden heat, capped by the long weekend of arousal. She'd never felt more ready.

She heard the zipper, and felt the new warmth of his bared flesh against hers. It galvanized her into renewed struggles, but he slapped her hard on the ass. "Be still, and maybe I won't hurt you too bad."

The next moment, Sylvester grabbed her ass cheeks, spread them apart. His cock prodded deeply between her thighs, then her pussy lips. She felt the large, blunt head of it slide over her clit, and she tensed, all thought fleeing her head before the violence he was preparing to do. "Please god, don't do this, don't do this . . ." A force seemed to envelope both of them, an unholy harbinger that made her clench her body, struggling to keep him out. Even as she fought hard, she shuddered with the excitement of being violently breached.

She could hear his breath come fast. His thick fingers felt clumsy and hurtful as he kicked one of her legs until he'd spread her open to him.

Then his cock plowed into her, driving in and up until he'd lodged so deeply it hurt, and his balls lodged against her mound.

She screamed.

He grasped her hips as he withdrew slightly. Then rammed it home again.

The pain and the fullness couldn't be denied, wished away, or transmuted into something loving. He hurt her, pounded into her repeatedly. "Stop," she gasped, crying. "Please, it hurts."

Instead of answering, he did it again, and again, humping her with savage grunts. The width of him stretched her, and as the length slid in and in to her most personal space she felt violated anew. Made dirty. Each time, she cried out, her tears running freely down the sides of her face to drop into the dirt. Debased. Horribly used.

She felt him tense, and his cock throbbed and grew even larger within her. "Yeah, that's it. That's what you're good for."

He was coming within her. Sudden heat. Slipperiness.

Despoiling her. She felt the orgasm rocketing up through her at that most intimate of thoughts.

When it hit it made her entire body convulse with a pleasure scraped from the depths of the abyss, magic shooting up to take the deliberately obscene actions of Sylvester's abuse and transform it, on waves of shattering joy, into the sweetest, purest gift he could have given. This was her fantasy, her rapture, and he was the perfect lover who'd given it to her.

He trembled, still within. He whispered in her ear, so soft it might have been in her mind: "Thank you."

After, he cradled her.

He brushed her hair back from her moist brow with fingers so delicate it felt like the gentlest of night breezes. How was it possible to feel so cared for, so cherished after what he'd done? This counterpart to violence, this thoughtful caring, held an exquisite sweetness that touched her as deeply. She murmured drowsily. "Is this your aftercare? I love it. You said it would be 'long and thoughtful.' I hope it goes on and on and on. . . ."

"As long as you want," Sylvester promised. "Anywhere in the world, anytime you wish."

As she smiled against his warm chest, content, she heard Mistress Kiana's brass bell begin to clang.

18

Epilogue

"Ryan did the same thing to Black, when she went to check on Osmond. Waited until she had her back to him, then smashed her over the head with a ceramic bowl. Knocked her out."

Nora curled one leg under her, sitting on one of the two cozy velvet-covered chair sets that made Sylvester's living room such a comfortable place to hang out, even when a body had the run of the entire huge place.

Well, except for Mage's loft, of course. But that wasn't where she wanted to be.

Nora picked a grape from the platter Little Peter had left with her, before departing with Mistress Kiana. "Is Black okay?"

Sylvester closed his laptop. "Yes. White says the doctors reported no concussion, no lingering effects beyond a bad headache. Which I can relate to." He looked at her.

"I'm sorry. I'm so glad he's gone. I can't believe Ryan did that to both of you."

"I can." He patted the laptop, then pulled his chair closer to hers. "But let's talk about you. Do you realize you've managed to do most of the things on your checklist? It was a tiny list, but still."

She threw a grape at him.

He picked it up from the ground, placed it on the low, carved teak table in front of the two chairs with no change in expression. "You're welcome to stay here as long as you wish, Nora. But what about your job? Vice president is a big deal."

How did his voice both soothe and stimulate? She had to admit it. She was well and truly infatuated. The subject of her company's executive options felt foreign, and unwelcome next to the option of staying at Twisted Wood for as long as she wished.

The feel of his lazily circling thumb on the nape of her neck made it hard to concentrate. Or maybe she just didn't care as much about her career climb as she once did. Not if it meant giving up such bliss.

She tried to focus. "I can't go back to twelve-hour workdays and no time off to speak of. And I don't want to keep looking at all the places I'll never get to go. Being vice president there would seal my fate." She was surprised to feel so strongly about it. "I guess I've decided to say 'no' to their promotion."

She checked out his reaction. Neutral? Indecipherable. Of course.

Mildly piqued, she said, "Also, I'm going to quit my current position and be a travel writer instead. Travel writers get to go all over the world, and we always need good ones to send back photos and reports. I mean, *they* do. The company."

"Mmm." Still neutral. Uncaring?

"Means I'll finally have the time to do what I've always wanted to do. Stop the workaholic insanity. See the world." Pointedly. Was he actually yawning? He was! Discreetly, but still.

She wriggled away from his fingers. "Not that you're interested in my boring career choices or anything."

He immobilized her by grasping a fat handful of her hair. "No, you don't. I'm interested in every damn thing about you. My goal in life is to make you happy, or haven't you figured that out yet?" His eyes glinted with pleasure as he watched her halfhearted struggle to free herself. When she stilled, he released her to resume the slow, sensual movement of his thumb. "This connection, *us*—it's the most important thing in my life, Nora. Never doubt it." She felt like purring, but he was continuing. "Why don't you just quit? More flexibility in your—our—destinations that way."

She considered. If she threw the career advancement out the window, what was left? Her work satisfaction once lay in successfully portraying exotic locations as alluring destinations. But that pleasure paled next to the excitement of actually visiting the destinations. She answered truthfully. "I'm good at the job—the descriptions, the photos. I like the idea of freelancing. But the biggest reason I can't up and quit is the usual one."

"Money? Not an issue."

"It is for me. Trips around the world aren't cheap."

"Neither is your new boyfriend. No, don't argue. If you want to work, work. If you don't, don't. I respect your choice either way."

She stared at him. "How rich *is* my new boyfriend?"

For the first time, he seemed awkward. He looked away. "Quite well off, actually. Had some good fortune at a dot-com start-up, and invested well afterward . . . you know."

"Sylvester?" She looked at him wonderingly. He was blushing. She'd never seen anything more adorable in her life. How astonishing, that a man who spoke unflinchingly of flesh hooks and nipple clamps could be made abashed by mention of filthy lucre.

She would enjoy investigating his many layers.

But for now, she would change the subject.

"France has the most lovely lavender fields, and the food is nothing short of exquisite."

"The Chez Kink B and B is in France."

She looked at him sideways. His blush was gone as if it had never been. She nodded. "Fun. I've always wanted to see the tulips and windmills in Amsterdam as well. They're astonishing in the springtime. Did you know Keukenhof, near the town of Lisse, is the largest flower garden in the world? It's a massive park that's open only in the spring. Maybe we could go on a river cruise on the Rhine. Wouldn't that be glorious?"

"The Dark Tulip B and B is in Amsterdam."

She tried unsuccessfully to suppress a smile. His own lips curved in a gentle smile as well, though she felt sure his thoughts were anything but gentle. "Another fun destination would be New Zealand. Many people don't realize there are special *Lord of the Rings* tours to showcase the stunning scenery in those movies. And Milford Sound looks like one of the most beautiful places on earth."

"Master Don's Xtreme B and B is in Auckland."

"You're impossible. I give up." She threw up her hands in mock exasperation. "A one-track mind." She stood, turned her back, and started to walk away from him.

She heard the disturbed air as he moved, and a split second later strong arms lifted her, captured her.

Joy radiated through her as his grip changed, grew expert. He cradled her firmly to him. "I do not"—he kissed her head— "have a one-track mind. I'm fairly certain there must be at least two or three tracks." She reveled in the strength and warmth and affection she felt from him.

He carried her toward his master suite. It reminded her of her first visit with him there. They'd sat in his private library, talking about her checklist and what she found desirable. She'd done her best to ignore her attraction to him. Suppressed the forbidden fantasies about him flinging her onto that enormous four-poster bed she could see in the next room.

She snuggled closer to Sylvester.

Happiness washed over her, a warm, tingling river of pleasure. They hadn't even tried the bed yet.

She snorted laughter as he carried her through the doorway.

"You remember your safe word, right?" he inquired. Polite. She nodded.

How she relished the feel of his enormous erection when he released her legs but not her torso, controlling her slow slide down his body. She couldn't miss the fierce gleam in his eyes when she tried to break away and he prevented it. His large hands gathered her wrists into a cruel grip, crossed before her chest.

She tried hard, but couldn't break his grip.

Her whole being flooded with desire. Exhilarating. "No. Please don't," she gasped, her voice quivering with need and something more. He grinned in response. He kicked the heavy wooden door shut behind him.